DATE DUE

AG 8 97			

DEMCO 38-296

THE MEMORIES OF
Ana Calderón

❧❦❧

A Novel
by
Graciela Limón

Arte Público Press
Houston, Texas
1994

...........gh grants from the National
Endowment for the Arts (a federal agency), the Lila Wallace-
Reader's Digest Fund and the Andrew W. Mellon Foundation.

Arte Público Press
University of Houston
Houston, Texas 77204-2090

Recovering the past, creating the future

Cover design by Mark Piñón
Original painting, "Seated Girl in Ruffled Dress" (mixed medium),
by Nivia Gonzalez

Limón, Graciela.
    The memories of Ana Calderón : a novel / by Graciela Limón.
        p.   cm.
    ISBN 1-55885-116-X : $19.95
        1. Mexican American women—Fiction. 2. Women—United States—
    Fiction. 3. Mexican American—Fiction. I. Title.
    PS3562.I464M46 1994
    813'.54—dc20   94-8663
                                                          CIP

The paper used in this publication meets the requirements of the American
National Standard for Permanence of Paper for Printed Library Materials
Z39.48-1984. ⊚

To

Minerva Preciado
who was first my student and is now my friend

ACKNOWLEDGMENTS

I especially thank my friend, Mary Wilbur, who took time to read the manuscript of *The Memories of Ana Calderón* with care and diligence. It is to Mary that I owe the fine tuning of the circumstances and congruity of events of this novel. I also am grateful to Sister Martin Byrne, friend and colleague, who assisted me in detecting the flaws that marked the original version of the manuscript. And I am indebted to Dr. Nicolás Kanellos, Publisher of Arte Público Press, whose editing has made possible the final version of my novel.

G.L.

...el ángel del Señor le dijo,
"Agar... ¿de dónde vienes tu? ¿y a dónde vas?"
Ella respondió,
"Vengo huyendo.."
el ángel del Señor le dijo,
"...el Señor te ha oído en tu humillación..."

...the angel of the Lord said,
"Hagar...where have you come from and
where are you going?"
She answered,
"I am fleeing..."
the angel of the Lord said to her,
"...The Lord has heard you in your humiliation..."

Genesis 16:8, 11

THE MEMORIES OF
Ana Calderón

❧❧

ॐ❧

*My name is Ana Calderón, and my story begins in a pala-
pa close to Puerto Real in southern Mexico. Even though many
years have passed, my recollections of the hut often come to
me. Its roof was made of long interlaced fronds which were
lashed to a supporting frame of poles hacked out of palm trees.
Its floor was the black sand that had been washed ashore ages
before our time. Our palapa was on the fringe of a cluster of
dwellings, and even though we weren't really a part of the port
city, still, its lights could be seen from where we lived. We
could even see the ships that came down the coast from
Veracruz.*

*My father's name was Rodolfo and like all the men of the
village, he was a fisherman. My mother was named Rosalva. I
don't remember her as well as I do my father, and that's
because she died when I was twelve years old, but I know that
I loved her very much. Although I have memories, even vivid
ones of when I was a child, I've always thought that my life
really began on the day that my little brother, César, was
born. That happened on the day I turned ten.*

*I was listening to my Aunt Calista's voice calling out for
me that afternoon, and even though it sounded heavy with
frustration, I pretended not to hear her. I was sitting under
the shade of a small palm tree, wiggling my toes in the sand,
with my knees drawn tightly under my chin as I gazed at the
emerald-colored water. I used to dream most of the time when
I sat by the ocean.*

*When I heard Tía Calista calling me, instead of running
to where she was, I closed my eyes trying to forget that my
mother was having another baby. I didn't want to think of it. I
knew that it meant that I would have to take care of another
sister because, of all my mother's children, only the girls lived.
Each of the boys had died. That began to happen after I was
born.*

*Ever since I could remember, everyone always reminded
me that I must have done something bad to my mother's
womb when I was inside of it because after me two boys, one
right after the other, died. It wasn't until Aleja came along
three years later that we had a new baby. But even after her
there was another boy, and he died too. So everyone convinced
me that it had been me that had done it.*

11

They said that no boy could live where I had lived. I knew my father resented me for what I had done to my mother's insides and that made me feel very lonely. So from as far back as I could remember, I tried to let everyone believe that I didn't care what they said. But I did care. Sometimes I even shook all over just thinking of what I had done. So I decided, when I was very little, that I would live inside of myself, down deep where no one could blame me for what had happened.

Of the sisters, I was the oldest, and because of that I was expected to take care of the smaller ones. I didn't like it, but when I complained I was told that all girls were born to have babies, or to take care of them. My Tía Calista, my mother and my father really believed that, but even then I knew that there was another reason for what they told me. My mother had to wash clothes for the people of Puerto Real to help my father feed us, so somebody else had to watch my sisters. But I told myself that it wasn't that bad because when they reached two years or so, each one would go off on her own during the day. I don't remember exactly where they went. I think they spent their time playing with the neighbor children.

I had only turned ten, but already I knew how to deliver a baby and how to take care of it from the beginning until it began to walk. The only thing I couldn't do was feed it. For that I had to take the little girl to wherever my mother was washing clothes. I didn't have to say anything because she knew why I was there. She would stop what she was doing and sit under a tree. With her arms still dripping soap, she would uncover her breast and stick its rose-colored nipple into the baby's mouth. I remember that my mother's breasts were large. They were round and brown. They reminded me of the clay jugs in which we kept the water we drank.

Alejandra was born when I was three years old, and after her the ones that lived were five girls. My father, I think, had lost hope of ever having a son until César came. He was the only one able to live to be a young man. Then when he was born, my mother stopped having babies.

There was also Octavio Arce. We called him Tavo. He was not my brother. I don't remember when he first came into our family. He was an orphan, and although no one in particular took him in, he spent most of his time with us. He even slept in our hut. He, Alejandra and I were like triplets. I mean, we were hardly ever apart one from the other. That is, until we were grown-up people.

On the day of César's birth, Tía Calista was calling me, but I was dreaming of becoming a famous dancer, so I pretended not to hear her. Alejandra and Tavo were with me, but I had that special way of going inside of myself to be alone with my plans. I used to do that because I wanted to prepare for the day when I would show my father that I could be just as good as the son he longed for. I wanted to do that every day, but he hardly ever looked at me except to let me know with his eyes that he hated me because I was not a boy, and that he believed that I had poisoned the way for the brothers that followed me. But one day, I knew, I would make him see that he had been wrong.

On that day, I could hear my aunt's voice. I didn't want to answer because in my mind, along with my imaginings, I was also seeing my mother's legs spreading out. I could see the syrupy liquid that leaked out of her body, and even how it stained the rough sheet under her, making it stick to the sandy ground. I didn't want to go to the palapa, *but I knew that if I didn't I would be sorry for it later on.*

☙❧

"Ana-a-a-a! Ana-a-a-a!"

The voice cracked under the strain of shouting.

"Where are you, *muchacha?* Ana-a-a-a! Your mother's time has come! *Por Dios, ¿dónde estás?* I need you! If you don't come right now, I'll beat the skin off your behind. Ana-a-a-a! I know you're out there somewhere. The baby is coming, and I need you!"

Ana gazed at the shimmering water and the foamy waves as they slapped against the embankments of the harbor prison, far away. She could hear her aunt's exasperated call, but she didn't want to interrupt her thoughts. Ana could also hear Octavio's and Alejandra's giggling as their bare feet poked her rump, prodding her to run to the hut. Several minutes passed.

When Ana finally decided to respond, she pulled her legs out of the sand and, sprinting up as she always did, the girl danced from one palm tree to the other, from one low fern to the next. Nothing in her body or face indicated that she was in a hurry, or frightened, or worried. Instead, she jumped, springing as high up toward the tops of the trees as possible. At the height of each leap her body was suspended in mid-air, back arched, one leg poised straight out in front, the other gracefully held behind as she lifted her arms in a wide curve above her head. When Ana landed in the sand after each leap, her feet touched invisible springs that again pushed her straight up into the turquoise sky.

By the time she came within view of her family's hut, Ana slowed down, dragging her feet and tracing long tracks in the sand with the tips of her toes. When she crouched through the low entrance, her nostrils expanded with the pungent smell of her mother's body combined with the acrid smoke from the earthen fire crackling in the far corner. As soon as Calista saw the girl standing in the opening, she moved toward her and spoke in a muffled voice. She pinched the girl's underarm, making her flinch with pain.

"*¡Muchacha condenada!* Where have you been? You know that I need you! I suppose you've been dreaming again. Don't bother to answer. Just bring over those sheets, and put more water in the pot. *¡Muévete!*"

The girl moved with familiarity towards the corner her aunt had pointed out in the gloomy hut. When she found the sheets, she brought them to Calista. Ana crouched on her haunches to get a closer look at her mother, who was sweaty and dusty. She had both her hands clenched into fists, and she was biting one of them so that she would not scream.

"Scream, 'Amá, scream. They all do it. Why don't you?"

"*Cállate, malcriada!* Don't you see how much your mother is suffering? She went through the same thing just for you, and look at you! As if nothing were happening. Just wait until you have your own kids. Only then will you under-stand."

"I'm never going to have children, Tía."

"Ha! When we're young, we women all say the same thing. But in the end, no one asks us what we want, or don't want. Come, *Hermana*, push, push, just a little more, and it's over."

Her aunt's voice was husky with fatigue and what Ana thought to be resentment. Ana knew that the baby was close to coming. She was glad because she hated her aunt's words that assured her that she would be just like the other women in her family. These thoughts troubled Ana. She wanted to escape; she could hardly wait until she would be able to run out to the beach again.

Suddenly the smeared tiny body appeared from between her mother's legs. Calista took hold of the child while cutting the cord. A shrill cry tore at the gloom. Calista turned to look at Ana. It was an intense glare; her eyes were filled with a meaning that the girl was unable to understand. Calista saw the girl's bewilderment and, sighing heavily, looked down at the baby.

"*¡Santo Dios!* It's a boy! *Hermana, ¡es un hombrecito!* Maybe this time..." Calista bit her lip and murmured to her niece, "Here, take him. You know what to do. But be careful with him, and give him right back to your mother."

Ana took her baby brother from Calista's hands and moved to the light where she could look at him. This was the first boy she had really looked at. As she wiped his body, her eyes lingered on his genitals, and she thought that his penis looked like a tiny handle. She felt a surge of affection for him, remembering that he had come into her life on her birthday. She told herself that he was a gift for her, and she hoped that he would not die. That would prove to everyone that she had not done anything wrong.

Ana slowly wrapped the boy in the threadbare blanket that had been used for each of the babies that had come before him. She was aware that her aunt was cleaning her mother, and she could hear the two women murmuring. But she could not make out what they were saying. When she was finished cleaning her brother, she took the child to her mother.

"Here, 'Amá. Can I leave now?"

Calista sucked at her lips in irritation. "*¡Muchacha, buena para nada!* You can hardly wait to go out and jump around like a *burra*, can you? You know how special it is to at last have a boy, and here you leave your mother..."

Ana didn't hear the rest of what her aunt said because she was out of the hut, sprinting toward the beach. She felt her heart beating, but she knew that it was not the running that was causing the pounding. It was because she did indeed see how special it was that their family now had a boy. Ana told herself that he had come to save her, and because of that he would be just like her. She and her brother had been born on the same day for a special reason. She was born to become a famous dancer, and he would grow to be someone important, too. Ana ran as fast as she could to find Alejandra and Octavio to tell them the news.

She knew where to find them. The three children had a favorite cove where they spent their time playing in the sand whenever they could escape from their hut and the dreary chores. They would go there especially during the months when the priest who taught them how to read and write traveled to other villages to marry couples and baptize their children.

Ana arrived breathless. She found Octavio and Alejandra lying face up on the sand playing a game in which they pointed at clouds that looked like animals or plants.

"It's a boy!"

Ana's voice startled her sister and Octavio, causing them to jump to their feet. Neither wore shoes nor much clothing. Alejandra was the first to utter what sounded like a groan.

"Ahhg! Is it dead?"

"No! He's alive, and very pretty. Come on! Come and see him!"

Alejandra was annoyed. She stood erect, glaring at Ana, showing her dislike for her. She resented Ana's self-assurance and offishness, but most of all Alejandra was jealous of her sister's looks, which were so different from her own. Whereas Ana's skin was a coppery brown, hers was white; this was the legacy, said Calista, of a French grandfather. Ana's body was thin and sinewy, and her limbs tapered, as if she had been cast in a porcelain mold. Alejandra, on the other hand, was round and supple, and even though she was only seven years old, her small breasts were already beginning to protrude underneath her shear cotton dress. Ana was still flat-chested. Her body retained the look of a boy rather than a girl.

Ana returned her sister's disapproving gaze for a few seconds. Then, suddenly disengaging her eyes from those of Alejandra, she turned to look at Octavio who was standing with his arms hanging limply by his sides. His mouth was open and he blinked his eyes, not knowing what to say. He blurted out the first thing that came to his mind.

"What do you think his name will be, Ana?"

Her answer was brisk. "I think I heard them call him 'César.'"

Octavio's skin was dark and his body was beginning to show that he would develop into a tall man. Although people guessed that he was only nine years old, there already was a transparent fuzz over his upper lip that glistened with perspiration from the excitement of hearing Ana speak. Whenever she spoke, his heart inexplicably beat faster.

Ana was staring at him. "Come on! Let's go see the new baby!"

It was Alejandra, however, who responded. "No! We can see him later. We're in the middle of playing a game. Come on, Tavo! I'm ahead of you."

Octavio looked at Ana as if expecting her to say something. Whenever he gazed at her, his face took on a faint smile, not so much with his lips as with his eyes. He felt drawn to the girl's energy and ability to recreate imaginary worlds that were beautiful to him. Secretly, he preferred the games devised by Ana to those of Alejandra.

"Well, why don't we change and instead play the game Ana was telling us about. The one with the Aztecs and the princess who is going to be sacrificed."

"Oh, no! I hate that one. She's always the beautiful girl who dies after she dances her head off. I think it's boring!"

Alejandra was showing irritation with both Octavio and Ana. She sensed that he liked her sister better and that whatever she did or thought of doing was wonderful for him. Alejandra, however, wanted him for herself, just like when Ana was away. Unable to think of how to get rid of her sister, Alejandra shouted out. "Ana, I think Tía Calista is calling you again."

"No, she's not. You're right, Tavo! Let's do the Ritual of the Humming Bird. You're the High Priest, and I'm Huitzítzilin..."

Ana, forgetting the baby and her mother, leaped through the air, her sheer cotton dress flowing in the warm breeze. Despite her young age, she had already invented a number of dances, each with a title, story line and characters. She often organized her sister and Octavio as part of her troupe, directing them to jump and kick and twirl.

Alejandra protested more than ever to the humming bird dance, knowing that it had two leading parts. The only role she could play was toward the end of the piece when she appeared briefly as an old sorceress. "Oh, no! Not that thing again! Huit...Huit...I can't even pronounce the dumb word! I'm fed up with you being the lady-of-the-something-or-another, and Tavo is always the warrior who's in love with you."

Ana and Octavio disregarded the girl's objections. Without an introduction or warm-up, they whirled about in the sand as the declining sun cast golden sparks in their hair. At first Alejandra sulked, plopping down on the sand with arms folded over her chest. Then she made faces at them as she mimicked their movements. Finally, losing patience, she jumped to her feet, stuck her tongue out at the dancing couple and ran off towards the hut where she knew she would find her mother, her new brother, and at least one of her other sisters or cousins with whom to play.

The two dancers didn't notice Alejandra's mocking gestures. Instead, they continued their ritualistic dance, just as Ana had imagined a high priest and a sacrificial virgin would do. They sprang and turned until their breath came in spurts and their chests heaved from the exertion. They ran from one end of the cove to the other, waving their arms in the air, gesturing and posturing until Ana, re-enacting the death scene, collapsed on the sand. Octavio, knowing his part, fell at her side, first on his knees, then finally on the imaginary onyx knife with which he would take his life after sacrificing the princess.

He was so out breath, however, that he lost his balance and fell on top of her. He had not meant to do that, but when he felt her body beneath him, an unexpected urge kept him there. Octavio felt bound to Ana, and he didn't want to be separated from her. He realized that he had never before felt such a sensation, but he liked what he felt, and he remained without moving.

She was also surprised and remained motionless for several seconds. Then, not knowing what to do, she wiggled to one side until Octavio slid off from on top of her. Still, their faces were very close and their breath intermingled. They were both quiet until their breathing stabilized. Then Octavio placed his hand on her chest, and without thinking he said, "Ana, I wish we could be this way always."

As if his voice had been a musical note marking her next step, Ana jumped to her feet, laughing and swirling her dress. She ran away, shouting words that seemed aimed at the tops of the palm trees rather than at him. "We will always be this way."

ॐ◌ॐ

My mother died in the middle of a scream. No one really knew exactly when it came, or the name of the sickness that afflicted her. I only remember that it began one morning when she whispered, "¡Aye! My head hurts so much!" She wasn't speaking to anyone in particular. She said it as she handed César a cup of chocolate.

In the beginning, the pain in her head made her sigh almost constantly. Soon after, her sighing turned to moans; sometimes they sounded like short gasps. But the time finally came when her groans turned to screams that tore at the night like a sharp invisible knife.

Tía Calista came to be with my mother during those terrible days and nights, but no matter what brews she prepared, my mother's screaming only grew louder. All through those times, we children sat outside our hut along with our father as Calista and other women tried their concoctions, hoping to lessen my mother's pain. I asked my father several times what we would do if she died, but he kept quiet. He never answered my questions; he only stared at me with his resentful eyes. I remember that I didn't cry, despite the big hole growing in my stomach with each minute that passed.

On the last night, my mother let out a wail that I have never been able to forget. It was so loud and so desperate that its vibration caused the owls to flutter up from their roosts in the palm trees. I remember their dark silhouettes as they rose, angrily flapping their wings against the sky that was lit only by the brilliance of the stars. After that, my father was left alone to bring us up. César was two years old.

ॐ◌ॐ

Ana's mother died in 1932. It had been a bad year for the fishing communities living near Puerto Real. The fighting and killing in central Mexico had overflowed Sierra Orizaba, spilling onto the shores of the Gulf and spreading from northern Tamaulipas down to southern Campeche. People trapped in poverty talked of moving away to find a new way to live. No one seemed to know exactly what was happening. The weekly newspaper in Puerto Real described the executions of priests and collaborators who had been found to be in defiance of the constitution. Later on, drifters coming in from different parts of the country countered those reports with stories of their own. A stranger one day walked into the cluster of huts shouting *"Long Live the Cristeros!"* but few people really understood what his words meant.

Rodolfo Calderón was not involved in those events. His mind was taken with the grief of losing Rosalva and with the worry of caring for his eight children. Like everyone else, he saw that things were bad, that the situation around them was deteriorating day by day. Adding to his personal sadness, after his wife's death, bad luck afflicted Rodolfo even more when his boat struck a reef and was damaged beyond repair. The *panga* had been small, but it had provided him with a way to feed his family. Now, even that was gone. His two brothers offered to help him, but he saw that their lives were even more miserable than his. His sister-in-law Calista was helpful with the children, and he was grateful, but that wasn't enough.

He began to visit the busier streets of the port town in search of work. Instead, he found countless men without means of supporting their families as well as women who no longer could find a way to help their husbands. When he spoke to any of them, each seemed to have troubles greater than his own. At first, Rodolfo thought that it was their fault for not wanting to break away from the old ways. When he approached the cannery for a job, however, he discovered that wanting to work was not enough. He was rejected because he was unskilled with machinery and inexperienced in packing. He then turned to the cantina and restaurant, offering to be a waiter or even a cook, but he found out that there were several men ahead of him, waiting for just such a job to come up.

After several months, he gathered his children in the hut. Calista was there also. They sat in a circle on the sandy earth as if they were going to share a meal. No one spoke; they seemed to understand that something important was about to happen. The only sound was the crackling of a few twigs burning in the brasier.

As he peered into the face of each of his daughters, Rodolfo felt a tightness in his stomach. His eyes lingered so long on Ana's face that she began to bounce her crossed legs up and down nervously. It was a gesture she repeated often, and it annoyed him as did most of her traits. He turned away from her, trying not to think of the feelings that assaulted him whenever he looked at her, or even thought of her. Ana was his first child, and he knew that he should have loved her above the others, but he couldn't. He found it impossible to explain why he resented her, especially after his sons had died one after the other. He felt that the disappointment and bitterness that flooded him after each death had infected his heart, making him hate Ana as if it had been her doing.

Rodolfo stared at Rosalva, thinking of how brown her hair and skin were, and that she looked just like her mother when he first saw her. His eyes rolled over to Alejandra, and her determined look unsettled him; something in her eyes usually made him uncomfortable, yet she was his favorite. He turned to Zulma, and he told himself that she seemed filled with the energy of the ocean. He felt a little afraid. Rodolfo's eyes then met those of Jasmín and his heart leaped at the beauty he saw there. But he remembered how often she was ill. He stared at the two youngest, the twins Pilar and Cruz, as he began to speak in his usual quiet manner. "We're going north. I hear there's work in the fields of Sonora and plenty of jobs for everyone on the plantations."

Each of the children, from Ana to César, looked first at their father and then at each other not knowing what to respond. None of them had ever thought of life beyond the familiar shoreline between their hut and the town. Only Ana had dreamed of leaving Puerto Real, and even she was quiet. Tía Calista, astounded, was the first to speak.

"*Compadre*, no! It's a mistake, believe me. What are you going to do all the way across the world? You're from here, from this very sand on which we're sitting. The cord that connected you to your mother's womb is buried out there, right alongside this *palapa*. It's there, just like the cords of these children. I should know; I buried them with these hands. And what about the boys? Even though they didn't live, they're still your sons, and they're out there, too. *Compadre*, you can't leave them...or Rosalva."

Calista stopped speaking, but her breathing was hard; everyone could hear it. When Rodolfo didn't respond, she said more. "Besides, you're a man of the ocean. You'll die if you go where there's only dirt everywhere you look. I mean...what do you know of beans, or whatever it is that they plant up there?"

As if controlled by a single force, the eight small faces snapped from looking at Calista over to their father's face. Fastening their eyes on him, they waited for his response. Rodolfo's head, however, was hanging low over his chest, and it took him a while before he lifted it to speak. "I know nothing of seeds or of how to plant them in the earth, *Comadre*. But I must try. For their sake."

Rodolfo's face was covered with sweat and it glistened in the dimness of the hut. His children were looking intently at him. They saw his broad, bronzed face taut with worry. They sensed that he was thinking of their mother and the dead boys. The thatched roof cast a shadow accentuating his brow; it appeared to be cracked by a deep crevice that cut downward from his hairline elongating his nose. Rodolfo's dark mustache seemed to droop more than ever over his thick lips, and his slanted, black eyes had narrowed like slits in a brown mask.

"Listen to me, *Compadre*." Calista felt compelled to speak again. "Hear my words as the older sister of your wife, God keep her in His company. Things will change, I'm sure. At least you know how to go about living here. And what about your brothers? Are you just going to leave them never to see them again? And, don't forget, *Compadre*, that even though I can't help provide the tortillas, you have me to help at least with the children. Except for Ana, they're all yet so little... *¡Por Dios!*...and all of them useless girls except for this one."

Calista put her arms around César, who was sitting next to her. The girls were familiar with being called useless, but they had never before seen their aunt's face so intense. Somehow it looked darker than ever. In the darkness of the hut, the deep wrinkles of her cheeks seemed like fissures in the brown coral they knew well, and her aquiline nose dipped sharply toward her chin.

Rodolfo again looked around at his brood, but he remained silent. The only movement in his face was when he nibbled at his upper lip, nervously tweaking his mustache.

"I have thought about it long enough. I've sold what was left of my gear, and with that money we'll have enough to take us to Veracruz. From there we'll make our way northward until we reach the Río Yaqui, where the planting is plentiful."

Calista had nothing more to say. She nodded vaguely, rose to her feet and left the hut. Rodolfo's children were silent, still not knowing what to say or do. Alejandra was the only one to speak. "What about Tavo?"

"What about him, Aleja?"

"Well, 'Apá, we can't just leave him. He's part of our family."

"I only have enough money for us. He'll have to stay behind."

Alejandra's head jerked to one side as if she had been slapped. Her face was filled with shock and disbelief because she could not even begin to imagine life without Octavio. "Then I'll stay, too." She was close to tears as she blurted out the words to her father.

"Alejandra, hush. It's impossible for you to stay. We're a family and we're staying together, and there's no more to be said."

After a few moments in which they all sat without saying anything, Rodolfo stood up and left the hut. As soon as she was sure that he was beyond hearing her, Ana sprang to her feet and let out a howl of joy. The other girls and César, not knowing how to react, also stood up and began to giggle. Only Alejandra remained squatting on the sand. She looked up at her older sister and said, "We can't leave Tavo behind."

Ana stopped in the middle of a whoop. "He'll come with us, silly. Nothing will hold him back."

Then, not knowing exactly why, the other girls and César began to yell and screech in wild joy. Inexplicably, they were elated at the prospect of leaving the place in which they had been born.

❧

My dream was beginning to come true. I didn't know where we were going, but I felt that each step away from the palapa *would lead me to the fulfillment of what I knew was my destiny. And I would show everyone that I could do some good, after all.*

Unlike me, Alejandra was sad. She didn't share my joy, especially when she saw that our father would not allow Tavo to come with us. On that last night, both of them begged my father to let him come with us. She cried and said she would not come unless he came along. Even Tavo wept as he asked over and again for the permission. But my father was firm; the answer was no.

When we were finished with the packing, we laid down to sleep. Alejandra and I shared the same mat, so I was able to feel her turning over from one side to the other. I couldn't sleep either, not because of Tavo, but because I was so excited. After a few hours, I felt Alejandra leave the mat. I opened my eyes and saw that she had crawled over to where Tavo was lying, and I saw that she put her arms around him. He put his arms around her, too, and I knew that they would stay that way for the rest of the night.

Before the sun came out, we heard my father moving on his mat. When he blew his nose, we knew that it was time to rise and say goodbye to our aunts and uncles and cousins. I knew, also, that it was time to begin the road that would lead me to the world that I had imagined.

☙◈❧

The sun was rising as Rodolfo Calderón and his eight children walked toward the bus station in Puerto Real. He was at the head and the children trekked in single file behind him. He wore overalls, thick sandals, and a *morral* bag in which he carried a pouch with each child's baptismal certificate. He also had a photo of the family when César was baptized. With the exception of the two smallest, each girl had a bundle strapped to her back; in it were a few pieces of clothing and an extra pair of shoes. In a pouch sewn out of an old blanket, Ana carried César on her back, along with her belongings.

They walked in silence, and as the sun rose, its golden light elongated the shadows cast by the Calderón family. Not far behind came Octavio, who tip-toed and crouched, taking small, hesitant steps because he feared being seen by Rodolfo. The boy would not stay behind despite the older man having forbidden him to follow them. Octavio felt that they were his family, the only ones he had really known, and he loved them, especially Ana and Alejandra. So he darted from behind trees and bushes, hoping that a miracle would happen at the last minute.

When the family arrived at the edge of town, Rodolfo pointed in the direction where the buses were stationed. They were battered, scratched vehicles; the hand-printed signs on their sides were so faded that most were unreadable. The children giggled and stared wide-eyed at the disheveled bus drivers. Only Alejandra was withdrawn; she seemed to be somewhere else. Ana had taken César out of his pouch and put him on the ground. She held his hand, but he began to cry, motioning to her that he wanted her to pick him up in her arms again.

Rodolfo turned to Ana. "Wait here. I'm going in to buy our tickets. Make sure no one strays away."

When Octavio saw this, he rushed from behind the squat building that served as the station office. "Chsst! Ana...Alejandra...I'm here!"

Everyone was caught off guard. They had already said goodbye to him and no one imagined that he had been behind them all the time. Alejandra, her eyes inflamed and blurry, let out a yelp of joy. Ana, still holding her brother in her arms, didn't seem surprised, however. "I told all of you he'd come." Turning to Octavio, she said, "What are you going to do now, Tavo? We don't have money to buy you a ticket."

"I don't know, but I can't stay. I want to be with you."

Alejandra, whose face had drained of color, was biting her lip, trying to hold back the tears that were again assaulting her. "Ana, please think of something. Please!"

The other girl was looking around her as if searching for the answer. Then, smiling broadly, she pointed to the bus she supposed they would be taking. "Well, just wait until the bus gets going, and then you can hang on to that ladder that's stuck on the back of it. I've seen lots of kids like you doing that. No one will know until we get to the next town, and then 'Apá will have to let you come along with us."

The girls all gawked at the built-in ladder meant to be used for loading baggage on the roof of the vehicle, and their eyes grew rounder with each moment as they grasped the height that Octavio would have to manage. His eyes, too, were riveted on the highest rung. He ran his tongue over his lips before he spoke.

"I...I...yes...I've seen boys do that...but just around here, on these short streets."

"Oh, well, if you're scared to do it..."

"I'm not scared, Ana." Octavio hesitated, trying to decide what to do. He finally blurted out, "Yes! I'll do it that way!"

"Tavo, what if you fall?"

"I won't fall, Alejandra. I promise."

When Rodolfo reappeared, Octavio dove for cover behind the bus. The boy began to stretch and flex his short fingers in preparation. He had nothing to carry; he was wearing everything he owned. But he regretted that he was wearing shoes because they were beginning to hurt his feet, and because he was unused to wearing shoes he felt as if he would lose his balance. He plopped down on the dirt and removed them. Then, tying them by their laces, Octavio wrapped his shoes around his neck. He felt secure now, knowing that he could use his feet and toes to help his hands stick to the ladder. No matter what happened, he knew that nothing would knock him off the bus.

Rodolfo gave them instructions. "Hold each other's hands." The children obeyed him, and they followed him to a bus which was warming its engine. Once at the door, he lifted up each girl, beginning with the smallest. When Ana with César on her back stepped onto the running board, Rodolfo muttered, "God help me." He handed the fares to the driver as he hoisted himself aboard.

Once on the bus, they saw that it was nearly filled to capacity. But the passengers were kind and some of them even changed places so that the family could sit together. Alejandra insisted on sitting at the rear of the bus, but her father instructed her to stay with the rest of her sisters. She became despondent and seemed close to tears, even though Ana kept giving her glances that said that Octavio would be fine.

The bus lurched forward, bouncing on the rough road that headed up the coast to the port city of Veracruz. The vehicle steadily picked up speed once it reached the highway, which was also filled with bumps and holes. Alejandra became paler with each impact, and when Rodolfo noticed her sickly look, he leaned over the others to speak to her. "Hija, come over here so you can put your head on my shoulder."

She moved over to his side and buried her head in his shirt. Some time passed and the road seemed to become even worse. When Alejandra could no longer control her anxiety, she began to cry.

"*¿Qué pasa*, Aleja?" Rodolfo called her by the name he used to show her affection. He wanted to know why she was crying.

"'Apá, he's back there and he's going to fall and get killed!"

Startled, Rodolfo put his hand under the girl's chin and lifted her face so that he could look more closely at her. "Back there? Who's back there?"

"Tavo. He's hanging on to the bus, but I think he's going to fall and get killed."

"Octavio!..." There was disbelief in Rodolfo's voice.

Her father moved Alejandra away as he turned in his seat to look to the rear of the bus. He rose and groped his way back to the dingy window where he could get a view of the outside of the bus. His breath skipped when he was able to make out two small hands gripping one of the rungs of the ladder. He could see that the knuckles were a grayish brown. That was all Rodolfo could make out because of the cloud of dust being churned up by the speeding bus.

Rodolfo tripped over bundles and boxes as he rushed up the aisle to the driver. He vaguely heard disgruntled muttering telling him to watch out, to be more careful. "Señor, my son is hanging to the rear of the bus. Please stop!"

"*¿Qué?*"

"I said, please stop the bus! Please stop it slowly or he'll be killed."

The driver muttered obscenities, but he began to apply the brakes as his eyes searched for a flat spot on the side of the road. The passengers craned their necks, looking in every direction, not knowing why they were stopping in the middle of nowhere. Their first guess was that the tall man talking with the driver had to get off the bus to rush over to the first clump of bushes. Some of the people began to snicker, criticizing him for not being able to hold on until the next town.

When the driver pulled the lever opening the door,

Rodolfo leaped out, not bothering to use the steps. He ran to the rear of the vehicle where he found Octavio, his hands still clinging to the rung and his toes nearly welded to the ladder. The boy's body was gray with dust, his eyes were shut tightly, and his head dangled backward. He seemed close to fainting. Rodolfo took him in his arms, but the driver, who by that time was right behind, had to unclasp the boy's fingers one by one.

When some of the passengers began to get off the bus, the driver shouted at them to return to their places. Still muttering and complaining, he glared first at the boy and then at Rodolfo. "This will cost you another fare, you know. Now, let's get going. We're late enough as it is!"

As Rodolfo made his way down the aisle with Octavio in his arms, everyone stared at him, wondering where the boy had come from. They whispered to one another, wagging their heads, some in disbelief, others in disapproval. When Rodolfo returned to his seat, Octavio began to stir, and the girls clustered around him, rubbing his cheeks and chest. He finally opened his eyes and looked up at Rodolfo. He smiled so broadly and with so much happiness that the older man could not help himself when he hugged the boy close to his chest. A man seated close by passed a jug of water to Octavio, who took long gulps, spilling water down his chin and onto his dusty shirt. As the bus gained speed, Ana turned to Alejandra. "I told you 'Apá would let him come along."

I remember our trip north as if it had happened yesterday; what is uncertain to me is time. I don't recall how many hours, or even days, it took the bus to arrive at Veracruz. I suppose that it was a hard trip for the grown-ups, who seemed to feel the bumps and curves in the road. They seemed to sweat more than the children as the heat seeped in through the windows and pounded the thin metal roof of the bus. But those of us who were kids didn't mind it. Alejandra was happy since Tavo was with us. As for myself, I sometimes thought of Tía Calista and what she would be doing. I recalled my mother, too, and how she was buried down deep under the dirt

*with her little sons. But most of all, my thoughts carried me
forward to the years when I would be free to dance out all the
feelings I had inside of me.*

*My sisters thought the trip was exciting. Every time we
stopped at a village or small town, someone always bought
peanuts or a bag of oranges to share with us. Only 'Apá, I
remember, looked very sad. He never said anything about
money, but Alejandra, Tavo and I knew that he was worried
about making it all the way to the valley watered by the Río
Yaqui.*

*From Veracruz we took another bus headed for the capi-
tal. This time was different because the bus had to climb a
giant mountain, the Orizaba. No one laughed on that part of
the trip because most of us were sick. I hated every minute of
it. I remember looking around and seeing that everyone's face
was a grayish color. I imagined that my face must have looked
like a bag filled with sour milk. My little sisters and César
cried a lot. They wanted to go home to Tía Calista and they
begged 'Apá to take them back. I think that this only made
him sadder.*

*When we arrived in Mexico City, my father told us to hold
hands and not let go of one another. I was so tired, though,
that when I tried to put César on my back, I found out that I
couldn't. 'Apá took him from me and carried him all the way
as we walked to a part of town everyone called Tepito. We had
an uncle there who would let us stay with him for a few days
to rest.*

*We were scared because we had never seen so many cars
and people all in one place. There were a lot of beggars, too,
and they frightened us even more. But 'Apá seemed to know
exactly where he was headed as he led us around corners and
across streets and finally to a small store owned by our uncle.*

*My Tío Sempronio and his wife, Tía Olga, were waiting
for us when we arrived at their store. We got there after dark,
so the place was scary; it was lit only by a kerosene lamp
hanging from one of the rafters. The place was tiny, and I
remember that it smelled funny. I couldn't tell what it smelled
of because it was like a mixture of many things. As I looked
around, I saw a sack filled with rice and another one with
beans. Above me, on the counter, there was a large basket
filled with eggs, and next to it another one filled with onions
and red chilies. High up on the ceiling, hanging from hooks, I*

saw a ham and a big chunk of raw meat.

*We stayed there several days, and during that time my
father and Tío Sempronio talked for hours. They sat at the
small kitchen table with their faces so close that their noses
almost touched. Years later I found out why they spent so
much time whispering. My Tío, who didn't have much money,
had agreed to help us enough so that we could travel north to
Sonora and the Río Yaqui.*

*During those hours, Tía Olga would take us out to see her
city. She told us that it was a very large place where it was
easy for children to get lost or run over by a car. But we were
never able to see how big the city really was because she only
took us to the Shrine of Guadalupe, where she made us pray a
rosary each time. This happened every time we left the store.*

*I didn't like the Shrine because it was spooky and the
buzzing of prayers frightened me. But Tía Olga said that if a
family prayed the rosary every day, that family would never
separate, and much less would they commit serious sins. So I
tried to concentrate on the Hail Marys and on the Our Fathers
even though my knees hurt from kneeling on the stone floor.*

*We were at the end of our prayers during one of those days
when I noticed a woman hobbling on her knees toward the
main altar. She was dressed in black, and she wore a long
shawl that covered her head and most of her face. When she
came close to me, I was able to see that her face was puffy and
blotched from crying, and that her eyes were so swollen that
they looked liked tiny slits. I watched her as she made her way
to the railing and clung to it as if to keep from falling onto the
cold stones. Her hunched shoulders heaved as she sobbed
silently. Now and then she looked up to the picture of the
Virgin of Guadalupe, and I could hear her mutter words that
I couldn't make out.*

*The crying woman scared me so much that I felt my heart
pound, and I looked over to Tía Olga who, as if reading my
mind, said, "She is a sinner." I looked again at the woman,
wondering what sin could be so great to cause such sadness.
When we returned to the store, I asked Tía Olga about sin and
why it had made the woman cry so much. But all she said to
me was, "Life will give you the answer."*

*When it was time for us to leave Mexico City, my Tía Olga
packed us a basket filled with food and fruit for the trip which
we were to make, this time on a train. Although I was excited*

about our trip, I felt sorry to leave my aunt and uncle. They were good and they seemed to like us. The rest of the girls wanted to stay, but Alejandra and Tavo could hardly wait to know what it felt like to get on a train.

We said goodbye and walked to the station, again holding hands to make sure no one got lost. After my father bought our tickets, someone showed us the part of the train where we were to travel. I remember that my heart started beating when I saw that it wasn't just one train as I had imagined. It was several trains, or coaches, as I found out later when I was growing up. It was so long that I couldn't begin to understand how we would be able to get from one end of the train to the other. Each section seemed to come to an end where it was joined to the next car by a big chain.

Once inside the coach, we saw that the only place to sit was on a long bench attached to each of the sides. By the time we got in, all those places were taken, so our family had to sit on the wooden floor of the car, even 'Apá. That's how we traveled all the way to a city none of us had ever heard of. Its name is Hermosillo, in northern Mexico.

It was hard sitting and sleeping for so many days on that floor. The hardest part was that the car didn't have a toilet, so we had to wait until we reached the next stop. The girls cried, and César did it in his pants. I remember hurting a lot, but I tried to forget my pain by remembering that at the end of the trip would be the place where I could get dancing lessons, and that soon after that I would become a famous dancer.

At night as we crossed mountains and flat plains, the wheels of the train whirled, grinding against the rails, and the sound lulled me to sleep until I could see myself in a dress of white lace. In my dreams I danced and pirouetted in the center of a large stage where an elegant audience looked at me with admiration. Several times, though, this dream was interrupted by the image of the woman I had seen crying at the Shrine, and in that dream I asked her what she had done that was so bad. Each time, the woman would turn to me and say, "You, too, will commit my sin. You, too, will do what has been forbidden." Her words filled me with so much fear that I would wake up, and because César slept in my arms, I would cradle him until the woman's flushed, tearful face disappeared.

When we finally arrived in Hermosillo, we were all disap-

*pointed. It was hot and dusty, and no one paid attention to us.
'Apá looked worried, but again he seemed to know what to do
next. Later on he told us that Tío Sempronio had told him
where he would find the trucks that took campesinos out to the
fields for the harvesting that was going on. And so, although
we were all exhausted and hurting, my father put us aboard a
big truck, where we were squeezed in with dozens of men,
women and children, all heading for the fields and work.*

"*¡A la pisca!* To the harvest!"

Truck drivers competed with one another, each trying to
out-shout the next in an attempt to get as many people to
climb aboard his truck. The dilapidated Ford flatbeds were
there to transport as many workers as possible to the fields
where the tomato harvest was at its peak.

People milled around trucks and drivers, trying to get the
best fare. Men, whose weathered faces reflected a lifetime
spent in fields, clung to bundles and boxes packed with mea-
ger possessions. Women of all ages stayed close to husbands
and children; many of those women were pregnant, others
where carrying babies only a few months old.

The shouting grew in intensity as men and women
became more anxious with each minute. Many of them had
migrated from as far south as Yucatán and now, when so
close to the place that promised the opportunity to work, they
feared being left behind. They pushed and tugged, forcing
others to do the same. As their shuffling feet ground into the
powdery desert sand, clouds of dust lifted, making children
sneeze and cough.

Rodolfo, with César clinging to his back, held on to the
twins, one in each hand. He had to raise his voice to be heard.
"Ana! Aleja! Tavo! Each one of you take hold of one of the
girls, and don't let go of her no matter what! Follow me!"

The older children did as they were told, but as the family
clustered together, they were pushed back and forth. Jasmín
yelped in pain when someone stepped on her foot; she began
to cry. Ana kept her eyes on César and saw that he wasn't
scared. He seemed to be enjoying the rocking and bouncing as

his father struggled to keep his balance. Rodolfo finally made his way to one of the drivers.

"We're ten. How much?"

"Ten cents a piece."

Rodolfo didn't have time to barter or complain because when he looked behind him, he saw anxious people waiting for him and his group to either jump aboard the truck or get out of the way. He turned to the driver and nodded in acceptance. The driver helped lift the girls onto the flatbed while Octavio climbed up the side of the truck. Rodolfo rapidly reached into his pocket and pulled out the one peso bill that would pay his and the children's fare to the camp.

They felt relieved and safe once on the truck, but soon they realized that the driver, anxious to get as much money as possible out of his load, kept packing more passengers aboard. Rodolfo had to lift the twins onto his shoulders in order to protect them from the squeeze. They hung there, twisted grotesquely, side by side with César. Because they too were tiny, Rosalva, Zulma and Jasmín clung to the three older children, trying to keep their feet and chests from being squashed.

People shouted at the driver to stop, but he seemed oblivious to their screaming. Most of the men and many of the women, too, were forced to perch children on their necks and shoulders. The pregnant women, especially, screamed and pleaded for those nearest to them to give them just a little space. Ana looked up to her father's face and saw that it was dirty and streaked with sweat. Her view was partially blocked by squashed sombreros and wrenched arms and necks, but she could see that the muscles of his jaw were quivering nervously. Ana turned to look at Octavio and she saw that his face was so caked with dust that only the whites of his eyes seemed to be clean. She realized that she, too, was so dirty that she must have looked like a monkey.

The driver and another man finally closed off the rear of the flatbed with wooden panels. Mud-smeared, frightened faces looked at one another. Most of them were embarrassed to be squeezed in so close to an unknown man or woman. As the truck bounced onto the dirt road that led to the crops, the swerving and bumping became intensely painful. Most of the smaller children were crying out loud. Their bawling mingled with the mumbled obscenities of some people, and with the groans and incoherent prayers babbled out loud by a few others.

Ana, who had been pressed into one of the corners of the flatbed, managed to twist her body so that she was finally facing the outside. Her cheek was mashed against the frame when she was forced to put her face against it, but she didn't mind because she was able to look out at the passing landscape. The side of her face hurt, but she was grateful, knowing that others smaller than she were trapped. She imagined that all they saw and smelled were the rumps and thighs of those pushed up against them.

The sun was beginning to decline, and Ana gazed at the long, dark shadow cast by the truck. Her eyes became fastened onto that black form that seemed to wiggle before her eyes like a worm crawling along the reddish, sandy earth. Then, feeling an intense desire to be away from the pressing flesh that was nauseating her, she slowly maneuvered one of her arms away from her body and stuck it out between the railings. She felt the rush of fresh, desert air flow through her outspread fingers, making its way up her arm and funnelling through her thin cotton blouse. The wind's coolness curled into her armpit, making her feel free.

The trip took only two hours, but at its end all the passengers were numbed and hurt; their cracked lips showed extreme thirst and nausea. Some of the children had fainted and were passed from hand to hand in order to get them off the truck. Everyone showed signs of being frightened at what lay ahead.

Rodolfo pounced down onto the ground from the high flatbed in a single leap, his three smallest children still clinging to him. When he finally clustered all of them around him, he paused for a long time before saying or doing anything. Then the questions began.

"'Apá, where are we?"

"When are we going to eat? I'm hungry."

"Where's the toilet, 'Apá?"

Rodolfo's chest was heaving with anxiety. He rolled his eyes in every direction, as if looking for a door through which he and his children could escape. He tried to ask others what to do next, but everyone was just as terrified as he was. They either yanked away or just shrugged shoulders; no one could pay attention to the misery of others. This went on for some time before a man dressed in khaki pants, a plaid shirt, and high leather boots spoke out. He had a bull horn placed to his mouth to assure that he could be heard.

"*¡Bienvenidos al Rancho la Concepción!* If you want work, this is where you'll find it. We pay five *centavos* for each bucket of tomatoes you pick, except if they're bruised or damaged. Over there to the right you'll find toilets and water. To the left of that is a store where you can buy the goods you need. You can find the buckets right there, too. And back there is the space where you can set up your tents to live in. Work begins at four in the morning and ends when the sun sets. In the meantime, I want you to know that I'm the main foreman, and standing here to my right and left are my associates, Señor Donato Sánchez and Señor Evaristo Mendoza. They will deal with paying you as well as with any act of disorderliness. If anyone doesn't like it here, you can walk back to Hermosillo. It's in that direction."

The man pointed in a westerly direction, and without waiting to answer questions or give any further information, he turned abruptly and walked away from the stunned crowd. He then drove off in a dusty Packard that had been waiting for him.

There was silence for a few moments before everyone realized that hardly any of them had blankets, much less tents in which to take shelter. A minute passed. Then the stillness was broken by a spontaneous outburst as all realized that the space pointed out by the foreman was limited, and that a family could be left without a place to sleep.

The impact of this possibility made everyone panic. At first, they shuffled from side to side, uncertain of what next to do. Then one man broke away from the crowd, and as if a signal had been given, the rest stampeded like disoriented cattle in every direction. Men, cursing and spitting out insults, pushed and wrestled with one another over a few feet of dirt. Women, too, were using their fists, teeth, fingernails and feet to throttle, shove, grab until they could lay claim to at least a bit of space. All of this happened amid the din of screaming adults and squalling children. Dust churned by trampling feet rose high above, enveloping men and women and children. All the while the foremen looked on, evidently accustomed to what they were witnessing.

Ana and Octavio were the first to reach a small patch of ground where they threw themselves down, spread eagle,

instinctively understanding that this would signal possession. Seconds later, Rodolfo reached the same place and
together with the rest of the girls fanned out in a circle,
claiming the area. They dug their bundles into the soft dirt,
as if they had been fence posts lashed together by invisible
barbed wire. The Calderóns had taken hold of that spot of
dusty earth and laid claim to it against any intruder who
might dare to trespass.

When Rodolfo and his children were finally able to flop
down to catch their breath, all of them, except César, were
gasping for air as their lungs returned to normal breathing.
Their bodies were encrusted with dust and sweat that had
turned into blobs of mud. Their lips were chapped and dry,
and each one of them was starving.

"'Apá, let's go to the store. I heard the man say that we
could buy things there. We're all so hungry."

Alejandra had finally caught her breath and her voice
was filled with pain. No one else spoke, but most of them nodded their heads in support of what she was saying. Rodolfo,
too, agreed as his hand reached deep into his side pocket.

"Ana, you and Aleja stay here with the little ones. Tavo,
you come with me."

As Rodolfo and Octavio groped their way around knots of
people, some of which had already started fires out of twigs
and leaves, they saw expressions they had never seen before.
The boy began to feel fear for the first time since they had left
Puerto Real. Doubt began to creep into Rodolfo's heart as he
looked around at faces overwhelmed by sadness and fear.
Many were weeping, even men. The stench of sweat and
urine was beginning to foul the air, and the crying of babies
told of desperate hunger which a mother or a father was powerless to relieve.

Rodolfo and Octavio had to wait because a line had
already formed at the door of the dingy shack that was the
company store. From where they stood, they could hear murmuring, then loud words and finally shouting, as a man complained because of the unheard of price that was put on tortillas and a few pieces of cheese. They didn't hear a response.
What they saw, however, told them what was happening. The
man was grabbed by the two foremen, arms twisted behind
him, and thrown face down onto the ground just outside the
store and in full view of the waiting customers. One of the

foremen made an obscene gesture at the prostrate man, and looking at the rest of the men, he said, "You'll get the same if you misbehave."

Someone, however, had the courage to speak out. "But what if we don't have enough money? Are we supposed to let our children starve?"

"Of course not. The *patrón* is not inhuman." The words were charged with sarcasm. "All you have to do is get a little credit, that's all. You'll all find that Don Chicho—that fine gentleman that runs this store—will set you up without any problem. All you have to do is ask in a courteous way and not like an animal, like this one." The foreman pointed at the man who was still laying face down. Rodolfo looked away, but Octavio could see that the muscles of his jaw were clenched.

When they finally entered the store, they encountered an obese, bald man who appeared to be around fifty years old. He wore a tiny mustache and his eyes, Octavio thought, were like those of a pig.

"*Caballero*s, what will it be? I have canned goods as well as dry goods. Rice, beans, onions, whatever you desire. I have tortillas—not too fresh—but still very delicious. And, of course, I have plenty of tequila. For medicinal purposes, of course."

As he howled at his witticism, his belly wobbled up and down and from side to side. Rodolfo glared at him in silence. "Give me a kilo of tortillas, some of those chorizos and a jug of water."

After placing the items requested by Rodolfo on the counter, the fat man scribbled a figure on a scrap of paper and handed it to him.

"¡Ten pesos! You're crazy. That's more than a month's wages back home..."

"Take it, or get out of here. You saw what happens to troublemakers. On the other hand, the store will give you credit if you want. Just put your mark on this paper."

Rodolfo, fighting the urge to strike out at the man, controlled himself, remembering his children. He would be able to pay later, anyway. What was important now was to keep everyone strong enough to work. Then the money to pay the bill would follow. Rodolfo put his initials on the bottom of the bill without saying a word.

When they returned, Ana and Alejandra had built a

small fire around which the children were huddling. As their father produced the package of food, each one stuck out a hand that could hardly wait for a taco of sausage followed by a gulp of water. When they finished all the food, they were still hungry, but because they were also exhausted, they clustered against one another and immediately fell into a deep sleep. The only sounds in the camp were the hootings of the owls and the crackling of the fire. Ana, holding César tightly, began to wonder for the first time if this were really the place where all her hopes would come true.

We worked in the fields of Sonora picking tomatoes for almost three months, but we got nothing in return. My father kept getting deeper into debt with the company store. Even though we were seven workers, we were never able to gather enough tomatoes to pay for what we ate each day. Don Chicho, the fat man, never denied anyone what they wanted, but people understood that at the end of the harvesting season, he would present a bill that more than likely no one would be able to pay. It meant that those people would have to move over to the other side of the rancho where the corn was ready to be picked, and work there in payment of the bill.

Saturday evening was payday. The men, my father included, lined up at the two tables from which the foremen paid the wages earned that week. Each of the supervisors had a tablet in front of him with a count of the buckets brought in by each man. The work that the women and children did was credited to the man of the family. My father, who had six workers to his name, sometimes came out a little ahead of the other campesinos. But not always, because if there was at least one tomato that showed a bruise or a cut, that bucket wasn't counted. Since Jasmín, Zulma and Rosalva were still little, they sometimes dropped their buckets and damaged the tomatoes.

There was another reason why at the end of the season most of the families owed the patrón money. It was because on Saturday night Don Chicho put out bottles of tequila and invited the men to treat themselves. "It's your just dues, isn't that so, caballeros? You've worked like mules all week long,

*haven't you?" He reminded them of this as he laughed hearti-
ly, his belly shaking and his thin mustache glistening with the
oil that dripped from his cheeks.*

*The men became drunk every Saturday night. Most of
them, and many times my father, spent everything they had
earned during the week on tequila. I disliked my father most
of all when he was drunk. He frightened me. He glared at me
for hours as I crouched with the rest of the kids by the small
fire. He often grumbled under his breath at me and most of
the times I felt that he wanted to hit me because I wasn't a
boy.*

*I made up my mind that I would show him that I could
work as much as Tavo, and even more. Besides, I wanted to
make up for what my little sisters couldn't do in the fields, so I
worked without stopping sometimes. My hands and fingers
became blistered and my back always hurt from stooping over
the tomato plants. But no matter how many buckets I filled
during the day, my father still seemed to resent me, especially
when Saturday night came around.*

*Tavo worked hard, too, but many times he and Alejandra
would fool around, wasting their time. They made faces at me
when I reminded them that it was work, not play, and that we
needed the money to pay for our tortillas that night. But they
didn't care. They were as playful as they had been back home.
I wondered at those times why I was different. I still went into
myself to become an elegant and well-known lady, but I did
this now only at night when I was falling off to sleep.*

*Along with my father's resentment of me, what I hated
about those days was what we had to do to César and the
twins. We had to leave them at the edge of the field with one of
the many grandmothers who were too old to work. It was
another expense because she charged ten cents for the care of
each of the kids. Spending the money was not what bothered
me because I knew that I alone picked enough tomatoes to pay
that bill. What hurt me the most was to hear César cry out
after me when I left him with the old lady. It didn't seem to
matter to him that his two sisters were there with him. All he
knew was that I wouldn't be around to hold him. Even when I
was in the middle of the field, I could still hear him crying out
my name. And this hurt so much that sometimes tears
squeezed out of my eyes.*

The worst thing that happened to us was that Jasmín

became very sick. First she stopped eating; we couldn't even force her to swallow a piece of tortilla. Then we saw that it was difficult for her to move, so we had to leave her with the old lady who took care of the other children. By this time, I could see that my father was growing desperate. He didn't know how he would pay the money he owed the patrón, *and he could see that Jasmín needed a doctor. It was at that time that I saw him whispering several times with some of the other workers.*

We all knew what was happening, and the few days that followed turned into nightmares for each one of us. No one laughed or played anymore, especially me, because on top of everything, something suddenly happened that changed my life. I had known about it for a long time and I knew that it came to all women, but I suppose that I had thought that I would be different.

It occurred one day when I was stooped over a plant and I glanced down at my ankle. Blood! It was dripping from between my thighs. By the time I looked, small blobs of it had already mingled with dust at the top strap of my huarache.

I still can't understand why this hit me as it did, except that up to that moment I had supposed—I had hoped—that this would never happen to me. That trickle of red liquid forced me to accept that I was like other girls after all. I straightened up and looked around at the women; I knew that some weren't much older than me. I watched them toiling under the relentless sun. Like dumb animals, they mechanically yanked the red fruit from the vines. I looked at the soiled, dusty bandanas that covered their hair already streaked with gray. I saw their bony faces marked by grayish blotches, their eyes sunken and sad, their skin aged beyond its years.

The darkened palapa *and my mother's body, legs spread apart, took shape before my eyes, shimmering in the transparent desert air. I heard my voice: "I'm never going to have children, Tía." Then Calista's words rang out in my memory, even stronger than when she had first uttered them, "When we're young, we women all say the same thing. But in the end, no one asks us what we want or don't want."*

I knew that in just a few years, maybe even less, I would be the same as the women surrounding me. I saw that what I had desired—my hope of being a dancer, of being famous—

*was nothing but a fantasy; the silly, empty dream of a child. I
felt something inside of me shatter, and I could hear the pieces
clashing against one another as they cluttered up my insides.*

*I couldn't help what happened next because I wanted more
than anything to be little, to become invisible. Lowering
myself, I burrowed as far as I could under a plant. I rolled up,
bringing my knees close to my chin and I clasped my body
with my arms. I stayed there for the rest of the day.*

৵৵৻

Rodolfo squatted on his haunches; his voice was tense as
he whispered to the children. "We're leaving tonight after all
the campfires die out, so don't fall asleep! It'll be like this.
First Ana will pretend to take the twins to the toilet. What
she'll do is go far behind it, over there to where the oak tree
is. She'll hide there and wait. After a while you, Tavo, will
wait until I give you the signal to do the same thing with
César..."

"No, 'Apá! He'll cry if he doesn't go with me. He'll wake
everybody up!" Ana pleaded with her father.

Rodolfo sucked at his teeth. *"Bueno, sí,* you're right. Then
you'll have to pretend that you're taking all three kids to the
toilet. That means that Aleja will have to do the same with
Zulma and Rosalva when I tell her to go." Turning to her, he
said, "You're not scared to do that, are you, *Hija?"*

Wide-eyed, Alejandra nodded negatively. Rodolfo continued with his plan as he turned to Octavio. "That leaves you
and me. After we're sure that everyone is behind the tree, I'll
carry Jasmín. You stay close by my side." He looked at all of
them as he rasped out his whispered words. "We can't rush
because we might stumble over somebody or something. If
that happens just say you're sorry and that you've got to
hurry to the toilet before you do it in your pants."

The children giggled, but were cut short by their father's
scowl. Rodolfo continued whispering, telling them what they
would do after they made it to the oak tree. His brood huddled around him, listening intently. He didn't have to say
more; they knew what it was all about. Each one of them
understood that they had been unable to make enough money
to pay their bills, that Jasmín was very sick and that they
had to get out of the camp. They also knew that they were

surrounded by people in the same situation. That fear had gripped the *campesinos* and their families in a deadly vise, and that instead of trying to help one another, there was likelihood of being denounced if seen trying to escape.

The night was dark as the Calderón family waited for the moment of their flight. The moon was a tiny slit in the sky and the stars sparkled like diamonds, clustering so closely in some places that they created white patches against the velvety blackness. Ana was wide awake. She felt her heart pounding with anticipation and with hope of getting out of that place which had brought them only misery. Now and then she prodded the children with her foot or with her hands when she saw that, overcome by fatigue, they were drifting off to sleep. The only one she rocked and swayed trying to put into a deep sleep was César. Ana feared that he would let out one of his powerful squeals once they began to make their way out of the camp.

Ana closed her eyes, not because she was sleepy but because they seemed to be on fire. She was keenly aware of the different sounds around her. She could hear humming and a lilting ballad at the far edge of the camp. She heard forks scraping against tin plates, children whimpering, muffled conversations here and there interrupted by laughter; she wondered what anyone had to laugh about. Soon, however, those sounds began to recede until there was only an occasional banging of the outhouse door. When Ana opened her eyes, she saw that the camp fires had burned down to embers glowing in the middle of circles of bodies covered with *sarapes* and cast-off flour sacks.

When she looked to where her father crouched she was able to make out the whites of his eyes and Ana saw that they were glowing almost as brightly as the dying embers of their campfire. She knew that he was ready; and she, too, was ready. Wordlessly the signal was given to one another. It was time to go.

Taking only what she was wearing, Ana rolled César tightly into a gunny sack. Then she slung him over her back and tied the material around her chest and waist. Accustomed to her body, the boy didn't wake up. She took Cruz and Pilar by the hand and slowly, as if walking on something fragile, made her way around and sometimes over bodies. As they moved farther away from their family, the three silhouettes seemed to float toward the outhouse until they disappeared into the night.

Rodolfo, clenching his teeth, forced himself to let a minute pass before he turned to Alejandra. He shuddered, however, when he caught the glimmer of tears on her face. He crept close to her, and as he took her hand, he realized that it was cold and that she was trembling.

"'Apá, I'm afraid!" He had not counted on anyone being afraid. Rodolfo paused, apprehensive, feeling the air siphoning out of his stomach. Suddenly he turned to Octavio. "You'll have to do it." Then, looking at the girls, he whispered, "Come here!" He took Zulma and Rosalva by the hand, pulling them close to him. "You'll have to stick with Tavo. Don't be afraid. You saw how easy it was for Ana. All you kids have to do is follow her. Remember, she's behind the tree waiting for you. Ready?"

Three heads wagged in affirmation. Rodolfo took the hands he was holding and pressed them, one each into Octavio's hands. He knew that the boy was also scared, but that he wouldn't lose his nerve. "Quietly and slowly, Tavo. Remember all the times you've had to go to the toilet at this time and nothing has ever happened. Think that I'll be coming right after you and that you'll be safe."

Holding hands, the three children cautiously inched their way toward the outhouse. Everything seemed to be going right until the noise of clanking tin tore at the silence. One of the children had stumbled on a plate. There was stirring, and someone grumbled, "Damn kid! Watch where you're going!" Rodolfo, holding his breath, caught sight of the three forms vanishing behind the outhouse. Then there was silence.

Again forcing himself to let time slip by, Rodolfo took Jasmín into his arms. He was unable to know if she was asleep or unconscious. His heart sank, however, when his fingers and forearms felt that her small body had become so thin and frail that it weighed hardly anything. Shocked, he cradled his daughter against his body as he felt the bones of her rib cage dig into his flesh. He had known for days that his daughter was ill, but it wasn't until that moment that he realized how close she was to death.

These sensations instantly diffused the fear that had been building up inside of Rodolfo. The few seconds that had elapsed between the moment he had taken Jasmín in his arms and his understanding of her condition forced him to become acutely aware of only one thing, and that was that he had to take his child to where she could be helped. He moved swiftly to his feet and began to make his way toward the outhouse. Alejandra followed him nervously.

Without thinking, he cast away all the precautions he had mapped out for himself; he didn't even bother to crouch or to step carefully and quietly. He was indifferent to whatever he might step on causing a commotion, or what he might trip on, or that he might awaken this or that other person. At that moment Rodolfo was aware of only one thing: that if anyone blocked his way, he would kill that person. Nothing, he realized, could stop him from taking this child as well as the other ones out of that camp of wretchedness and degradation.

No one noticed the man holding the skinny child in his arms. Rodolfo and Alejandra made it to the outhouse and beyond to the oak tree, where the others were waiting for them. Without speaking, he led his brood, walking away from the ranch toward the road leading to Hermosillo. The night became less dark as time passed, but the dust churned up by their feet began to make everyone cough.

"'Apá, where are we going. I'm tired."

"We're almost there. Just a little bit more."

Finally, they turned a bend in the road and came up to a battered Model-T truck. The driver jumped out from his seat and approached Rodolfo. They spoke for a while, apparently haggling, almost arguing in a low tone of voice. Ana now understood what her father's whisperings over past days had meant. It had all been part of a plan to get them away from *Rancho la Concepción*.

The stranger looked at the children who stood in a circle around him. "*¡Vámonos!*"

Rodolfo laid Jasmín on the front seat of the cab, then the men helped the rest of the children onto the rear end of the truck. The driver, Reyes Soto, told them to hang on tight because they were going a long way, and that when they woke up next day, they would be on the other side of the border in a town called Nogales.

Their names were Harry and Opal Carney, and it was the first time we had ever seen people like them. They looked different and we couldn't understand their language, but they were kind to us when they saw that Jasmín was sick. They even got a doctor for her, but it was too late. My sister died a little bit after we arrived in Nogales.

When we had crossed the border, Reyes stopped at a gas station while we went to the toilet. Everyone except Jasmín. I think it was then that Reyes became frightened because when we returned, he said that we had to get help for her right away. He turned to a frame house across the street from the station and told us to wait a minute while he went for help. In the meantime, my father took Jasmín out of the truck and ran after Reyes. The rest of us followed him. When a tall, thin, white lady came to the door, we were all standing at the bottom of the stairs looking up at her.

She looked surprised when she opened the door, but she was friendly because, instead of telling us to go away, she stepped out onto the porch and spoke to the driver. Reyes was a pocho, so he could speak her language. But that wasn't necessary because her eyes landed on Jasmín almost immediately. The lady went over to my father and led him into the house. From where I was standing I could see a man, just as white and almost as thin as she was. There was a kid, too, who looked a few years older than me.

While my father was in the house, the rest of us sat on the steps not saying anything. The lady came out in a few minutes, and with her hands and eyes invited us into her kitchen where she sat us around a table. She was warming soup that she first took to Jasmín in another room. Then she returned and served us each a bowl.

Before eating, we looked at each other not knowing what to do. We were just a little bit scared because we couldn't see where our father was. But we were so hungry that soon we forgot that we were frightened and began to eat. We had never tasted that kind of soup before, and we all thought that it was delicious.

Then we saw the boy run in the front door with another man behind him, and we noticed that he carried a small suitcase in his hand. We saw that he, too, disappeared into the same room where we knew Jasmín and our father were. It wasn't long before my father stepped out of the room and we

*could tell that our sister had died because he leaned against
the wall with his eyes closed. I left the table and went to stand
by his side, but he seemed not to notice me. I reached out to
put my hand on his arm, and even though he moved away
from me abruptly, I stood looking at the wall for a long time
wishing that I could tell 'Apá that inside of me I knew what he
was feeling.*

*We buried Jasmín in a plot of ground in the cemetery out-
side of town. Harry and Opal Carney collected enough money
from their neighbors and from several churches to buy the
grave and a coffin. All of this happened so fast that none of us
were able to understand, and it was Reyes Soto who explained
to us that there was no special reason why those people were
helping us, except that they just wanted to help us.*

*Immediately after Jasmín's death, Señora Carney contact-
ed all her women friends and neighbors and got them to come
to her house for a meeting. She invited us children to come
and sit in the front parlor as the ladies squeezed into it. None
of us knew what they were saying, but I recall that we weren't
afraid because their eyes were kind and they smiled at us
when they asked one of us to sit nearby. We were amazed at
how they spoke in soft tones as they passed small cups of tea to
one another.*

*Soon after their meeting, the women went up and down
the streets until they collected clothes for us to wear at our sister's funeral. We knew that the dresses and things we got were
used, but they looked almost new. Tavo got a nice suit, and
even though the legs were too long, its brown tweed color made
his skin look better than ever. The rest of us, even César, got
things to wear, including shoes. Mr. Carney lent my father a
hat and a black jacket to wear over his overalls .*

*When it was time to bury Jasmín, the Carney family and
all their neighbors accompanied us to the church where a
priest named Father O'Dawd said mass. I was surprised that
everyone went with us because, even then, I knew that they
had a different religion. From the church, everyone walked
behind the priest and the coffin to the cemetery.*

*Before we arrived, Pilar pulled at my hand and said, "I
think the box is too small. What will happen when Jasmín
grows more?" When I told her, "Our sister isn't going to grow
anymore," Pilar began to cry. I put my arm around her as we
walked because I didn't know what to say.*

Summer was ending by then and there was a cold wind blowing in our direction; it came from the desert. As our procession entered the cemetery, I looked up to see the eucalyptus trees that surrounded the grounds. They were swaying in the breeze, making a hissing and rustling sound. The sky was so gray that I told myself that soon it would begin to rain.

When we arrived, the priest motioned to my father and us children to come close to him. Then he waved his arms, telling us to form a half circle behind him. As we got near to him, we saw that a hole had already been dug. The sight of this startled us so much that we instinctively drew away from the place. None of us had ever seen such a deep pit, not even the one in which our mother had been buried. I looked at my father and saw that his face was like a wooden mask. His mouth was tightly sealed and his mustache drooped downward, hanging limply on his chin. His eyes looked tiny, flinty; he seemed filled with rage and pain.

Father O'Dawd finished the prayers and handed my father a small crucifix that had been taped to Jasmín's coffin. He took it from the priest without saying a word and put the cross into his hip pocket. Then the priest came close to the rest of us, saying something that we couldn't understand. But when he realized this, he turned to Señora Carney and said the same thing to her. She followed his instruction by placing her hand on the coffin, and as if it had been a signal, two men began to lower the box into the deep hole.

The twins suddenly let out a howl so shrill and loud that everyone seemed jolted out of their place; our bodies flinched without thinking. The girls' weeping intensified with each second, growing more and more disconcerting. Their mouths were wide open, and no one, not my father or me or Señora Carney, could convince them to stop their wailing.

Pilar and Cruz wrapped their arms around me and cried, their small bodies shaking uncontrollably. I could see that everyone was deeply touched by my sisters' grief because men and women began to pull out handkerchiefs, even though no one had known Jasmín. I looked up to my father and saw that he had turned away, hiding his face.

I was the only one who didn't cry because I didn't feel like it. I was happy for Jasmín. I felt joy that she would not live to be worn out like the women we left behind in the Río Yaqui desert, nor would she ever commit a sin that would cause her heart to break, as had happened to the woman at the Shrine. Down deep I was glad that my sister would not be like our mother, who had died screaming from pain caused by something that slowly grew in her head. Instead of feeling sorrow, I wondered if Jasmín had ever had dreams like those that I used to have, even at her age. I told myself that if she did have those hopes, at least now she would not see them crushed, as I had seen mine destroyed when I realized that I was like all other women, and that I would never be loved by my father because I wasn't a boy.

I returned to Nogales about fifteen years ago. I went to the Carney family house only to find that it had been torn down and that in its place a small county library had been built. I visited the cemetery that used to be on the outskirts of town and discovered that it was now surrounded by houses and factories. I spent a long time walking through the grounds, reading the headstones and plaques until I found the place where Jasmín was buried. The wooden marker placed by the Carney family was collapsing and the writing on it was no longer legible. Before leaving the city, I ordered a new marble headstone. I had it erected to mark the place where Jasmín, still a little girl, had lain for so many years."

❧

Reyes Soto was born and raised in East Los Angeles, where he had lived all his life. He had only gone as far as the eighth grade in school, but he was able to make a good living because he could do just about anything with his hands. He could paint a house, fix its plumbing, tape a couple of wires together so that a light bulb would go on, replace or repair broken auto parts, and weld pieces of metal together so efficiently that they would stay in place, never again to split apart.

Reyes' main business was scouring East Los Angeles junk yards to retrieve salvageable parts and sometimes entire engines. He repaired and overhauled those things, and when he had a truckload of water and gas pumps, engine blocks, axles, pistons and rods, he headed south of the border. The huge Sonora ranch spreads were his usual markets because there he had built up a solid reputation for his goods. Whatever parts Reyes Soto sold, he stood by. The ranchers, whose tractors and irrigating equipment were in constant need of repair, knew that whatever they purchased from him worked.

On return trips, Reyes sometimes gave one or two riders a lift up north of the border. He didn't do this for money; the only thing he asked from passengers was to chip in for gas, and for what they bought to eat on the road. It was on one of these trips that Reyes came in contact with Rodolfo Calderón. It had happened indirectly through the words of a *campesino* who had told him of the family and of a sick child.

In the beginning, Reyes had hesitated because he realized that they were probably running away from the *patrón* of *Rancho la Concepción*. Reyes understood the situation, but the fact that it was only one man with his hands full of kids did something to Reyes. He wanted to help.

He agreed to ferry them north, but only as far as the Arizona side of Nogales. With Jasmín's death, however, he became personally involved with Rodolfo and the children, and Reyes began to have doubts about leaving them behind. He had been, after all, the one who had taken the risk of running up to the Carney house looking for help. It had been he who had translated for Rodolfo and who had contacted the priest who immediately went to work with the Carneys to scrape up money and clothing for the family.

Reyes began to think that if he left them in Nogales, the Calderón family would have no other alternative except to head east to the cotton fields of Texas, or toward Colorado to the beet harvesting. He concluded that if that happened, more than likely the rest of the children would die off one by one, just like Jasmín.

After the funeral, Rodolfo and Reyes stood in front of the Carney house. Reyes, his head hanging low and his hands plunged into his pockets, was distractedly tapping the tip of his boot against the front tire of his truck.

"Look, Señor Calderón. I never do this, and I wouldn't except for the kids. Why don't you come to Los Angeles with me? Things are real tough, but I know that you'll be able to make a living for them. There's a school where I know they can go."

Reyes spoke with a lilting, up and down rhythm. The

Spanish he spoke was interlaced with English words, as well as with expressions that were a combination of English and Spanish. Some of it escaped Rodolfo, but most of it was clear to him. His face, which up to that moment had been cast in sadness, lit up for a moment.

"That city is on the coast, isn't it? I'm a fisherman, you know."

Letting out a shrill, whistling sound between his tongue and teeth, Reyes said, "Look, *ese*, you got it all wrong. I'm talking of East Los Angeles and, believe me, there ain't no fishing there!" He emphasized the word *East* as if trying to engrave it on the other man's mind. However, when Reyes saw confusion and disappointment on Rodolfo's face, he continued speaking. "You have strong hands, Señor Calderón. I know you'd be good with a hammer, or a screwdriver, or with a pick and shovel, wouldn't you?" Reyes was very close to Rodolfo's face as he spoke. His eyes reflected his emotion; his fear that the other children would also die.

"Sí, Reyes."

"Just call me Ray. All my friends do."

Rodolfo's voice was soft as he answered, disregarding the nickname. "Reyes, let's go thank Mr. & Mrs. Carney."

The whole group walked up to the front door. This time it was Rodolfo who knocked at the door. Again Mrs. Carney appeared and, smiling, asked everyone to come in. Her husband and son were standing in the middle of the parlor.

"Reyes, please tell this family how grateful I and my children are for all their kindness and for helping us. Without them and their friends, we would have been lost. Tell them, please, that one day we'll be in a position to thank them as we should. For right now..."

"Hey, Rudy, just a second! I can translate just so much at a time." Reyes interrupted Rodolfo, using the nickname that would cause him much irritation later on. Reyes turned to the Carneys and paraphrased Rodolfo's sentiments. He added also that the family was coming with him all the way to Los Angeles and that they would begin the trip immediately.

This time Rodolfo broke in while Reyes spoke. "Tell them that I and my kids have one last favor to ask them. Would they please take flowers to Jasmín's grave on her birthday? It's the fifth of December."

When they understood what had been asked of them, all

three Carneys nodded their head in affirmation.

Once in the truck, Reyes sat for a long time without speaking and without moving, as if listening to a voice. A few minutes passed before he said, "Rudy, we're going to do this right. I don't want the *Migra* to come sniffing around my porch later on. You got the kids' papers on you?"

"Papers? What kind of papers?"

"Anything! A birth certificate, or something like that to prove that they're yours."

Pushing César onto the seat next to him, Rodolfo pulled out the sweat-soiled pouch from under his shirt, using both hands to draw open the thick cord that held it together. He withdrew a few pesos and the photograph that by now was crinkled and badly bent. Next he pulled out a folded wad of yellowed papers, and unfolding it, he handed it to Reyes.

"Let me see. Okay, Rudy! These look like baptism papers. That ought to take care of business. *¡Vámonos!*" Cranking on the motor, Reyes made a screeching U-turn and headed back toward the border.

It was a short drive to the front of a small office which had the words "U.S. Immigration" stenciled on the window in large, white letters. When the group filed into the office, it was empty except for a uniformed man seated behind a scratched wooden desk. The suddenness with which the group entered startled the man.

"Whoaa! What have we here?"

Reyes, somewhat nervous, approached the official and stated their wish to be legalized in the U.S. He explained that they were traveling with him to Los Angeles, where a job was waiting for the father. As he spoke, Reyes partially turned to Rodolfo, indicating with his hand that this was the person in question.

"Hmm. It's a bunch of them, you know. But, just a minute. To begin with, let me see some papers from you."

When Reyes produced the small, crinkled card from his wallet, the man scrutinized it. "Born in the U.S.A., huh? Where?...Oh, never mind...it's all the same." Nodding his head in the direction of the family, he said, "You sure you're going to stuff them all into your house? They can't be on the streets, you know."

"No, sir."

"Well, for openers, let's get a look at their papers."

When Reyes gestured to Rodolfo for the papers, he handed them to the officer. The official spread them out in the
order in which Rodolfo had given them to him. He placed the
documents on the desk top one by one. He took time, carefully
looking at each certificate. As he did this he called out the
name inscribed on the paper, despite his difficulty with pro-
nunciation. He paused to look at each girl as she responded,
"*Aquí, señor.*" When he read out Jasmín's name, no one spoke
up, and there was an uncomfortable silence. Wrinkling his
brow, the official called out César's name as he looked directly at Octavio. But when everyone pointed instead at the little
boy, the officer became confused.

He got to his feet, taking the few seconds he needed to
collect his thoughts. He was a tall man, well over six feet, and
when he stood at his full height, Reyes and Rodolfo looked up
at him in unconcealed amazement. The children, open-
mouthed and head bent back as far as their necks would
allow, looked at him as they would have a giant.

The man, placing his hands on his waist as he wrapped
his fingers around his leather belt, stuck out his chin in their
direction as he blurted out, "Just a minute, here! Let me get
this straight. It sure looks like we got us a problem, you
know."

Everyone froze. The tall man continued speaking as his
penetrating blue eyes looked straight at Reyes. "According to
what I see in front of me, we've either got an extra boy and
one missing girl, or...or..." The children, sensing that something very serious was about to happen, audibly sucked in
their breath. "...or that kid's name," he pointed a thick, long
index finger at Octavio, "is Jasmín!"

Somehow, they all understood his meaning. They seemed
relieved and the girls laughed at Octavio, who looked painfully embarrassed at being confused for a girl. Reyes snapped
his head over to Rodolfo, half-whispering. "Do you have anything for the kid?"

"No. He's an orphan. No one knows where he came from,
much less who his family is, or when or where he was born."

"Hey! Cut out the jabbering and give me an explanation."

Reyes responded immediately. "Look, officer, here's the
story. First, the girl Jasmín died; just yesterday. We buried
her a while ago. If you don't believe me, you can call Immacu-
late Heart Chur...."

The inspector held up the palm of his hand, signaling Reyes to stop speaking. He pursed his lips together as he lowered his head in thought; his forehead was wrinkled. After a few moments, he spoke. His voice had mellowed. "No. It's not worth the phone call. I believe you." Raising his head, his eyes scanned the children's faces; the man appeared to have softened. "I believe it. It's no wonder they're not all dead. I don't know how they do it."

Then returning to his seat, he said, "We've still got the problem about this kid's identity. How do I know if he's not here against his will? I can't let him go through just like that." He snapped his fingers. "Ask Señor if he's got anything that will prove to me that the boy's been with the family from the beginning."

He waited, this time patiently as Reyes whispered to Rodolfo who, as if suddenly struck by a completely new idea, remembered the picture that he was holding. In it was Octavio. Grabbing it from Rodolfo's fingers, Reyes turned to the inspector. "Look, he has a family picture that shows the kid right up there with them. This picture's not even two years old."

He handed the officer the photograph. He peered at it, looking up and checking each child's face as his finger moved across the picture. He paused on one face and muttered, "This must be the mom. Dead, too, I'll bet."

After rubbing his eyes and cheeks, the officer continued speaking, "Okay. You're all lucky we're still doing it this way. Soon crossing will get tough, you know. Anyway, the registration fee for each one of them will be six bits. Here, take these forms over to the other room. Fill them out. We need a picture of the father and each kid. That'll cost a nickel a piece. In the next room you'll find Artie Hess. He's the court photographer, you know."

The man, finding this last remark funny, laughed out loud, heaving his mid-section in and out. The group filed out of the room, and it took several hours before they were handed a group visa. It was a large document. On it were printed words none of them could decipher; a large, spread-out eagle was stamped at its top, and each of their pictures was pasted to the bottom of the paper. César was taken in the same shot with his father. Pilar and Cruz were also paired off. On their own were Octavio, Zulma, Rosalva, Alejandra and Ana. Only

Ana's eyes burned with a strange brilliance that even the years that intervened between the time of that photo and when she became a grown woman would not diminish.

~∞~

As things worked out, Reyes Soto and his family became so close to us that people thought that we were cousins, aunts and uncles. I've never known why he did so much for us at a time when he could have walked away from us. What's important, however, is that he didn't. I mean, he didn't leave us in Nogales where we probably would have had a life much different than it turned out to be.

He was a man about my father's age. When he came into our lives, I think he must have been around forty, maybe just a little less, or a little more. He was a short man and, because of this, he held himself very straight, with his shoulders arched up as if trying to stretch himself just a little more. He had bushy brown hair that coiled upwards, each hair seeming to be a separate curl. His face was round and so were his eyes, which were cheerful most of the time. He wore a thin mustache that was dark when we first knew him, and later on it turned gray, just like his hair. Reyes was one of those men who lived his entire life without becoming bald.

As the years passed, he liked to tell everyone that he was a pachuco. *He even tried to adopt the words and expressions such as "Ese Vato Loco" when speaking to men, and "Esa Huisa" when speaking to women. But no, Reyes was never a* pachuco. *He was was from East Los Angeles, but he was never one of those angry young men who dressed up just so that someone could come and attack them.*

I know that for us he was a hero because he rescued us from the desert, and from a trap that would have destroyed us. Reyes guided us from that terrible place to where we finally made our home. There are some parts of that trip that brought us to Los Angeles that I've forgotten, and others that I'll always remember. I'll never forget that even though my father's money ran out before we even got to Yuma, Reyes continued to pay for the gas and for what we ate on the road. I remember the desert we had to cross, and how Reyes put a big

*canvas cover over us, trying to keep the sun and sand from
hurting us.*

*The girls couldn't help themselves; they cried a lot because
of the intense heat that burned their skin during the day and
because of the cold at night. When darkness overtook us at the
end of each day, Reyes stopped the truck and we had to spend
the night out in the desert, in the middle of nowhere. We had
very little to eat, but he was careful to make sure that we had
enough water to drink. I think, however, that my sisters cried
mostly because they were afraid. Octavio and Alejandra didn't
seem to mind any part of that trip; they played their usual
games. Most of the time they were oblivious to the rest of us
and to what was happening.*

*When we crossed over into California and into the
Imperial Valley, Reyes stopped at the Salton Sea. We all loved
it there because it was the first time we had come close to
water since we left Puerto Real. I looked around, however, and
saw that behind me was all desert, and that it was different
from the cove of my memories.*

*We went to Coachella and Indio, and when we got to the
orchards where the fruit of the palm trees is cultivated, Reyes
made a special stop just so we could taste that fruit.*

*As we moved closer to Los Angeles, I noticed that more
and more people looked like the Carney family and the officer
who had scared us because he was so tall. I liked to listen to
those people speak; I liked their language. I didn't know then
that soon I would be able to speak with them.*

*'Apá became more silent; he spoke very little and he
seemed to be shrinking. He never spoke to me except to tell me
to help César or to move over in the truck. He didn't look at me
at those times, either. I mean, he didn't look at my face when
he spoke to me, as if I had been invisible. Now and then when
he did look into my eyes, I knew that it had been an accident
because I could feel the icicles that were inside of his eyes.*

*When we got to Riverside, Reyes told us all to relax
because soon we'd be in Los Angeles. He didn't call the city by
its name. Instead he always said L.A., so we lived for years
thinking that we lived in a town named L.A.*

*My first memory of the fringes of Los Angeles is of long
tracks of flowers on the left side of the road as we headed for
Reyes' house, and to the right of us were sloping hills that
looked soft and golden in the declining sun. With the desert of*

the Yaqui River Valley still in our mind, the sight of those
strips that alternated in red, white, lavender, amber, and then
red again filled us with excitement. There were so many flow-
ers that none of us could see where they ended. Jasmín came
back into my mind because I remembered that 'Amá once told
me that she had named my sister after a flower because she
was born at dawn, when the sky was the color of lilacs and
lilies.

As the truck slid alongside the flowers, I stretched my neck
over to the driver's side of the cab and shouted to Reyes, "Is
this where we're going to live?"

"No," he yelled back. "It all belongs to Chapos. They're the
people who grow flowers and sell them at the main market in
town."

I told myself that I would like to work with those people,
even though at that time I didn't know what a Japanese per-
son looked like.

When Reyes saw how excited we all were because of the flow-
ers, he stopped the truck and stuck his head out the window.
"This road is called Floral Drive because of all the flowers."

Soon after, we went down a steep hill to where the truck
made a turn on Humphrys Avenue, and there Reyes stopped.
He jumped out and announced, "We have arrived!" He shout-
ed out his wife's name, and in a minute a very pretty woman
came out of the front door. She was followed by several chil-
dren, girls and boys, and they all looked just like Reyes.

હેબ્ર

"It's only a garage, Rudy, but you and the kids can stay
here until we find you a job. Tomorrow I'll take you over to
some of the junk yards. I think something will turn up."

"'Apá, where are we going to eat?" Zulma blurted out
what everyone was thinking, but her father ignored the question.

Rodolfo, with the children huddled behind him, stood in
the middle of a rickety garage with a dirt floor. "Gracias,
Reyes. I'm grateful. As soon as I can work, maybe we can find
a house."

"Yeah." Reyes looked at Zulma and said, "You can eat in

the kitchen with my kids. We got a lot of rice and beans."
Then turning to Rodolfo, "In the meantime, my wife told me
that the older kids better start off in school right away."

"'Apá!...'" Several voices shouted out in protest.

"We don't know how to talk the way they do here. How
can we go to school?" Alejandra confronted Rodolfo. "Why
don't we work with you? That way we can get a house right
away."

Rodolfo and Reyes looked at one another and then at the
children. "No, Aleja, you need just a little bit of school. After
that, you can start working."

It was late September when the Calderón children joined
the rest of the barrio kids who walked to Hammel Street
School. Ana and Octavio were placed in the sixth grade and
Alejandra in the third, and their fear of not knowing how to
speak English disappeared once they saw that most of the
children were just like them.

Ana felt older than the other children in her class, but
she liked school. It was difficult for her to forget the tomato
fields and the women who had worked by her side. Her mind,
however, was captivated from the beginning with learning
the new language, and she concentrated on how her teacher
used pictures and the blackboard to teach new words.

At the end of the first day in school, as Señora Soto was
serving them dinner, the Calderón and Soto children jabbered about their experiences. When the noise got so loud,
the woman was forced to shush them into silence. After a few
minutes, the talking began all over again.

Ana looked at Octavio and said, "I learned to say some
words in English. How about you?"

Octavio smiled at her, exposing the contents of his stuffed
mouth, but he didn't answer her question. Alejandra made a
face of disgust as she said, "I hated it. I don't want to be by
myself with a bunch of kids I don't know. I wish we could go
back home. I liked it better there."

"Ana and me were put with the older kids because we're
smarter than you." Octavio laughed, showing her that he
liked being in the same classroom with Ana. But Alejandra
resented it when he bragged about himself and Ana. She felt
insulted and could only glare at him as she mumbled,
"*Burro!*"

Ana thought of the cove back home, the palm trees, and

how she, her sister, and Octavio spent most of their time playing by the water. She looked down at the plate in front of her and wondered why she felt so different now. Not much time had passed, she told herself, and yet she didn't want to play with either Octavio or Alejandra any more. She spoke up again. "I liked the teacher a lot." Looking at Alejandra, she explained, "Her name is Miss Nugent, and she told me that if I try, I can learn right away."

"Liar! How could she tell you that if she doesn't know how to speak like us?" Alejandra challenged her sister's remark.

Ana stopped, fork in mid-air, wondering how it had happened. "No. I'm not a liar, and even if I don't know how she told me, still, I understood her."

Alejandra jumped out of her chair with the pretext of putting her plate in the sink, but once she was behind Ana, she put horns over her head, making everyone laugh.

The days that followed turned into weeks and months. Ana became fond of school. She learned new words every day until she began to put them together, and by the end of the term, she was able to stay after school to talk with Miss Nugent while helping to clean the blackboard and dust off the erasers.

Octavio, on the other hand, was not interested in learning anything, and from the first day, instead of concentrating on what the teacher was showing them, decided to become the class clown. He had a winning way about him, so much that he even became the teacher's preferred student almost immediately, despite his disinterest in her lessons.

He noticed his impact on girls, and when he realized that there was something about him that made them like him, he fooled around, intentionally making them blush and giggle. He liked that very much, and he soon understood that he had a special personality, one which made him admired even by the boys.

He was taller than most of them, and his features were already striking. His skin had a rich, dark mahogany tone and his hair, also dark brown, was wavy and shiny. His eyes were slanted and large, like those of a cat. His brow was medium-sized and his nose tended to be long and slender. His mouth was sensitive, and it appeared to be developing a sensuousness that would intensify as he grew older.

The months passed and by the time the first year of

school ended for the Calderón children, Rodolfo was able to rent a small house across the street from the Reyes place. He needed help, however, and when most of the families of the barrio migrated up to Fresno and Salinas for the summer harvesting, he told Ana, Octavio, and Alejandra that they had to join the others and go to work.

"'Apá, let me stay here to look after the kids." Ana didn't want to return to the fields, to the outhouses, to the drunken Saturday nights. When her father turned his face away from her, she pressed him with more intensity. "I can cook for you and the kids, really I can. Please let me stay and…"

"No! You have to earn your keep. Don't think you're fooling me; I know that the only reason you want to stay is to read more books. You're a lazy girl, Ana, but you don't fool your father. When you return in September, I expect you to bring money enough to pay for your food during the year."

"But 'Apá…"

"*Silencio!*"

Ana did as her father ordered, and she did this each summer until she ended the tenth grade in school. During the school year, however, she was able to read and keep in contact with her grammar-school teacher, Miss Nugent. But the more she learned, the more separated Ana felt from Octavio and Alejandra. And, she felt her father's resentment growing with each year.

$$\mathcal{L}\!\!\ll\!\!\mathcal{D}$$

Just as the tenth grade was ending, 'Apá told me that I had to quit school. He said it to me as he was passing through the kitchen on the way out the back door. At first I thought that I hadn't understood what he had said to me because he spoke, as he always did, with his face turned away from me. I stood for a few seconds staring at the soapy water in the sink before running out to the yard where he was standing.

My voice was shaking, but I asked, "What did you say, 'Apá?"

He repeated his words. "You have to leave school to go to work. I can't feed and clothe all of you on my own anymore. It's up to you and Octavio to share the responsibility."

Without thinking, I began to cry. The desert fields of the Yaqui Valley and the hot orchards of Fresno appeared in my mind. I saw the campesinas; *their haggard, blotched faces were turned looking at me as if waiting for me to join them. Far behind them I saw Miss Nugent inviting me to join her, but she began to grow smaller until she disappeared.*

I pleaded with my father. "'Apá, only two more years, please! That's all I need to finish. After that, I'll be a different person. I can get a good job; maybe in an office." While my mouth formed those words I was thinking of Miss Nugent and how she had shown me that she believed in me and in my ability to learn.

'Apá turned his eyes to look at me, but his eyes were like hot coals. They burned my face, and his words hurt me even more.

"You can't go on thinking that you're better than the other women of the family. A head filled with foolish thoughts means empty hands not only for the woman, but for everyone else around her. Your mother worked with her hands as had her mother, and her mother. She did what God had put her on earth to do: to work and have babies. It's now your time."

I confess that in my heart I longed to raise my hands to strike him, hoping that my fists would be like iron. I wanted to scratch my frustration and disillusionment into his face with my nails, to force open his eyes with my fingers, making him understand once and for all that I was not like my mother and her sisters. But instead of showing him what I was thinking and feeling, I became stiff, frozen, and my mouth was blocked, as if a rag had been stuffed into it. I was remembering the penitent woman at the Shrine, and I wondered if her sin had been that of disobeying her father.

I wanted to run as far as I could, away from his hot, hard eyes, but even then I knew that I had nowhere to run. I lowered my head and went back into the kitchen.

⌘

It was early in the summer of 1937 when Ana and Octavio went to work at a shoe factory located on Alameda Street. Octavio's job was to oil the machines that stamped out leather that later would be fashioned into men's and women's sandals and pumps. Ana worked up front in the finishing department. She put in eight hours a day inspecting each shoe as it came off the conveyor belt, making sure that the stitching on the toe and heel was properly done.

A few days before beginning work, Ana ended her days in school. She had hardly slept since her father had spoken to her; the night hours dragged by as she tried to think of how to stay in school. At the end of each plan, her mind bumped into the cold glare of her father's eyes until she finally told herself that she had to obey him.

On the last day of school, Ana thought of walking away without saying anything to her teachers, not even to Miss Nugent. But after thinking it over, she decided that she couldn't just disappear; she knew that they would wonder, maybe even worry. She realized that Miss Nugent, especially, would be surprised not to hear from her again. She had demonstrated an interest in Ana over the years, even after she had left grammar school to go on to junior and high school.

Miss Nugent had seen to it that Ana would come twice a week to her classroom for more books. It hadn't been easy because Mr. Calderón had objected, protesting that his daughter should not be out of the house after school hours. He insisted, through Reyes Soto's interpreting, that books were of no use to any of his daughters because they would not help with the feeding and clothing of the family. It was instead, he claimed, a waste of time for Ana, and would only end by giving her false ideas of what life is.

This is what Mr. Calderón emphasized to Miss Nugent. She, on the other hand, persisted in asking that Ana be given permission to continue reading with her for just one semester. When he grudgingly approved, the reading sessions kept up, term after term, until that day in the Spring of 1937 when Ana approached her teacher.

"Miss Nugent, I can't come for my reading session any more. I have to get a job to help out the family."

"What? Ana, what are you talking about? What about your other studies...You mean, you're even pulling out of your regular classes at the high school?"

"Yes."

The teacher was perplexed, even shocked. Her face mir-

rored disbelief at the thought that someone like Ana should
be be yanked out of learning, cut off before she could even
begin to reach her fullness.

"But!... This can't be! I'll talk to your father..."

"It's no use. He told me that he's been patient enough,
that this should have happened a long time ago. Maybe he's
right, Miss Nugent. I mean, look at all the time I spend at
home reading, and...well..."

"Well, what, Ana? Look, you've got talent. God gave you
something special; you have brains. Brains, you hear me? But
they have to be developed and that can only happen here, in
the classroom, and in the library."

The teacher put her hands on the girl's shoulders saying,
"Listen to me, Ana. How old are you?"

"I'm seventeen."

"Well then, hear my words and remember them. If you
give up preparing yourself for a life that is bound to be better
than the one your family left behind, you'll live to regret it.
Believe me. Working can wait. How have all of you got along
up to now, anyway? What changed all of a sudden to make it
necessary for you to drop out of school just a couple of years
before you finish? What's going on, Ana?"

The girl was overwhelmed by her teacher's questions; she
couldn't respond to any of them. She knew that her life was
changing, that its course was now pointing her in a direction
she did not want. She felt powerless, frustrated, but there
was nothing she could do. She realized that there was no way
Miss Nugent could understand, and she closed her eyes
because she was unable to sustain the intensity of her
teacher's gaze.

"I have to do what he says, Miss Nugent. He'll throw me
out of the house if I don't."

"Is there anything I can do, Ana?"

"No. It's no use."

This conversation happened in early June, and through
one of Reyes Soto's contacts, Octavio and Ana began as
laborers in the shoe factory soon afterward. In the beginning,
Ana was overcome by the intensity of the long hours during
which she had to keep up with a conveyor belt. It never
stopped, not for one moment, and many times its constant
motion and purring nauseated her. Until she became used to
the machine, her head throbbed almost constantly during the

first weeks of working at the assembly line, and once her stomach was so upset that she had to leave her place to run to the ladies' room to vomit. When she returned, her supervisor reprimanded her, saying that several shoes had been damaged because of her carelessness.

Octavio easily adjusted to his new way of life. He didn't mind leaving school, and he was pleased, telling himself that now he could work and become a man. He was confident that Ana would see him in a different way, and that the silliness of reading books that had filled her head for so long would disappear, leaving him as the most important thing in her life.

When he went on the job, Octavio was accepted by his fellow workers; they liked his clowning and his usual cheerfulness. He had a good voice for singing Mexican love songs in the men's locker room during his shift. Despite the loud machine noise that made even speaking difficult, his singing could be heard above the din.

Although he was kept busy by his job of going from one machine to the other, Ana thought that his job was easier than hers. In fact, she was convinced that the jobs allotted to the women were all heavier than those of the men. She saw that the women had to be at the end of conveyor belts and had to keep up with their ceaseless, rapid pace. The men, on the other hand, pulled levers, or inserted material, or loaded bobbins of thread. Octavio, she saw, spent eight hours squeezing oil out of a small can.

When the five o'clock hour finally appeared, Ana was so exhausted that she could hardly speak. Octavio, however, seemed ready to leap out onto the street and do something exciting. He prattled gaily as they waited for the streetcar that took them to the bus that finally landed them at the corner of Floral Drive and Mariana Street. He didn't seem to notice Ana's fatigue, much less her depressed mood, and instead he talked about himself and of how happy he was to be working.

Alejandra hated the idea of Octavio and Ana working in the same place, and she begged her father to let her quit school so that she, too, could bring in money. After all, she told him, she was almost fifteen years old, much too old to be in school. Besides, she explained to him, she was bored; she still hated being cooped up in a room with a bunch of stupid kids.

She stopped speaking to Ana because she couldn't help being eaten up by jealousy. She resented that her sister was with Octavio all day long. She detested the way he tried to make her laugh, and Alejandra hated, above all, the manner in which her sister seemed to ignore his efforts. Alejandra saw that the less Ana noticed Octavio's advances, the more intent he seemed on gaining her sister's attention. At the same time, Alejandra saw that he was losing interest in her, and that he was treating her as if she were a little girl, one that should stay out of his and Ana's company.

Nearly two years passed before Ana became accustomed to the factory. She realized one day that her head no longer hurt nor did her stomach churn until she was sick. The depression that had gripped her for almost two years had become less intense, and she found herself thinking, not of the future as she used to before, but more about Octavio. She was surprised, because they had lived together ever since she could remember, and never had she spent time thinking of him.

In the beginning, she forced herself to stop thinking of Octavio, but this became more difficult with each day. Ana noticed new things about him. Her attention was often caught by the way his face had developed. What had been a transparent fuzz had now turned to hard bristle, mostly around his chin and over his lips. She was surprised when he once playfully picked her up in his arms and whirled her around for several seconds. His action was not what startled her, because he had done things like that even when they were in Puerto Real. It was, rather, the strength that she felt in his arms as he took her off her feet. She was astounded at the hardness of his chest and stomach, and she couldn't help feeling that his body and arms had grown, tightened, stretched.

These experiences and sensations made Ana look closely at her body. She noticed that she wasn't flat-chested any more; her breasts had filled, and they were round and firm. Even though her sisters knocked loudly at the bathroom door each morning, she often gazed at the reflection of her naked upper body in the small mirror over the hand basin. She also took time to stand on top of the toilet bowl to look at her lower body in the mirror because she was curious about the course, fuzzy hair that had grown over the mound separating her thighs.

Ana realized that her body had changed. But what engaged her interest most of all were the transformations that she felt inside of her, like the heat she felt gripping the tiny bead buried inside the lips of the hairy mound when she touched herself there. At those times, she discovered that her fingers caused a feeling so intense that her legs shivered.

During the winter months of that year, when the days were short, she and Octavio rode in the streetcar through the dark Los Angeles streets on their return trip home. More and more, Ana found herself enjoying those moments when she forgot how tired she was, and she began to like Octavio's way of laughing, especially how he was able to make a joke out of anything. She found out that she liked to feel his body up against hers when the streetcar filled with people, when they were forced to stand so close to one another that they could feel each other breathing.

By springtime, she and Octavio were inseparable. On Saturdays, when the work shift ended at two in the afternoon, they usually walked slowly from the bus stop to their house. It was on one of those afternoons that Octavio suddenly stopped and said, "Ana, I have a great idea!"

She looked at him, smiling. Recently, it was impossible to look at him without showing how happy she was to be with him. "Oh, yeah? What big idea do you have now?"

"Let's walk all the way up to the hill. It's not a long walk, and we can watch the sunset. Maybe we can even see the ocean from there."

"The ocean! *Ay*, Octavio! I think you've been working too hard." Ana was nearly laughing when she spoke, but her eyes had already accepted his idea.

"Really! Just look at that sky. It's beautiful, and we haven't been up there in a long time. Besides..." Octavio's voice trailed off.

"Besides, what?"

"I mean...it's April."

"I know it's April. What's so special about that?"

"It's my lucky month!"

Octavio took her hand as they walked up the incline to where the small frame houses became more widely separated until they disappeared altogether and the road turned to dirt. They walked in silence, listening only to the soft breeze that hummed as it sifted through the swaying new grass. Above them was a canopy of blue sky.

When they reached the crest of the hill, they found a spot they liked, and without speaking they sat on the grass, which was still warm from the day's heat. Ana and Octavio sat facing the declining sun; its long rays cast golden patches on their hair and cheeks. They breathed in the cool air of the early evening. He held one of her hands as he placed his arm around her shoulders. He drew her close to him because neither of them had ever felt what they were feeling at that moment.

☙❧

When his lips touched mine, I loved Tavo and I knew that at that moment he loved me, too. As we laid on the sweet grass, its fragrance mixed with our breath. We were both intoxicated by desire, and neither one of us wanted to stop it. When we kissed, I felt the earth spin uncontrollably, so much that I thought that Tavo and I would be thrown off its surface to drift away into empty space. I didn't care because I would have given my life to spend eternity with him caught up there where no one could ever reach us.

At first his hands were soft and warm on my body, but soon they began to tremble as he fumbled with my clothes. I felt myself shuddering when he inserted his fingers between my thighs, and even though I knew what would happen if I let him go further, I could not stop. A voice in my brain reminded me of the sinful woman begging for forgiveness at the Virgin's Shrine, but the sound was remote and it gradually grew so still that soon I stopped hearing it.

I was unconsciousness of everything except that Tavo was between my legs, plunging in and out of me, and that what I was feeling was the reason for which I had been born. Everything around me was in motion; I felt the dirt and grass beneath me quake and shift. Then, in a few seconds, the world exploded, giving me a pleasure that I had not imagined possible.

Tavo whispered over and again that he loved me, and I said the same thing to him. When it ended, we remained on the hill locked in each others' arms until darkness covered us.

The crickets began a song that has stayed with me ever since.

As spring turned into summer, Ana and Octavio climbed the hill every evening to make love and to talk about their future. For the time being, they decided to keep their relationship a secret until they had saved enough money for a place of their own. Keeping what they were doing from the others was easy because they had been in each other's company almost constantly for the last two years. However, Ana could not help noticing Alejandra's growing moodiness and her continued refusal to speak to her. But she told herself that as soon as her sister knew that she and Octavio were to be married, she would like the idea and they would be friends.

When she realized how often Alejandra whispered in the kitchen with her father, Ana began to sense that the two of them had noticed something. This feeling grew to apprehension when Ana began to suspect that she was pregnant. June had come and gone, and she had not menstruated. She forced herself to calm down by remembering that her body had probably developed a new pattern now that she was being intimate with Octavio. When July passed and nothing happened, she couldn't conceal her fear. One day on the hill as they watched the sun's last rays, she decided to tell Octavio. He was holding her hand in one of his, and caressing her breast with the other.

"Octavio, when are we going to tell 'Apá that we're going to be married?"

The question startled him. He gawked at Ana as if they had never spoken or planned to tell Rodolfo. He dropped his hands, looking stunned and confused. "What do you mean when are we going to tell him? He'll kill me if he knows what you and I have been doing!"

Ana felt her breath catch in her throat. "What do *you* mean?" She tossed the question back at him. "We've been planning to get married all these weeks, haven't we? How do you expect us to do that without telling 'Apá? Besides, he doesn't have to know about this..." Ana waved her arm, taking in the slope.

Octavio, caught off guard, didn't know what to say, so he placed his elbows on his crossed knees as he cupped his chin in his hands. He clenched his jaw and stared out across the city to where he imagined the blue of the sky connected with the ocean.

Ana looked up and saw a tiny star, the first one for the night. It was twinkling brightly in the gathering darkness. "Tavo...I'm...I think I'm pregnant..."

She stopped speaking, suddenly intimidated by his eyes that snapped in her direction as she stumbled over her words. Octavio glared at her, obviously struggling with emotion because his mahogany-colored skin took on a pinkish hue and his eyes filled with tears. Ana sensed intense fear and anger in him when he leaped to his feet.

"Jesus!...No! Why didn't you do something?...Pregnant! Tell me this isn't so!"

"I can't tell you that it's not true because it probably is!" Ana's voice had also risen; it was filled with apprehension and confusion. "Besides, Tavo, so what if I am pregnant? We're going to get married, aren't we?"

He had turned his back, and Ana, still sitting on the grass, could see only the back of his legs. Octavio was digging one of his heels into the earth. She repeated her words as she looked up at the back of his head, "Aren't we?"

He whirled around, looking down at her. "Not yet, Ana! Not yet!" He was almost shouting. "I thought that we would wait a couple of years..."

He was interrupted by Ana, who had by now also gotten to her feet. "A couple of years! Tavo, what do you think we've been doing here all these weeks? I can't wait a couple of years, you hear me? I can't even wait a couple of months before 'Apá and everybody else knows what's inside of me!"

Ana sat down again. She drew her knees up to her chin while she covered her face with both hands. She was silent, her body was hunched over, overwhelmed by an invisible weight. The wind made a soft sound as it curled through the long grass. Far away, the echo of a barking dog drifted towards them.

After a few minutes, Octavio crouched next to her in an attempt to make her feel better. "Look, Ana, no use worrying so much over this thing. I guess I'll tell your father..."

"When, Tavo?" Ana turned her face up, bursting in on his words.

Her eyes frightened him; he had never seen such intensity. He didn't like what he saw, and he disliked Ana even more for looking at him that way. He resented the growing feeling of being trapped and of having to do what she wanted, when she wanted.

"Soon, that's when." Without another word, he got up and began walking down the hill, not waiting for Ana, who remained sitting for a few minutes. Even when she called out to him to wait for her, he pretended not to hear her and, almost running, he scrambled down the road, arriving alone at the house.

Ana and Octavio hardly spoke to one another during the following days. They communicated rarely on their way to work and said nothing to one another while at the factory. In the meantime, Ana's fears mounted with each day. She had no doubt now that she was pregnant, and she was intensely aware of Alejandra's scrutiny. She sensed that her father, too, was studying her, keeping his eyes on her while she was not looking. This happened especially when she was in the kitchen, during her turns to cook or wash the dishes.

Except for the constant chatter of the younger children, conversation was strained between the older ones, and Octavio, whose face was tightly drawn and nervous, hardly spoke to anyone. The days dragged by for Ana until she couldn't tolerate the strain of not knowing what to do next. During one of their lunch breaks at the factory, she asked Octavio to sit alone with her.

"If you're afraid to tell 'Apá, I'll tell him."

"No! Are you, crazy or something, Ana?" Nearly jumping up from the bench, Octavio hissed the words through clenched teeth. His brow furrowed with near terror. "I said I would tell him, and I will! Jesus...Ana...why are you trying to push me around? Give me time, please! I promised that I'll tell him, and I will!"

"I don't have time, Tavo, don't you understand? Here, look for yourself." Ana lifted the apron she was wearing. A noticeable bulge raised her dress at the waist. "This is growing every day...every minute!"

"¡Ay, Dios!" Octavio groaned as he wrung his hands.

When he didn't say anymore, Ana spoke, "What's the

matter with you? I don't understand why you're afraid to tell 'Apá. He knows that all of us are eventually going to get married and have babies. That's all he's been telling me ever since I can remember. He'll say it's okay for us to marry. Honest to God, Tavo, I don't understand why you're scared."

"Because I'm like your brother, that's why. Your father will kill me! He'll say that's why he didn't want me to come with the family when you left Puerto Real. Besides, what will Alejandra say?"

Octavio's claim to be as close as a brother faded when he mentioned Alejandra's name. Stunned at what he had just let out, she felt as if her breath had been knocked out of her. "Alejandra! Alejan...What does she have to do with this? Tell me, Tavo! What does my sister have to do with this?" Ana had raised her voice so that several of the other workers began to stare in their direction.

Intimidated, Octavio made shushing sounds as he tried to calm Ana by nervously patting her shoulders. At the same time, he smiled sheepishly at the people looking at them. He lowered his voice, almost to a whisper, "Forget I said that, Ana. I didn't mean it."

She looked at the floor, thinking about what Octavio had just said. Suddenly she stood; her voice was calm and steady. "It's an excuse. This brother thing is just your way out, isn't it Tavo? You have something going on with my sister, don't you? That's why you don't want anybody to know about me and you."

Ana took a few steps away from Octavio, but then she turned, coming close to him again. "Well, whatever it is, Tavo, I'm going to tell you one thing. This is yours," she pointed at her belly, "and you're not going to get out of it."

She worked the rest of the day as if in a dream. She was numb and her body seemed to be made of stone. She felt nothing; the only sensation she was aware of was coldness. Her insides were freezing, as were her hands, but her forehead, despite her shivering, was beaded with perspiration. During the hours she passed in inspecting shoes, Ana resolved that she wouldn't do or say anything. She decided that there was nothing she could do to change things or to avoid whatever it was that was going to happen to her.

Two months passed and still Octavio said nothing. He and Ana no longer met while alone, and when they were on the bus or the streetcar, they separated, he in one seat and she in another. She noticed, however, that he seemed relieved as time passed, as if he believed that she had invented the entire thing. She saw, too, that he was regaining his usual playfulness, except now it was directed at others and not at her. And she knew that he spent most of his time chatting and giggling with Alejandra, who strutted around the house showing Ana that she was relaxed and happy.

❧❦

My pregnancy was becoming more apparent, and I had to wear baggy dresses and sweaters so that no one could see how my body was changing. I couldn't be like Tavo, who decided to be a clown. Instead, sadness was devouring me and it became deeper each day because I knew that sooner or later my father would notice my growing belly. On that day, I was positive, all the anger and bitterness against me which he had kept trapped in his heart would overflow.

❧❦

It was cold and windy on the Sunday morning of Ana's turn to make breakfast, and everyone was still asleep. She had been unable to sleep that night, so when the first glimmer of gray light broke through the shade in her room, Ana left the bed that she shared with Rosalva. She dressed quietly, making sure to slip on the oversized sweater that she now wore constantly.

When she went into the kitchen she was startled by Rodolfo, who was sitting at the table staring out the window. Through it he could catch sight of the alley that bordered their back yard. Nothing was moving out there; everyone in the barrio was asleep. He seemed not to notice when Ana came into the kitchen. She deliberately clanked the coffee can against the sink.

"*Buenos días*, 'Apá."

Rodolfo remained unmoving and silent. He sat erect, poised, as if waiting for something. Ana noticed this, and,

sensing that she was to be the target, began to retreat. She
was about to back out of the kitchen when he bolted out of
the chair, noisily knocking it over. As he lunged, Rodolfo
grabbed her wrist with one hand, and with the other he took
hold of the hem of her sweater. He pulled it up around her
neck with a yank, then he planted the outstretched palm of
his hand on her belly.

Rodolfo's face was a mask, and his eyes slanted more
than ever. Ana was overcome by fear. She tried to pry her
wrist out of her father's grip, but couldn't because his hand
was like an iron vise that squeezed and wrenched the bones
of her hand. A moan escaped her.

"¡Cabrona!"

Rodolfo hissed the word through stiffened lips. Taking
her shoulders with both hands, he slammed her against the
stove. A half-filled pan fell onto the floor, splashing its contents, clanging and bouncing against the wall. Ana tried to
escape, but a sudden blow to the side of her face threw her
against the table, which screeched under her weight.
Stunned, she groped with her arms in an attempt to find a
way out, but just as her hands landed on the door jamb, her
father's fist caught her at the back of the head. The force of
the rabbit punch sent her skidding headlong against the door
leading to the front yard.

"¡Hija de la chingada! Leave my house! Pig!"

Ana had not screamed or made noise during her father's
attack, but the metallic clashing of falling pots and the crashing sounds of overturning chairs pulled everyone out of bed.
Alejandra, in her nightgown, stood at the bedroom door, her
hair disheveled and her eyes blinking as she tried to make
out what was happening. Behind her crowded the startled
faces of the other girls. From the service porch on the other
side of the kitchen, Octavio and César scrambled out. Both
were still in their shorts.

It was César who reacted. Realizing what was happening
to Ana, he lunged forward and screamed, "No! No! 'Apá,
please stop!" Without thinking, César tried to intervene, and
even though he stood barely above his father's waist, he was
able to intercept the next blow. But Rodolfo was blind with
rage and taking the boy by the jaw lifted him off the floor,
smashing him against the wall. César was knocked out by the
impact and he flopped inertly onto the floor.

His intervention, however, had given Ana the few seconds she needed to make an escape out the front door. Stumbling over the rickety porch steps, she made it outside. Rodolfo was enraged. He unbuckled his heavy leather belt, sliding it off his waist with one pull. He wrapped one end of it around his wrist leaving the metal buckle dangling. Then he went after Ana, catching her just before she could open the wire gate leading out to the street.

He took her again by the wrist, and he held her at arm's length as he beat her. The belt whizzed through the gray morning air, striking Ana's body each time with a dull thud. He aimed at her face, but she was able to twist and turn so that sometimes the blows fell on her shoulders, others on her breasts, and yet others on her buttocks. She was mute; only involuntary groans escaped her, and her silence provoked and infuriated Rodolfo even more. When her legs could no longer support her, she fell to her knees while her father continued to lash her, this time striking even her face.

By this time, the other girls had run out the door and onto the porch. Except for Alejandra, they were crying out hysterically, screaming to their father to stop. Octavio had also come outside; his face had turned the color of ashes, but he did not move or utter a sound. Rodolfo kept up the barrage, whipping his daughter as he screamed.

"Who is the father, whore? Tell me who is the bastard, so I can kill him the way I'm killing you!"

Rodolfo kicked Ana with all the force of his leg. He had aimed at her stomach, but she contorted her body, and when his foot landed instead on the small of her back, her mouth opened wide, letting out a groan.

The girls' howling brought frightened neighbors to the Calderón house. The first was Reyes Soto. When he realized what was happening, he crashed through the gate in an attempt to take hold of Rodolfo's arms, but his strength was not enough. As he struggled to intercept the belt, Reyes received several stinging lashes. Twisting his head, he yelled at Octavio, "You son of a bitch! Come! Come! Help me!" But when he saw that Octavio was not going to help, he kept shouting until other men came running to help him.

Octavio was paralyzed with fear, and he stayed nailed to the porch while the other men assisted Reyes. They were finally able to disarm Rodolfo by wrenching his swinging arms behind his back. They knocked him off his feet, but even though he was face down, he kicked at them and resisted by contorting his body, wiggling as he bellowed obscenities and curses.

When Ana, dazed and close to losing consciousness, realized that the attack had ended, she was crawling on the dirt. She was disoriented and crept about in circles. She couldn't stand up, or see anything to hold onto for balance. Her clothes were in tatters, as if she had been attacked with scissors, and her face was a mass of cuts, as were her arms and hands. She cupped her hands to her face as she coughed through her fingers, and she saw that the dribbling saliva was filled with blood and mud.

It took two of the neighbor women to slowly move her first onto her haunches and then, with their help, up to their shoulders so that they could lift her off the ground. Her last recollection before fainting was seeing Octavio, still standing on the porch. His face blurred until it disappeared.

∂∞⌒

I regained consciousness when Reyes, with the help of several men and women, took me to his house. Once there, however, he realized that it would be the first place that 'Apá would come looking for me. Everyone had heard him vow to find and kill me. The Soto house filled with neighbors, each one wanting to help, but everyone, I'm sure, was secretly afraid of my father.

No one could think of what to do to help me until Doña Hiroko Ogawa made herself understood. She was a Japanese woman, the owner of the grocery store across the street on Floral Drive. No one in the barrio could pronounce her last name, so she was known only as Doña Hiroko. Like the rest of the grown-ups, she hardly spoke English, but when Doña Hiroko understood the problem, she let Reyes know that they could take me to her home. She was the only one brave enough, and, nodding her head in insistence, she showed them the way.

When I was taken to her home, her voice was the only thing I could make out, and I sensed the pity that she was feel-

ing for me. I was frightened and confused, and I wanted to run, but my body was crushed; every part of me was hurting. I wanted to speak, but my lips were so swollen that speaking was impossible. I wanted to see, but my eyes were puffed up and shut tightly.

Doña Hiroko removed the tatters that clung to my body and she bathed me. I abandoned myself to her gentle hands, and while she washed the cuts and bruises, she spoke to me. I didn't know most of her words, but I understood their meaning. I realized that she was telling me that I had to be brave because now it was me and my child, and that we were alone.

I listened to the soft tone of her words, some in her language, some in mine. In my heart, however, I was thinking of Tavo, and that I hated him for his cowardice. He had stood by while my father tried to kill me, and he had not screamed out the truth about our baby. As Doña Hiroko spoke, I wondered if he, too, thought that I had poisoned my mother's womb, and that perhaps he was afraid of having a baby with me. There was no way I could say this to Doña Hiroko because I was incapable of saying it to anyone. The words kept repeating in my head, even though I tried to silence them in the days that followed.

I lost my job at the shoe factory, but the women of the barrio brought Doña Hiroko food and clothing for my keep. They visited me, chatted with me and tried to make me think that nothing important had happened. But something had occurred because my life had changed.

One evening Doña Carmelita and Doña Trini came to visit me. Because I was lying very still, they thought that I was asleep, but I heard them whispering.

"Doña Trini, something terrible has happened. I was still in the yard when I heard Señor Calderón raging."

I couldn't hear her very well, so I moved my head and ears in the direction where the women were whispering. I heard the rest of what Doña Carmelita was saying.

"He raised his clenched fist and cursed Ana and her unborn child! He swore that only wretchedness and tragedy would fill their empty lives. He commanded Heaven to fulfill his curse in his name. I have never in my life witnessed such a terrible thing!"

"A curse! No! Doña Carmelita, you must be wrong. Say that you didn't hear such wretched words!"

*"As God is my witness, I heard Señor Calderón condemn
his own flesh and blood."*

"Don't let her know what you've just told me."

*"She must know! Ana must beg her father's forgiveness if
she is to rid herself of the evil that will surely follow her and
her child for the rest of their lives."*

*Their words stunned me. Had my father really cursed me
and my baby? What would happen to us? I wasn't able to sleep
most of that night, thinking of the evil my father had wished
on me, but when I did fall asleep I dreamed of the penitent
woman. Again she told me that I would commit a grievous
sin, just as she had.*

☙◆❧

Everyone in the barrio knew that Ana was staying at the
home of Doña Hiroko Ogawa; everyone except Rodolfo. It was
a neighborhood secret because no one doubted that he would
fulfill his promise to kill her if ever he found her. So a net-
work developed to shelter Ana while she convalesced.

No one seemed interested or concerned to know the identity of the child's father. What mattered, they said, was Ana's
welfare, and afterwards that of the baby. Neighborhood people got together, putting out feelers to see where she could
get a job and also where they could get a small place for her
to live in. Doña Hiroko had already offered her home for that
purpose, but everyone agreed that it was too close to the
Calderón house.

Ana also worried about her future. As she regained her
strength she thought most of the day and many times into
the night about what she would do with her life. She went
through a long period of confusion. This was followed by a
depression that was so dense and so heavy that she was sure
that her sadness would never disappear. She missed her sisters, but she especially thought of César. Her last recollection
of him was seeing his body flying through the air and crashing against a wall.

Her thoughts of Octavio were disjointed and contradicto-
ry. At one moment she hated him for having abandoned her;
at another she felt that perhaps she wasn't good enough for

him after all. Most times, Ana would lose herself in memories of the hill where she and Octavio had loved one another, and where everything had been golden and sweet smelling. These recollections would vanish, however, when she remembered his nervous evasions, his childish ways with Alejandra, and how he had hinted that there was something between them. Ana admitted that she was especially confused and devastated by his refusal to admit that he was the father of her child, even when he saw that Rodolfo had intended to kill her.

Most of the times Ana told herself that she hated Octavio, that she detested him for having betrayed her, and that never again would she want to be in his presence. This attitude seemed to strengthen her because, she told herself, it was the truth.

As Doña Hiroko prepared broths and aromatic rice for her nourishment, Ana's body healed and her thoughts began to find order. It was at that time that the note came. César, who missed Ana more than anyone else, disobeyed his father's command that none of them was ever to speak to Ana, even if they knew where she was.

One day, the boy slithered out the back door of his house, climbed over the chain-link fence, and dashed across the alley to the other side of Floral Drive. He ran up the back stairs of Doña Hiroko's house and rapped on the door. When she opened it she knew immediately who the boy was.

"Come in, César."

"Gracias, Doña Hiroko. Can I see my sister? Please?"

"Yes. I'll get her for you. Sit there, please."

César smiled at the woman's strange accent, but understanding every word, he did as she had asked. It took only a few seconds before the bedroom door was flung open and Ana emerged. She and César embraced, and she rubbed his head and his cheeks, making sure that it was really her brother and not her imagination. As she left the room, Doña Hiroko told them to sit down and to talk for as long as they wanted.

Ana was surprised that she felt so much joy. She had thought the bitterness that had flooded her insides during the past weeks would never leave her, and that when she would again see any of her family, she would reject them, hate them. She discovered, however, that it was only happiness that she was feeling as she looked at her brother's face.

They talked, he in his little boy way, she as a young

woman. Ana evaded asking about her father or about Alejandra. She asked only for her other sisters. When César answered all her questions, he said, "Ana, aren't you going to ask me about Tavo?"

She was jerked out of her happy feelings, and she felt afraid and nervous. "Why should I ask about him?"

"Because he's been very sad since...'Apá...since that terrible morning."

When Ana sank into a long silence, the boy pulled a piece of paper from his shirt pocket. "He sends this to you, Ana. He wants you to read it and send him a note with me tonight."

Ana took the paper in her hands, holding it as if it had been a poisonous snake. She seemed afraid of it, or of what was written on it. "Why didn't he bring it here himself, César?"

"I don't know. I think...well, I think he thinks you're mad at him."

After a few minutes, she asked her brother to leave, explaining that she would read the note later. When César objected that he was supposed to bring her note with him, she calmed him down by telling him to return again the next night. The boy hesitated, thinking of the dangers involved, but he agreed.

When César left, Ana went to bed without reading the note. She tucked it still folded in a tight, small square under her pillow. But she wasn't able to sleep. It was as if the paper were burning through the pillow, singeing her hair, her scalp and her brains. After a few hours of glaring at the ceiling, she turned over and lit the small lamp by her bed. She pulled out the note and read it.

"Ana, please let me come to see you. I still love you, and I want you to love me. Tavo."

The tight, child-like scribbling seemed to have leaped from the crumpled paper and into Ana's heart. She felt as if the room were spinning and that, had she not been lying down, she would have fallen. Her balance was gone and so was the evenness of her breathing. Her heart began to palpitate and she felt the blood in her head pounding, trying to break the veins that contained it.

When César returned the following night, Ana told him she was not ready to write the expected note, but that she wanted him to come as often as he could. Her brother visited

Ana almost every night. He didn't seem to mind the danger of his father finding out that he had disobeyed him. The boy's only worry was that Rodolfo might find out where Ana was staying. He also reminded her, almost every time he came, that Octavio was waiting for a response.

After a few days passed, Ana decided to respond to Octavio, but not by way of a note. She asked César to tell him to come and see her face to face because she had convinced herself that once that happened, all would be over between them. When Doña Hiroko opened the door the next night, Octavio stood in the doorway.

Ana did not feel nervous or agitated. On the contrary, she felt a calmness she had not experienced since she had discovered that she was attracted to Octavio. He, on the other hand, looked sheepish, contrite and nervous. Before he was invited to sit, he compulsively put his hands in and out of his pockets, and he shuffled unsteadily from one foot to the other. He seemed tongue-tied, unable to speak, and when they were alone, they were wrapped in a stiff silence.

He finally spoke, "Ana...forgive..."

She didn't allow him to finish. The expression on her face silenced him, and he couldn't go on with what he was saying. Ana remained quiet, so he tried again. "I was a coward, but I couldn't help it! Honest to God, he'd kill me if he knew..."

Octavio began to cry, but despite this, Ana still did not talk to him.

"Ana, please tell me what to do. I'll do anything you tell me. Look here," he pulled a paper from his pocket and he unfolded it. "Look, do you know what this is? It's a license to get married. Yes! That's what it is! I went downtown yesterday and got it. Please, look at it! *Sí, sí!* Now all we have to do is go to Our Lady of Guadalupe Church and have the priest marry us. After that we can go on with our lives as if this nightmare had never happened!"

Words were spilling from Octavio's mouth as if they had been liquid. He slurred them, cutting some of them off so that one ran into the other. When he finally sensed that Ana was believing him, he began to gain confidence in what he was saying. As he saw joy welling up in her eyes, Octavio knew that this was what she wanted to hear.

To his surprise, however, Ana turned away from him. "What about 'Apá? Did he just all of a sudden disappear?

Didn't you say a few moments ago that he would kill you if he knew? What about that, Tavo? What about the baby? You haven't said a word about that, have you?"

"All right!...Okay...I did say that...I mean about your father. And about the baby...well...it's hard for me to even think of that...because..." He ran out of words and sat with his head cupped in his hands. After a few moments, he recuperated, raising his face to Ana. He said, "But what about this paper? Doesn't it say anything to you? Ana, if I didn't mean to marry you, I wouldn't have bothered to get this license. It's just as good as any promise. Look! If your father doesn't want to accept us, well then, we'll just have to live without him. I mean it, Ana. Please, believe me!"

Octavio's words began to persuade Ana even though her mind couldn't explain his sudden change. A few minutes before, he had been racked with fear and insecurity; he was crying as if he had been a little boy. Now he had changed, she told herself, right before her eyes. On the other hand, there was the license, and this said a lot to her.

Ana agreed that she would marry him, and they decided that it would be that Saturday. Octavio promised to make the necessary arrangements at the church. She was in the fifth month of her pregnancy, and when she went to bed that night, she fell off to sleep almost immediately, knowing that by the following week her life would be normal again.

કરુ

On the following evening, César brought me a note from Octavio explaining that he didn't want 'Apá to find out about our plans, and so he thought it would be better for him not to visit me. He said that Father Gutiérrez would marry us the following Saturday. He ended the note asking me to meet him in the church at four o'clock.

I was confused because I found it hard to understand why we needed to keep our plans a secret. I had expected that we would go up to my father and tell him about ourselves and our baby. When I spoke to César, just to see if he knew anything, I found out that Octavio had not said a word to anyone.

Still, I made myself wait for Saturday.

❦

Ana spent the rest of the week thinking about her and
Octavio's plans, but she couldn't get rid of a lingering sense of
apprehension. She nevertheless decided to put her doubts
aside and meet him as his note had asked. When Ana told
Doña Hiroko that she was to be married, she thought she
detected uncertainty mirrored in her face. But it was only
momentary because then she smiled and said that it was
good. She would, she told Ana, give her a new dress for the
occasion, and she and her sons would invite them for dinner
Saturday night to celebrate.

On Saturday Ana still wrestled with questions as to why
Octavio would not come to accompany her to the church.
Instead, he had asked her to go alone. She again repressed
her doubts and dressed. Doña Hiroko told her that she was
beautiful and that she would lend her one of her shawls with
which to cover her head. When she offered one of her sons to
keep her company on the short walk to the church, Ana
explained that she preferred to be alone.

She arrived at the front steps of the Church of Our Lady
of Guadalupe a few minutes before four o'clock. When she
entered the vestibule, it was dark, but she saw that the lights
on the altar were lit. As she walked up the center aisle, the
shallow echo of her footsteps bounced on the high vaulted
ceiling and her eyes caught the rays of the sun coming
through the brilliantly colored glass windows. She looked at
the stations of the cross, and for a few seconds her eyes lingered on the figures of a mob jeering at Christ.

Ana went up to the altar rail. No one was there. She sat
on the front pew and waited. The altar and its railing
reminded her of the Shrine of Guadalupe, but she forced the
image out of her mind by looking around her. Her eyes wandered restlessly as she looked at the white cloth on the altar
and the tall candles, which were lit. She looked over to the
side and saw the reflection of the chandeliers on the wine and
water cruets. The book from which the gospel would be read
was on the podium, and the missal was on the altar. As she
listened to the ticking of the large clock in the choir loft, her
concentration was suddenly interrupted by a hand tapping
her shoulder. She flinched involuntarily as she looked up. It

was the priest.

"*Buenas tardes, hija.* I'm expecting you and...I'm afraid I've forgotten the name of your husband-to-be."

"Octavio Arce, padre."

"Yes. I see that he's not here yet. Well, while he comes, I'll be in the the sacristy vesting. When he comes, please tell him to wait. I'll be out as soon as I can. I have confessions at five o'clock, so we have to be finished by then."

Ana smiled at the priest as she noticed his medium build, his bald head and the long black cassock which had evidently belonged to a taller priest. She saw that it was badly frayed at the hemline. A flush of relief at what he had said flooded her because it confirmed that Octavio was expected. She told herself that all would be well. She had been wrong to even listen to the doubts and questions that had hounded her during the previous days.

Nearly fifteen minutes passed before Father Gutiérrez emerged from the room at the side of the altar. He was garbed in a white robe cinctured at the waist by a cord. He also wore a colorful stole draped over his shoulders and a three-cornered barrette on his head. He looked surprised when he realized that Octavio was still not there, but with a shrug of the shoulders he sat on a bench by the altar. At his side was a prayer book which he opened and began to read.

Ana was again aware of the ticking of the clock. She twisted her head to look back at the time: four twenty five. She returned to her position facing the altar and tried to concentrate on her hands. She felt that it was her imagination when she thought that the ticking of the clock was growing louder, telling her that minutes were passing and that there was no sign of Octavio.

Father Gutiérrez suddenly looked up from his book as if he had just been struck by a thought, and he jerked up his left hand to look at his watch. He glanced toward the choir loft to confirm the time with the large clock. He frowned inquisitively and wagged his head. Then he sighed and pulled out a handkerchief from somewhere under his white gown and blew his nose heartily; the sound bounced off the statues of Saint Joseph and the Virgin Mary. After a few seconds, Ana again turned in her seat to look at the clock: twenty minutes to five.

She sat back in the pew because she felt her body tighten

with tension. Her mouth was growing dry, the palms of her hands were wet with perspiration, and her head hung so low over her chest that her chin was grazing the top button of her dress. She felt that each second was interminable, each minute intolerable. She winced when she heard the chimes of the clock uncoiling. One strike; two, three, four, five.

Her eyes were shut, but she sensed Father Gutiérrez approaching her. Ana looked up when she felt his hand on her shoulder. "*Hija*, I've got to begin hearing confessions. People are already lining up. I'm afraid I can't wait any longer." When the priest saw the agony that was tormenting Ana, he tried to comfort her. "I'm sure your young man is coming. When he does, come and call me. I'll be over there in the confessional."

Ana was riveted to the pew, although she was unaware of what power was keeping her there. Her mind told her that Octavio was not coming, and that no matter how long she waited he would never come. But her legs were unable to lift her body up and out of the church. She was ashamed. She knew that the people lined up for confession were looking at her, and she felt their eyes boring holes into the back of her head, making her heart fill with pain and humiliation. She knew, she understood. She now realized without a doubt that Octavio had never intended to keep his promise to marry her.

When the clock struck eight, Father Gutiérrez left the confessional and walked over to Ana, who was still seated in the pew; she was hunched over inertly. Without speaking, he patted her on the shoulder. Then, as he bent over to whisper something to her, she leaped to her feet, pushing the priest aside as she bolted down the aisle out to the dark street. Father Gutiérrez called out to her, but she didn't hear because of the loud, painful ringing in her ears.

When she reached Doña Hiroko's home, Ana dashed up to the second floor and knocked. The door opened onto a festively decorated front room. There were flowers in large porcelain vases placed on the low middle table as well as in different spots around the room. Red, blue, yellow and lavender candles lighted the room, their flames dancing gaily, casting shadows that leaped on the walls.

Doña Hiroko's face was joyful for a few seconds, but it sagged with confusion when she saw that Ana was alone. She and her sons became more embarrassed as each second passed; no one knew what to say. When Ana moved toward the bedroom, all four members of the Ogawa family lowered their heads.

☙◦❧

I felt cold and numb as I lay trying to sleep. My body was racked by pain caused by the battle raging in me. My arms and legs were wrenching away from their sockets; my heart pounded against my chest and my guts twisted painfully inside my stomach. I felt explosions going off in my head, blinding my eyes with sparks of shame. In my mouth I tasted the bitter poison of betrayal.

As I glared aimlessly into the darkness that surrounded me, I began to see first one, then three, then dozens of jeering faces. Some were of people I knew and others were those of strangers. There, to my close right, was the back of Doña Hiroko's head. Suddenly, it turned around with a snapping sound; her mouth was twisted with hideous mirth. On the other side, not far from me, was César's face, his mouth agape, his teeth exaggerated and pointy, and I could see that his laughter was so intense that his tongue bulged and vibrated. The blotched, puffy face of the weeping woman at the Shrine joined the others, nodding her head, reminding me that I was just like her.

Then from the center of the room, clinging to the the ceiling, I saw 'Apá's face. His eyes were slits filled with rage and shame at what I had done; his mouth was a terrible grimace filled with scorn. Then the apparition lunged toward me, coming so close that I began to whimper with fear. The mask did not speak, but I knew that it was repeating the curse my father had placed on me and on my child.

Those visages began to blur and swirl around me, multiplying endlessly until they became distorted and fractured pictures in a cracked mirror. They danced around the bed, bouncing from floor to ceiling, and the sound of their derision and mockery resonated without stopping until I thought my eardrums would burst. I tried to scream, to command those torturing faces to stop, but my tongue was nailed to the roof of my mouth, so I lay gaping helplessly at the sneering that sur-

rounded me.

When I could no longer resist the pain of their contempt, the grinning masks suddenly vanished, and in their place was a nothing, an emptiness that began to well up within me. I closed my eyes hoping to lose consciousness, to evaporate into the stale air of the room. Instead, I felt my mind separating from my body. I became aware of something inside of my brain beginning to grope, as if feeling around with soft, exploring fingers. It carefully touched first one side of my being and then another. I relaxed my body, abandoning myself to the probing tentacles of my spirit until, as if an invisible button had been pressed, a vile liquid secretly stored somewhere inside of me was released. The fluid seeped through my veins and arteries. I felt its ugliness wash over me, saturating my flesh, soaking my organs and my brain, until it inundated my mouth, forcing me to vomit.

My body convulsed painfully and I hung my head over the edge of the bed until my stomach had emptied. Now, after so many years, I know that the stench that rose from the floor was that of my own worthlessness, and the overpowering desire to die.

❧❧

Octavio had intended to keep his promise to marry Ana. During the Saturday half-day shift, as he did his work, he repeated over and again, "Yes, I will marry her. Yes, I'm in love with her. Yes, I want to spend the rest of my life with her." He noticed, however, that his stomach ached all day long and that his tongue was dry and bitter tasting. He told himself that it meant nothing because he had felt this way since he had spoken with Father Gutiérrez earlier that week.

As the hours passed, however, Octavio's resolve to keep his promise began to dwindle, to shake. The idea that perhaps he was too young to get married persisted, repeating itself even though he tried to dispel it from his thoughts. Alejandra's image also surfaced in his mind, and Octavio remembered how much he liked her pouting ways and the innocent manner in which she looked at him. On the other hand, he remembered Ana's constant attraction for him, a pull he had felt ever since they were children. He reminded himself how this feeling had become stronger, especially during the weeks and months before their intimacy up there on the hill.

When the buzzer sounded telling the workers that their day had ended, Octavio went to his locker where he folded his work apron. He withdrew a small hand mirror, and propping it against one of the shelves, he gazed at himself. He saw his hair, then his forehead, nose and eyes shadowed by thick eyebrows. He tilted his head back so as to see his mouth. He was young, Octavio thought, maybe too young.

He turned to look at the large clock attached to the wall above him. Two o'clock. He had two hours before meeting Ana at the church. He pulled out a sweater that hung on a hook in the locker, and then closed the door with a loud bang. He had to make the two-fifteen streetcar in order to reach the other side of town on time.

Octavio felt his feet becoming heavier with each step, but he made it to the bench where others were waiting for the trolley. He didn't realize that he was biting his nails and that his brow was furrowed by three lines that creased his forehead from one temple to the other. As he waited, Octavio shifted from one foot to the other, and as each second passed, his heart pounded louder, faster.

He had not intended to go home before making his way to the church, but Octavio found himself walking up the shaky steps and into the front room of the Calderón house. Everyone was in the kitchen, even Rodolfo, who motioned to Octavio to join them.

"Have something to eat, Tavo. You look pale."

"*Gracias*, but I have to leave in just a few..."

Alejandra broke in, not allowing Octavio to finish. "Come on, Tavo. I made some meat balls. You'll love them. Here." She didn't wait for his answer before she served him a plate of the meat with steaming broth. Octavio did not resist; he couldn't because he wanted with all his heart to stay there with those people who he knew were his family. He desired above all things to forget everything and to laugh and joke with the girls, with Alejandra especially. Octavio dreaded facing Father Gutiérrez and his kind but probing eyes. He was revolted by the thought of standing next to Ana, her abdomen visibly swollen. He admitted that he was ashamed of how she looked, and he knew that by marrying her everyone would know that he was the father of that child growing inside of her.

Octavio smiled sheepishly and, taking off his sweater, he picked up a spoon and began eating. Then everyone began to chatter almost at once. Alejandra sat staring at him, a wry smile on her lips. Each time he looked up from the plate, his eyes irresistibly turned to look at her. He returned her smiles because he felt his body relaxing as he did it. The jumpiness in his stomach began to go away, and the tightness in his neck was loosening.

When Octavio finished eating, Rodolfo signaled him with his head to follow him into the next room. They left the table and walked over to a couch in the front room where Rodolfo sat on a separate chair with his hands folded over his stomach. He was silent as he gazed at the floor.

He had been more silent than usual since he had beaten and thrown Ana out of the house. He seemed almost always lost in thought as if turning ideas over in his mind. Or maybe they were words that he never communicated to anyone. He had forbidden everyone to ever mention Ana's name, and it seemed to even the youngest of the children that their father spent most of his days erasing their sister's name from his mind.

Octavio sat in front of Rodolfo remembering that every second meant that four o'clock was approaching. Without even looking at the clock, he was sure that it was almost time. He knew that even now, if he jumped to his feet and sprinted to the church, he could still make it. But the older man's grim face kept Octavio riveted to the seat.

Rodolfo finally spoke up and he did so in Spanish. When Octavio responded, he did likewise, knowing that Rodolfo hated anyone to interject English when speaking with him.

"You're about twenty years old now, aren't you, Tavo?"

Octavio, surprised by the question, sensed that what they were about to say to one another was important. He knew immediately that it meant that Ana would have to wait for him. "Yes, sir, about that age."

"When I was your age, I was already married."

"Yes, sir."

"Well, what about you?"

He waited for Octavio to respond, but when he saw that

no answer was coming, he said, "Have you ever been with a woman, Tavo?" He didn't wait for an answer. "I think you have. Something happens to a man when he lays with a woman. There's a look in his eyes."

Octavio's head began to swim. His hands were clammy and the knot in his stomach returned, this time with flashing pain. His heart was racing with fear. "He knows," Octavio told himself. "He knows about me and Ana, and this is his way of telling me that it's my turn to be beaten, to be thrown out of the house."

He felt that he was about to faint when he heard Rodolfo's voice. "You look sick. Do you want a glass of water?"

"No, sir. I...think...I...that is, I just worked too hard today...my stomach hurts."

Rodolfo ignored the stuttering and leaned forward in his chair as if trying to look through Octavio's eyes into his stomach. His face was taut and stern as he uttered his words with care and deliberation. His voice was husky.

"It's your turn."

Octavio clamped shut his eyes, waiting for the first blow to fall, but he opened them when nothing happened. He saw the older man, his body slouched back in the chair, gazing at the wall above him. After a few seconds of confusion, Octavio realized with relief that he had been wrong, that he had misunderstood the whole thing, and that Ana had nothing to do with the conversation. Somehow, he told himself, Rodolfo had not connected her condition to him. He shuddered with joy and relief when he understood that the meaning of what was being said might lead in a new direction.

"It's my turn?" Octavio's voice was weak, little more than a whisper.

"Yes. Your turn to marry."

"But...I don't know of anyone who would marry me."

When Octavio heard his words, he felt his body shiver because he knew that he had again betrayed Ana. He recognized that this was his second chance to reveal the truth. A sinking, wobbly feeling held Octavio back. Wiping sweat off his forehead, he told himself that the older man would surely kill him if he spoke up, and that even Ana would not have wanted that.

Rodolfo leaned deeper into the chair, and his eyes squinted until they were almost shut tight. "I know that you have eyes for one of my daughters."

A hoarse gasp from Octavio's throat escaped him. He was again plunged into the mire of fear from which he had pried loose just a few moments before. His skin lost all of its luster, turning an opaque, yellowish beige. He opened his mouth to speak, but was cut off.

"I know, Tavo, that you love Alejandra. Your eyes almost scream it out, and only a blind man would not see that. And..." he held his hand up, palm outstretched when he saw that Octavio was about to speak, "I know that she loves you. I know because she has told me about it ever since she was a little girl."

Octavio felt that he was elevating, that his head was filling with something weightless and airy, and that soon he would be able to fly. His eyes grew larger as he gaped at Rodolfo whose face had suddenly, inexplicably, become soft, almost tender. Octavio hardly recognized him because he had never seen that face so filled with light, and he wanted to embrace Rodolfo, thanking him for having freed him from the captivity of guilt into which he had fallen. Octavio told himself that here was proof that it would have been wrong for him to marry anyone except Alejandra. It had to be so, otherwise this harsh, stern man would never look as happy as he did. By the time Rodolfo spoke again, Octavio had forgotten all about Ana and that she was waiting for him at the church.

"Alejandra is sixteen years old and it's her time. I want boys, even if they are to be grandsons."

"What about school..."

"She's a woman and has no more need for school."

When both men stood, Rodolfo put out his hand to Octavio, who grasped it, shaking it with a newly found energy. Alejandra was born for him, and he for her, and he knew that he had been foolish and stupid to have ever thought otherwise.

I couldn't get out of bed even though Doña Hiroko told me that I was not sick. I stayed in bed, just staring at the ceiling, not wanting to even open my lips. I couldn't speak or whisper.

I hardly did anything for myself except walk down the hall-
way to the toilet. I didn't comb my hair nor wash my face, and
I didn't want to take a bath. It was Doña Hiroko who came
with large basins of warm water with which to clean my body
and to wash and comb my hair. I remember that while she did
this she spoke to me. I didn't listen to her words. My heart and
mind had shut down.

☙

Doña Hiroko spoke in a low, resonant voice, but Ana
hardly responded. "Ana, in the land of my birth, the father,
too, is all-powerful. He has the power to caress or to strike a
daughter. My father chose the man whom I married, and I
was never asked what I felt or what I wanted."

The rhythmic strokes of the brush on Ana's hair filled the
silence of Doña Hiroko's pauses. "When the child comes, it is
the same everywhere because then the woman must live for
that new life. But let it be different with you, Ana. Live for
your own life"

She put the brush down on her lap for a few moments as
she gazed out the window. Ana turned her head slightly,
wondering why the words had stopped. Then the older
woman returned to her brushing. "When my first son was
born, I was a field worker. And every morning I used to tie
him to my back and go out to the rice paddies where I
worked, water up to my knees. I wondered even then if there
were any other kind of life for a woman."

She laughed quietly as she stood, and she looked at Ana
for a long time before leaving the room. "You must be brave,
because to be afraid, Ana, will lead you only to a living death.
You must be courageous for the child in you. It matters not if
it is a boy child or a girl child because they are equally important."

News of what had happened to Ana flashed through the
barrio, and during those days, César came only once to see
his sister because now, more than ever, he feared that his
father would discover what everyone else knew. He knew
that Rodolfo would stalk across the street to keep his vow to
kill Ana. César came to Ana's bedside and knelt there for a

long time before she opened her eyes. When she saw him, she smiled weakly, and when he took her hand in his, she pressed lightly against his strong squeeze. He couldn't speak, so he began to cry, and Doña Hiroko took him into the kitchen where she gave him a cookie while she spoke to him for a long while.

Other neighborhood women also came, hoping to shake Ana from her trance. One of them, Doña Trinidad, tried more than the others to strengthen Ana's spirit which, the woman said, wanted to die. She did this by reminding her of the women of Mexico.

"¡Ándale, muchacha! Get up! Remember that you come from good women, with strong blood. Some of them were even soldiers in the Revolution. Real fighters! Can you believe that, Ana? They were women who wanted to live. To prevail! Nothing stopped them! Not bullets or fear of dying."

Because there was no reaction to her words, Doña Trinidad would take Ana by the shoulders, shaking her and speaking loudly. "Ana! Ana! You came to this country for a reason. You didn't come all that distance, on buses, on trains, on foot through deserts, just to die of sadness rolled up in a bed. No, Ana! You're a fighter!"

Doña Trinidad usually began speaking softly, in barely a whisper, but as she was caught up by what she was saying, she became intensely agitated and her voice escalated in volume. She seemed convinced that by shouting, her strength would somehow fuse into Ana's heart, shaking her from the lethargy. The woman often ended her yelling and gesticulating by thrashing her brown, stringy arms in the air. Her voice always carried through the house, making Doña Hiroko run to the room to make sure that Ana was all right.

Nothing seemed to work. No one was able to penetrate the shell of Ana's withdrawal. When Doña Hiroko brought her food, Ana tried to please her by eating, but ended pecking at the food and shifting it around on the plate with the fork. As the days passed, she grew thinner. Doña Hiroko went to the women of the barrio, explaining her fear that Ana and her child might die if she continued in such a state.

They turned to Father Gutiérrez, who came a few times to visit Ana but was unable to make her speak to him. He spoke kindly and at length, but it always turned out to be a monologue. "Ana, what happened was not your fault, remember that." His words were met with silence, yet he persisted. "You must live. Please try! Touch your spirit, Ana, and tell it to live."

Father Gutiérrez walked away from those visits feeling that his hands were empty, and his concern for Ana gnawed at him as he filled with outrage against Octavio Arce. When several weeks passed and she remained fixed in the silent world into which she had locked herself, the priest decided to approach Mr. Calderón to advise him that his daughter's health and perhaps even her life were in danger.

Father Gutiérrez's conversation with Rodolfo lasted only a few minutes because the moment the priest first uttered Ana's name, her father sprang to his feet and angrily motioned his visitor toward the door. With his mouth clamped shut, Rodolfo took Father Gutiérrez by the elbow and forcefully pushed him outside. He slammed the door on the priest's face without ever having allowed him to say another word. The priest was not intimidated; instead he was incensed at Rodolfo's bitterness towards his daughter who he felt had done nothing to deserve such rancor.

The priest then decided to approach Octavio; he did it as the young man was waiting at the bus stop. Struggling with his voice so as not to let it betray his feelings of outrage, Father Gutiérrez opened up. "I think, Octavio, that you ought to know that Ana is very sick. You're responsible, you know."

Octavio was surprised by the priest's bluntness, and he felt his stomach react nervously. "I...I...What do you mean responsible? It wasn't my fault! I mean, how could I know she would misunderstand me?"

"What? Say that again? This is me, Octavio, the priest you contacted for the wedding arrangements! Señor Arce, I was a witness to how you left her waiting at the alter, remember?"

Emphazing his point, Gutiérrez poked Octavio's chest roughly, but Octavio only shrugged his shoulders weakly in return.

Before jumping aboard the bus, he turned to the priest. "It's not my fault. Besides, I'm going to marry Alejandra."

Trotting alongside the bus before it picked up speed, the priest shouted through the window at Octavio, "You'd better find another church, another priest for that wedding." It gladdened Father Gutiérrez to see Octavio's embarrassed face as the bus sped away.

After this incident, the priest decided to take action. He convened several of the neighbors at Reyes Soto's house and challenged them. "Which one of us has not sinned, eh? Which one? Speak up!" The priest's stocky body was shaking with pent-up anger at what was happening to the girl in Doña Hiroko's home. Standing with legs spread wide apart, his arms akimbo and his worn-out cassock limply hanging over his shoes, he glared at anyone who dared to return his look.

"When one of us suffers, we all suffer!" His voice was sharp, his words to the point. "What hypocrisy is this that we allow this child to bear the weight of a sin that many of us have committed? Eh, what is this? I want to hear an answer!"

"Padre, why are you angry with us? We have not turned out backs on Ana. It is her father that..." Reyes was speaking.

"Yes! Yes! I know! But what are you doing about it? Do any of you go over there, across that narrow street, and tell Rodolfo Calderón that his daughter is in danger of dying?"

"Look, Padre, we all know that you did, and begging your forgiveness, what did you get out of it? I don't mean to be disrespectful, but we all know that you came out with nothing. And if that happened to you, a priest, what do you think will result if one of us tries to intervene?"

Father Gutiérrez was forced to accept Reyes Soto's words as being true. He pressed ahead, however, this time in a more subdued manner. "Forgive me. Ana's condition has frightened me, and her father's coldness has terrified me. I don't mean to be offensive with any of you. I called you here, not to insult you but to see if all of us together can think of what to do for Ana."

Doña Carmelita spoke up; the tone of her voice was prophetic. *"Es la maldición, Padre."*

Instantly, voices shot out from different sides of the room. *"¡Ridículo!" "¡Absurdo!" "¡Qué estupidez!"*

Intimidated and humiliated, Doña Carmelita slouched back in her chair, sulking. Soon, from behind her, came someone's comforting hand which patted her on the shoulder. "Don't listen to them, Doña Carmelita," the voice whispered. "We all believe that a father's curse does terrible damage. They're just trying to pretend that they're modern people. Worse, they're trying to be like the *gringos* who don't believe in anything."

No one except Doña Carmelita heard these words. In the meantime, Father Gutiérrez and the rest of the group were thinking of what to do. After a long pause, Doña Trinidad spoke up. "The way I see it, we have to get her away from her father; away from this barrio. We have to find a place for her to stay until her baby comes and until she is able to work for the both of them."

Everyone, even Father Gutiérrez, nodded in agreement, but no one had a specific idea as to where such a place could be found for Ana. Again no one spoke while each man and woman searched inwardly for the answer to Doña Trinidad's recommendation.

The silence was broken by Doña Hiroko who, speaking haltingly, made herself understood with some difficulty. "I have a friend...Mrs. Amy Bast...who supplies my store with the eggs I sell. This lady and her husband have a chicken farm in Whit...Whit..."

She wasn't able to pronounce the word. Someone finished it for her, "Whittier."

Turning and bowing courteously toward the direction from which the word had come, Hiroko Ogawa continued with a smile on her face. "She will take Ana to her farm and let her stay there until the baby comes, and then..."

Everyone was sitting straight up in their chairs, bodies pressed forward, eyes riveted on their Japanese neighbor. They were intently trying to understand her heavily accented words.

"...She can stay or go where she is happier. Amy has already offered to take Ana to her place."

"¡Sí! ¡Sí! That's the answer. ¡Qué bueno! Gracias, Doña Hiroko."

The following day it was not Doña Hiroko who took a tray to Ana. It was Mrs. Amy Bast, the farmer from Whittier who had come personally to convince the young woman that she had to gather her energies soon, before she destroyed her health and that of her child.

She began by saying in a shrill voice, "Young lady, you're looking at me and I'll bet that I know what you're thinking. Yes, siree! You're thinking, 'Why, here's a woman who's skinnier than me!' That's what you're thinking, isn't it?"

Amy Bast was seated by the bed, a tray of food on her lap,

and she was responding to Ana's eyes that looked at her with surprise and wonder. Mrs. Bast had an accurate picture of herself because, as Ana's startled eyes noted, she was a tall, gaunt, angular woman. She had a stretched torso and lanky legs, and the length of her body was accentuated by the worn, faded cotton dress that hung loosely, almost reaching the high-top leather shoes she wore.

Amy's main characteristic was a long neck that was graceful and still beautiful despite her fifty-five years. Her face was small and lovely, even though it was creased by several deep wrinkles. Her short, straight nose was emphasized by lips that were thin but soft, strong yet gentle. And Amy had small, blue eyes that sparked when she spoke. Her manner of speaking made her special in the barrio because she talked with a strong Oklahoma accent in a high-pitched and drawled voice.

"I'm Mrs. Amy Bast, Ana, and I'm from all the way from Oklahoma. Yes, siree! Me and the Mister came out West when the Depression broke out. We lost everything back there..." Her voice trailed, pausing, then she continued, "We were able to set up a couple of hens and a rooster in a coop when we got here, and after a lot of strife and plenty of tears, here we are selling our produce to the good grocers of these here parts. It wasn't easy, girl, believe me! I been down in the big, black hole just the way you are right now. But I crawled out! And you're going to do the same thing! So, now, have this delicious meal Hiroko made for you and after that, up and at 'em! You and me got us a life to live."

Ana took the plate that Amy handed her. She picked up the fork and began to put morsels of food into her mouth. As she did this her stomach rejected the food, but she determined that this time she would prevail over her body. Amy's words had said much to her, but hers was not the only voice to which Ana was listening. The woman's presence had helped jolt her out of the depression that had gripped her, but so had that of Doña Hiroko, Doña Trinidad, Father Gutiérrez, and the rest of the neighbors who had come to save her from drowning. César's face, when he had burst into tears, came back to Ana, and that too had helped jar her from the overwhelming desire to die.

໓°◌⥈

*As I forced myself to eat, an image inside of me took
shape. It wasn't cracked and disjointed anymore. Now the
pieces were finding their place, showing me what to do. The
picture showed my father's face, but I wasn't afraid of him, or
of the curse. Behind that face and its evil wishes was
Octavio's, and I didn't fear him either.*

*I felt a weightlessness taking hold of me. I realized that
my father hated me because I had ruined the way for my
brothers. Yet, I knew that people had fought so that I could
live, and the meaning of their struggle came to me. I understood that in their eyes I had value, and knowing this filled
me with a desire to live.*

໓°◌⥈

Ana clumsily stepped off the running board of Amy's
Model-T Ford; her body was heavy with advanced pregnancy.
It was December, and a cold wind that skidded off the northern foothills cut through her sweater and thin cotton dress.
The trip from the barrio had taken Amy almost an hour. She
drove from Floral Drive over to Whittier Boulevard, and then
had gone eastbound until reaching the dirt road that led to
the egg ranch. After leaving the paved road, the bumps,
holes, and pools of mud made driving even slower and more
difficult.

It took Ana a few moments to regain her balance while
she stood with her legs and feet spread apart on the soggy
soil. As she looked around her, she saw that the Bast chicken
ranch was a bleak place. It was a five-acre spread covered
almost entirely by long chicken coops. In the center of the
property stood a house with a low roof and a short chimney
stack from which wisps of gray smoke spiraled. Ana craned
her neck and saw that behind the structure was the outhouse.

Amy Bast was cheery as she showed her new boarder the
way in. Once in the kitchen, she turned to Ana. "It's not luxu-
rious, but it's home. Over here will be your room. Come on in."

Ana followed her into a small room which had a narrow bed, a chest of drawers, and a small nightstand next to the bed. There was a window fringed by cheerfully colored curtains on the western side of the room. Under the window was a kitchen chair.

She liked the room. It was warm and comfortable, and for the second time in her life, she would have a bed to herself. She had grown to enjoy this while at Doña Hiroko's, and Ana was glad that she would be able to continue sleeping alone. As she picked up the small bag that contained her belongings, she turned to Amy and said, "Thank you, Mrs. Bast. This is very nice."

"Now, you just call me Amy. We're going to be friends. Mr. Bast—Franklin, that is—should be coming 'round in a while. He knows all about you and that you'll be with us for a spell. You'll like him, Ana, just you wait and see."

Ana found Amy's drawl interesting; she especially liked the way she pronounced her name. She had never heard it said in that tone, not even by Miss Nugent.

That evening Ana, Amy and her husband Franklin sat at the kitchen table finishing dinner. Amy spoke first. "Ana, you understand that both Franklin and I are very happy to have you. We never had children of our own, so you are very welcome. It'll be kind of like having a daughter. We know also that you're a hard-working young woman, and that you look on this whole thing just like you would a job. But we also understand that you'll have to wait until after your baby comes, so that you can really start helping us around here."

Ana listened politely. She looked at Franklin from time to time and saw that he, too, was paying close attention to what Amy was saying. She was impressed by his appearance; he looked, she thought, just like Amy. He was tall, lanky, blue-eyed and he, too, had a very long neck. The only difference that she could see was that he was bald. Her attention was suddenly drawn back to Amy when she paused, evidently to see if Ana had anything to say. When the young woman remained silent, Amy said, "I do declare, I think I talk too much."

"Yes, dear." Franklin spoke for the first time in an hour.

After that, Amy said that for that night they would retire immediately. Ana slept soundly except for a few minutes when she woke up sometime during the night. The silence of the ranch caused her to listen intently, as if expecting to hear someone calling out her name. She turned over and thought of the baby that was inside of her. Octavio's face flashed in her mind, and to dispel his appearance she forced herself to think of César, of her sisters, even of Alejandra. In her mind she pictured them asleep. She even thought she heard their deep breathing. But then she changed her position, and drifted off to sleep.

The next day was gray and drizzling, but Amy didn't allow the weather to interfere with what had to be done, so she went right to work.

"Ana, even though you're feeling uncomfortable, you've got to keep busy, otherwise you'll get bored, then homesick, and then just plain sick all over again."

"Yes, m'am."

She took Ana to the room where the feed was kept, then through the coops, showing her the light cords that had to be pulled so that the chickens would think it was daytime and lay more eggs. Amy prattled, indicating where Ana was to look for eggs and where to place them. Then she showed her the pile of crates destined to carry the product into town and finally into the hands of the grocers.

Ana was content. The hours had passed by so quickly that she was surprised when she realized that it would soon be dinner time. She had liked her first day on the ranch and had appreciated how Amy made sure that she took rest periods during the day, so that she would recuperate faster.

After dinner, the three of them joined in the kitchen clean-up. Ana was amused and startled to see Franklin washing dishes and pans. She had never seen a man with soap-suds on his hands, especially when washing plates, forks, and knives. She was astounded to see how cheerful he was, and that he whistled softly through his teeth as he wiped down the table with a large rag.

When they were finished, Amy dried her hands and looked at Ana. "Come on over and join me and Franklin here." She patted the table top. Ana saw that Amy had placed a large book with black covers in front of her. This was to be her first experience with a Bast tradition: reading from the Old Testament every evening after dinner. The ritual began with Amy saying, "Now, let's see what the good Lord has to say to us at the end of this day." She would then insert her index finger deep into the pages and open the text. Her eyes momentarily scanned the page until she decided what she would read. Sometimes Amy read long excerpts. At other times they were short chapters, or even random verses.

When Ana joined the Basts, her acquaintance with the Bible was scarce. She knew about Adam and Eve, but the extent of her knowledge was what she had learned as a girl when she and the other village children squatted on the sand to listen to the priest from Puerto Real. The few details about the Scriptures that she remembered were also what she had learned during Sunday mass. Bits and disjointed parts now drifted back to her: Jesus was born in Bethlehem and his mother was Mary. Saint Joseph was his father, but not really his father, and she recalled a few things about twelve men called the Apostles. She, however, had to admit that what Amy Bast read evening after evening was new for her, and very interesting.

As the weeks passed and Ana's pregnancy drew to its end, the evening readings became the highlight of her day. After finishing the reading, it was Amy's custom to ask Franklin and Ana what lesson they had drawn from what God communicated to them through the written words. One evening she looked at Franklin.

"Now, Franklin, here we have Moses coming down from the mountain after seeing God Almighty with his very own eyes of flesh, and what does he find? He finds all his folks partying and depraving themselves over some old statue of a calf. What do you make of such behavior?"

"Hmm. Well, dear, I think the meaning of it all is buried deep in my heart, where it'll have to stay for the time being."

Looking exasperated, Amy turned to Ana. "What about you? What do you think of such goings on?"

Ana was sitting with her hands folded over her swollen abdomen, and she giggled nervously, explaining that she did not know how to express what it meant.

The readings, however, occupied Ana's thoughts sometimes well into the night as she reflected on what she had heard. Ana was captivated, amazed and often puzzled by the stories that Amy conveyed with so much drama and warmth. She had not imagined that such a world of kings and prophets and shepherds had existed, and that those people had actually been in contact with God. She saw, however, that even though they communicated with God, they nonetheless murdered and warred and cheated on husbands and wives. The story of Bathsheba especially intrigued Ana, and she told herself that surely the woman must have known what the king had done to her husband.

Ana was fascinated to see how the songs and poems of those people were centered on God, and how, whenever one of them was in trouble—whether king or slave girl—from a bush, or a rock, or a spring of water a mysterious voice or an angel came to save them.

One evening, Amy's voice took on a special tone as she proclaimed her selection. Turning first to Franklin, and then to Ana, she said, "Tonight the good Lord will be speaking to us from the Book of Genesis, chapter sixteen, verses six to eight." Looking at Ana, Amy said, "Ana, this might just be a way for the Lord to be speaking to you, so listen real hard."

Taking a deep breath, she began reading. "Then Sara humiliated Hagar, and she fled from her. Afterward an angel of the Lord found her beside a spring of water in the desert, the spring on the road to Sur." Amy looked up, her small blue eyes bright with anticipation. After a moment, she returned to reading, "He said, 'Hagar, maid of Sara, where have you come from and where are you going?' She answered, 'I am fleeing from my mistress Sara.' The angel of the Lord said to her, 'You are with child, and shall bear a son; you shall call him Ismael...'"

Amy interrupted her reading when she saw that Ana was engrossed in what she was hearing. Putting down the book, she abruptly asked her, "Do you know the meaning of the name Ismael, Ana?"

"No, m'am, I don't."

"Well, I do. My Pa had a dictionary of Bible names and I just about memorized all of their meanings. Ismael means 'Let the Good Lord Hear.' Isn't that just something?"

Ana's mind was absorbing every word uttered by Amy because she felt that they contained a special message for her. How could a name have meaning? What did her own name signify? What name would she give her child when it came? She saw, also, that she was like the maid Hagar, humiliated and running away.

Her mind was racing, darting in different directions, when Franklin's voice broke in. "Amy, aren't you going to finish the reading? I mean, I think I remember that there's a bit more about Ismael."

"You're right, Franklin. I guess I just got carried away. It ends like this, 'He shall be wild, his hand against everyone, and everyone's hand against him; he shall dwell apart, opposing all his kinsmen.' There, that's all there is to the verse. It ends kind of mysterious, I must say. Why should anyone who's real ornery and who separates himself from family have the ear of the good Lord? That's what I always ask myself about Ismael."

"Maybe it's because it was to Hagar's pain that the good Lord listened, and not to Ismael himself. What if the angel gave that name to her son just to remind Hagar that she really wasn't alone, that God heard her crying?"

Ana was shocked to hear her voice blurting out words that had formulated in her mouth before she had even thought of them. Franklin and Amy sat up and stared at her as if she had just appeared in their midst out of nothing. Then they looked at one another, their eyes wide open. Long moments passed, their minds digesting what Ana had said.

"Why, Ana, that had never occurred to me." Amy's voice was soft. "I always thought that it was Ismael who was heard by the good Lord. But...Well...It could be so..."

Amy sat back in thought. When she finally spoke, her voice was filled with conviction. "No! Let's just wait a minute here! It really doesn't make sense that a slave girl should be more important than her son, because, you see, he's the one who went on to become the head of a big tribe, or something like that. That's why the good Lord saved her; only so that she could have the baby."

"I don't think so, Amy. It seems to me that the Lord saved Hagar because she was important on her own; because she was who she was. She came first, and God needed her so that her son could exist. That means that Hagar was more valuable than her son."

Ana, no longer afraid to say what she was thinking, spoke quietly. "Besides, I think that the story is of something more important than a tribe. What I mean is that maybe it's about Hagar, and about how God wanted to save her for something other than just having Ismael."

Amy leaned back in her chair, making it creak against her thin back. The light shed by the kerosene lamp hanging from the middle rafter cast bluish shadows on her hair and on her high cheekbones. The expression on her face showed keen interest. "Could it have been, then, that it was to Hagar's anguish that God listened, and not to her son's discontent? If that's the case, it's possibly as you say. Hagar is more important than Ismael."

Amy glanced over to Franklin who also seemed caught up with the new way of looking at a story he had heard over and again ever since he was a child. Amy suddenly said, "Franklin, had you ever thought of it that way?" When he remained silent, she closed the Bible, turned to Ana, and smiled, "Well, now, I'll just have to give this whole thing a bit more thought."

Ana slept fitfully that night. Visions of tents, tribes, and angels glided through her sleeping mind. She was Hagar and she had been cast into the wilderness not by Sara, but by her father. Laughing shepherds stood by jeering as they pointed at her distended belly. In her dream, she was dying of thirst in a desert filled with machines that made shoes, and where women workers mocked her with cracked, parched lips; their soiled bandannas flapping in the arid breeze. She screamed and asked for someone to rescue her from the sun that was burning her with shame and humiliation. But it was only Doña Hiroko and Doña Trinidad who heard her cries. One gave Ana a tiny cup of green tea to drink, and the other sheltered her in an embrace.

When Ana awoke, her pillow was wet with tears and saliva. She sat up in bed and saw that outside the night was still dark, and that it was raining heavily. She leaned against the iron bedstead as she pulled up the blankets to cover her chest and shoulders, then cupped her hand on her stomach for a long while, feeling the child move. She closed her eyes, sifting through her dream part by part, trying to decipher its meaning. And she remained that way for a long time until sleep overcame her.

The following morning as she joined the Basts for breakfast, Ana said to them, "If my baby is a girl, her name will be Hagar."

Franklin was about to take a sip from his coffee, but he stopped, holding the cup in mid-air. Amy slowly placed her fork on the edge of the plate as she tilted her head to one side. "What if it's a boy, Ana?"

"If it's a boy, his name will be Ismael."

❧

Ismael was born on a rainy night in early February of 1940. His birth was difficult because he began to make his way out of me a day and a half before he was born.

I was not like 'Amá, who bit her knuckles rather than cry out when she was giving birth to her children. I screamed and wailed with all the force in my body. Each time I let out a howl I was aware that the chickens were startled, and that they cackled in fear. Even the roosters crowed, although it was dusk and not dawn.

I was unconscious most of the time. I was not with Amy on the egg ranch; I was somewhere else. I went back to the palapa, and to the emerald ocean where I danced and dreamed; to where Tavo, Alejandra, and I played games of Aztec warriors and princesses. I saw myself sprinting toward the palm trees, ignoring Tía Calista's call to come help deliver the new baby. When I finally went into the dim hut, instead of my mother's spread-out knees, I saw mine. It was not her blood but mine that smeared the rough sheets clinging to the black sand, and it was my body that was being torn open, not hers.

In my delirium, Tía Calista's face appeared; it was still cracked by the ocean sun, and it was darker than when we had left Puerto Real. She made clucking sounds with her tongue as she reminded me that I had turned out to be like other women after all, just as she had said I would. In her eyes I could see a faint glimmer that said that all women are the same, and that we all end up with our legs spread apart enduring the pain of new life.

Suddenly Tía Calista's face was pushed aside by Miss Nugent, who sorrowfully wagged her head as she silently walked away. In her place I saw the women I had worked with, the ones in the tomato fields of the Yaqui Valley and in the shoe factory. Those faces were as I remembered them; their skin was blotched and their lips were drawn and sad. They gaped at me as their shoulders drooped to sagging, tired breasts that rested on their distended stomachs.

Behind them I could see Alejandra, the sister I knew had turned into my enemy. Her white skin was radiant, and her hair seemed fairer than I remembered. Her body was full of life, and she held herself so straight that her small breasts stuck out menacingly. She walked up to me, pointing at my convulsing belly, and she said, "Ugh, it's a boy! I'll bet you it's going to die. It's poisoned in there, you know."

I let out a scream so horrifying that Amy rushed over to me and placed a fresh cloth dampened with rubbing alcohol on my forehead. She stroked my arms and hands, telling me to relax, that it would soon be over. She didn't know that my cry had not been of pain, but of terror.

Alejandra disappeared and in her place was Tavo. My body suddenly became serene as I saw him gazing at the spot between my open legs. I saw that he had grown even more handsome since the last time I saw him; he was taller. His hair shone as it did that first time we loved one another on the golden hill above our house. Although his eyes remained fixed on the opening where the child would soon emerge, I knew the expression in them. I was sure that it was the same as when he laid upon me, smiling at me, kissing me, pressing himself over and again into me.

But I was wrong. When he finally looked up at me, his eyes were hard, filled with ice. Those pupils accused me of terrible things. "Everything has been a mistake, a misunderstanding." Octavio's eyes bored into me, saying that the child showing its slick, wet head between my legs was not his, and his glare told me what he felt. "I didn't have anything to do with it! You sneaked a seed between your legs and kept it there until it spawned. The baby is yours alone!"

"Get out! Get out!" I shouted over and over. Amy didn't know what I meant and she said that she had to stay with me, that she couldn't leave me alone. I calmed down and looked out the window where I made out Doña Hiroko and Doña Trinidad trying to coax my father into the room. I could only see his back, but I knew that it was him. A downpour made the three of them disappear.

Ismael finally came. He was alive, and he was beautiful. When Amy placed him in my arms, I saw immediately that he had gotten the white skin that ran through our family. Like Alejandra, my son inherited the color of the unknown French grandfather who had decided to marry a brown Mexican girl generations before us.

I felt strange when I first held Ismael in my arms. I looked at his face and an unexpected feeling, something like an iron hand gripping my heart, assaulted me. A sensation I had never experienced flooded through me, surprising me, leaving me confused.

I closed my eyes, waiting for my thoughts to clear. When I looked at my son again, I felt serene because I realized that there was a reason for the pain I had experienced for him. I looked out the window and I remembered what Amy had read in the Bible about Ismael, of how he would be opposed to everyone, and everyone to him. I made a vow that this would not happen to Ismael because I would assure him that he would be loved by all who would ever enter his life.

⤜•⤛

Two years after the birth of Ismael, on a sunny day in April, Alejandra and Octavio stood at the entrance of the church posing for photographs. They had just emerged; their marriage mass had ended and the organ was still bellowing out the triumphal wedding march. Outside, the smiling bride and groom were met with loud cheers and clapping accompanied by the joyful tolling of bells. As rice showered them, they giggled trying to dodge and shield their faces from the tiny grains.

Despite the war, everyone was in the mood to celebrate because there was more than a wedding for which to be grateful. Henry Miranda and Reyes Soto, son of the elder Reyes, had volunteered for the Navy the previous year, and both had been assigned to a ship that was attacked while in Pearl Harbor. When the news broke out, the barrio went into shock, thinking that two of their boys had been killed. Reyes Junior and Henry Miranda survived, however, and when word of their safety spread from street to street, from house to house, there were shouts of joy, and Father Gutiérrez made sure that there were thanksgiving rosaries for several nights.

Still relishing their relief and joy, the Reyes and Miranda families and everyone around them took the occasion of the wedding to prolong their feelings of happiness. Only a few of the older people grumbled when they saw that some of the young ones, girls as well as boys, were pretentiously made up in pachuco dress.

The young men, hair heavily greased and square cut in the back to better show off the cleavage of a duck tail, sported fancy tailored zoot-suits. The girls wore short tight skirts, and their hair was piled high on their heads, rolled up with supports they called rats.

"Look, *Comadre* Amparo. Over there. Isn't that a shame?"

"Is that little Tony? *¡Qué vergüenza!* Where did he get the money to have that suit made up that way?"

"Look, *Comadre.* Look at Esperancita and the way she's dressed. If I were her mother, I'd tear that rag off of her. Then they're surprised when men get fresh with them. Just look at her! You can almost see her *nalgas*, the skirt is so short!"

Alejandra and Octavio, oblivious to the heavy undercurrents that swept through the crowd, were resplendent. Alejandra wore a white satin gown that flowed gracefully to her feet; the soft folds of the dress accentuated the curves of her body. Her head was crowned with a wide white band interlaced with fresh orange blossoms and tiny artificial pearls. Attached to the band was a gauzy veil that floated gracefully in the noon breeze. This headdress made Alejandra's eyes seem larger, more brilliant, matching her smile which told everyone of her intense happiness.

Octavio was strikingly handsome, dressed as he was in a black tuxedo and white tie. The reddish brown tones of his skin contrasted sharply with the whiteness of his shirt. He had grown taller over the past two years, and the dark suit lengthened his height even more. He was keenly aware of the adulating looks that came his way, especially from the women, and his strong, evenly spaced teeth gleamed with each broad smile that he returned to his admirers.

Not once did Ana or her child cross his mind, even though Octavio was informed of their whereabouts. What mattered to him at that moment was that everyone around them was celebrating his and Alejandra's marriage. As Octavio looked around him, he saw only friends, neighbors, co-workers, and family. He basked in the applause that he heard each time the click of a camera sounded, especially when the photographer instructed the couple to kiss for the most important picture of all. As he gazed into Alejandra's eyes just after their lips separated, he heard a loud ahhh! coming from the crowd, and he was sure the sound reached up to the bell tower, soaring straight to the brilliantly blue sky.

Octavio saw Rodolfo at the fringe of the crowd. His face was glum, but there was satisfaction stamped on its expression. It had been his desire that Alejandra marry Octavio, and that wish was now fulfilled. When he had approached Octavio with the idea of matrimony two years before, he pulled Alejandra out of school and saw to it that she was given Ana's job at the shoe factory.

Rodolfo returned Octavio's glances; his eyes told him that everything was as it should be and that together with Alejandra he would build for the future with sons. Octavio looked at Alejandra and saw that she looked not only radiantly happy, but victorious as well. When she returned her husband's smile, her eyes told him that she thought she was the winner and that her sister Ana had lost. Octavio understood, and smiled in return.

As the wedding party rode back home in Reyes Soto's car, Octavio thought of the past two years. He and Alejandra had saved every penny so that they could be married in a ceremony such as this one. Together they had worked extra hours, sometimes even on Sundays, so that on this day she could wear the dress of her choice and he the suit of an elegant young man. The money they had put away, however, covered only the cost of their outfits and a reception to be held in Reyes Soto's garage. But it didn't matter to either of them that they would have to continue living with Rodolfo and the rest of the children because they couldn't afford a place of their own after these expenses. Neither did it seem important to Alejandra and Octavio that they would have to return to work the following Monday so that they could settle their unpaid debts.

Octavio sat back in the seat thinking that the bills didn't matter. What was important was that he had Alejandra and that he had followed her father's advice. "It's good for a young man to lay with a woman before marrying, because then he brings that experience to his wife and performs better as a man."

On the other hand, Rodolfo harped when telling Octavio

that under no circumstance should he marry a woman who was not a virgin. "If you marry such a woman, it is the same as eating another man's leftovers. Would you be content with garbage on your table, Octavio?"

These words were so engraved on Octavio that he once put Alejandra to the test. He invited her up to the hill to watch the sunset, and there he asked her to be intimate with him, but she shrank back shocked, insulted even. He ignored her reaction and reached under her skirt aiming to insert his fingers under her panties. Alejandra had been caught unaware. But she jerked away from him. She ran home alone, and didn't speak to him for several days until he apologized and swore never to do that again before getting married.

Octavio kept his promise. He, nevertheless, asked her again to come to the hill several times, but she declined each time. He liked this in Alejandra because he felt challenged and more desirous of her. He also remembered Ana, and the ease with which she used to take off her clothes and the abandon with which she gave herself to him. Whenever he was assaulted by feelings of remorse for what he had done to her, he told himself that she was not the type of woman meant to be a wife to anybody, that she was too easy; cheap even.

When the car drove onto the dirt driveway of the Soto house, it had been preceded by all the guests who were waiting for the bride and groom. Octavio and Alejandra got out of the car and glided through the crowd to the open garage as they were showered with shouts of "*¡Viva el novio! ¡Viva la novia!*" The place was decorated with satin streamers and large white cardboard bells, and to one side was a table already laden with gaily wrapped gifts.

As the newlyweds walked along smiling, shaking hands, and exchanging embraces, the guests pelted them with rice and confetti. A trio of guitar players crooned *boleros*, and soon there was dancing and drinking of wine amid shouts of "*¡Qué linda boda!*" A big cheer went up when the three-tiered cake was cut.

After a while, Octavio took Alejandra by the hand and together they crossed the street to the Calderón house and went into the bedroom that had now been set aside for their use. Without speaking, Octavio took off his clothes; Alejandra did the same thing. When she laid down on the bed, she was so still that he looked at her face to make sure she was awake. When he got onto the bed, he stayed on his back beside her for a few moments, then he rolled over on top of her and with one of his legs he spread hers apart. When he pressed himself into her, he felt her body shiver and he heard her moan. When it was over, he toppled back onto his back. His body still throbbing and agitated, Octavio felt an enormous relief because now he was certain that Alejandra had been a virgin.

I lived and worked with the Bast family after the birth of Ismael, and we became a family. Franklin loved my son, showering him with affectionate words and sounds. He often took Ismael in his arms, carrying him around the kitchen and outside when the weather was fine. Amy, initially surprised at her husband, often told me that she never dreamed that Franklin was capable of expressing so much warmth. She also loved Ismael, and she showed her affection for him by knitting him booties and sweaters. I know now that I grew to love Amy and Franklin as I had never loved anyone in my own family.

During the first months after his birth, Ismael was left indoors and cared for in rotating shifts by the three adults; one stayed with the boy while the other two went out to work. When he began to walk on his own, the pattern changed because now Ismael was allowed to accompany one of the three people as they went about working.

This pattern worked well until the day of their first argument. Franklin wanted to take Ismael along to keep him company while he counted sacks of feed, but Amy said that it was her turn to take the boy. Ana, under the impression that it was her day, protested. The conversation escalated to a near fight until Franklin, waving his arms in the air, came up with the solution.

"Let's be calm about this matter. I think that we can sit at the kitchen table and work out a schedule."

"Schedule! What are you talking about, Franklin? We don't need any such thing!" Amy showed her irritation at not being able to take Ismael with her on that day.

Ana broke in on Amy, "I agree with Franklin. Here's a calendar so we can write in the day each of us takes Ismael. All we have to do is follow the schedule."

"Oh, all right! All right! Have it your way, but we all know who the boy really wants to be with, don't we?"

They agreed to follow the schedule. So it was that Ismael went along with each of them, learning the different chores of an egg ranch before he was able to speak.

Amy and Franklin were happy with Ana's work because she seemed tireless. She worked so hard that at times they were compelled to tell her to come in to rest, to eat a sandwich or to let up for the day. Ana seemed to thrive on work, however, and she seemed impatient to get out to feed the chickens, to gather the eggs, and to pack them in cases. When Amy taught Ana how to drive the Model-T, Ana was anxious to drive her on their routes to distribute the crates to neighborhood grocery stores.

The practice of Amy reading from the Bible kept up, as did the periods of reflection, but now they were put off until Ismael had been put to sleep. Words that Ana had never heard often cropped up during those readings. Sometimes Amy or Franklin were able to explain the words, but it happened frequently that their definitions didn't make sense to her. So she asked Amy to stop off at a book store she had noticed on the road leading into East Los Angeles.

Ana bought a dictionary which she placed by her side each night after that. Whenever a word or an expression came along that she didn't understand, she wrote it down on a pad which she kept by her elbow. Now, when they finished the periods of reflection, she stayed up for a while to look up the unknown words. After a few months, Ana, who had missed finishing school by two years, began to develop a vocabulary that would eventually take her far beyond that expected of a high school graduate.

During the last years of the war, change became obvious to Amy, Franklin, and Ana. There was a rash of new building going on, slowly at first, and then at a quicker pace. They eventually noticed that structures began to show up near the boundaries of the ranch. While on their routes, Amy and Ana commented frequently about the increase they saw in car and pedestrian traffic on Whittier Boulevard. These changes were confirmed the day a couple of real estate agents approached Franklin, wondering if he would consider selling the spread. The government, they said, needed storage space. He declined the offer, but that evening the three discussed the matter even to the point of forgetting about the Bible reading.

"Cousin Mabel writes that her son, Kevin Thomas, has been assigned to a Navy yard out here. Says she and her husband are likely to up and move out here, just to be close to their son."

Amy spoke of her family in Oklahoma, how they too were noticing changes, and that folks were pulling up stakes and moving out to California. "That's probably why there's such a fuss going on out here. Time was that you could almost hear a pin drop. Isn't that so, Franklin?"

Nodding his head in affirmation, Franklin glanced at Ana who seemed especially quiet that evening. "Anything the matter, Ana? You feeling queasy or something?"

"I'm feeling just fine." Ana had unconsciously taken on the drawl with which Franklin and Amy spoke; now she used their words most of the time. "It's that I got to thinking about all this ruckus, and how maybe we could do something with it."

Franklin, sensing that Ana was thinking of something important, was the first to break in. "I don't follow your meaning."

"I mean, all we do now is deliver eggs to a few grocery stores, mostly between here and Los Angeles. It seems to me that maybe we can fan out, expand and sell different things other than just eggs."

Amy and Franklin sat straight up in their chairs, their necks elongated and tense, as was their habit whenever they were surprised. They stared first at Ana, then they exchanged an alarmed look with each other.

Amy heard herself speak, "Different...other than just eggs! What do we have to sell if it's not eggs?"

"I don't know, Amy." Ana paused as if to formulate words that were coming to her mind. "It seems to me that together we could make things, based on chickens and eggs..."

Amy burst in on what Ana was saying, "You mean food?" She appeared both interested and frightened, as if Ana were proposing that they again uproot themselves, just as they had at the beginning of the Great Depression. "No! I really don't think that would be a good idea. We're doing just fine as we are. No use getting greedy and bite off more than we can chew..."

"Oh, now, Amy. Just a minute! Let's give Ana a chance to speak." Franklin wanted to hear more of what the young woman was thinking. He had increasingly become impressed with her ways of figuring things out and the manner in which she was able to grasp how best to do something. He hadn't forgotten that it was Ana who had thought of relocating the coops so that there would be better drainage and less flies on the property. Turning to her, he said, "Go on, Ana. We're listening."

She smiled. "I was thinking of the Navy yards in Long Beach we've been hearing about, and the new factories for planes and things..." She paused as if searching, "I think they're out in El Segundo, or maybe Torrance..."

"Good God, Gertie!" Amy nearly jumped out of her chair just thinking of the distances that Ana was proposing. "How in the world do you think that we could get out there and back in just one day?"

Ana would not be intimidated. "That's why I got the map, Amy. Remember? Look, it can be done. In fact, people are beginning to do it more and more, going from one side of town to the other, that is. From here we can take Whittier Boulevard, then left on Atlantic, and then..."

"And what would we sell other than eggs at factories and naval yards? Why, they'd pelt us with our own product before buying raw eggs!" Amy turned to Franklin for support, but she glared at him when she saw his expression of interest and growing enthusiasm.

"I don't mean plain old eggs, but food, just as you said a minute ago. What I mean is that we can prepare things with eggs and transport them out to sell during the workers' breaks and lunch time. I remember when I was working at the factory, I would have given anything for something special to buy during my time off."

"Maybe the girl's got something!" Franklin was almost sold on the idea of catering to those far-off places.

"All right! I'm listening. Just what kind of things would we make?"

Ana spoke slowly, weighing her words, "We could begin by making *jericayas...*"

"Lord, God! What is that! I couldn't even begin to pronounce the word." Amy was becoming more contentious.

"A *jericaya* is a small custard that's made with eggs and a little milk. They're not hard to make. We could whip up a batch and drive them out to Long Beach just to test if the workers would pay attention to us. If they don't like us, then we come back home and forget this whole thing. But if they do...well then I can think of other items to make. Things like scrambled egg *burritos*, or even *rompope...*"

"Rom...rom!... What was that?"

"It's like the egg nog you make for Christmas, Amy. In fact, I think it is the same thing. It tastes real good and it gives a lot of energy. You feel like working after a few sips."

Ana, enthused by her idea, looked from Amy to Franklin, and then back again. She was sitting on the edge of her chair, her face flushed with excitement. She liked what she was feeling; planning made her heart beat fast and she felt happy.

"Well, now, I do declare!..."

Plunging ahead without hearing Amy's protestations, Ana looked at Franklin, "There's just one small problem...these things have to be kept cold, otherwise we take the risk of their melting, or going bad."

"I guess...yes! I think I can gear up something for you, Ana. Maybe some kind of ice chest. That would work, wouldn't it?"

Ana smiled again, especially when she saw that Amy was giving up on the obstacles. She had leapt to her feet and was scratching her chin as she always did when she was about to begin a new job.

The three of them plunged into the new enterprise. After the day's ranch work was completed, they worked together first to make the *jericayas*, the small custards that Amy cast in her muffin molds. They were forced to skip the Bible readings because of the time of night at which they finished. When Ana mapped out the route that they would take to reach Long Beach, they decided to concentrate on one job site in the beginning and wait to see how business went.

The ice chest devised by Franklin worked, fitting snugly

into the car's trunk. Equipped for business, Ana and Amy, with Ismael on her lap, drove to the coast and onto the docks where they parked the car outside the main entrance of one of the plants and waited for the lunch whistle to sound. Shortly after the blast was heard, workers began to emerge from the huge doorway. There were hundreds of them, men in denim overalls and women in slacks and plaid blouses, their hair caught up in nets and scarves. A handful of them caught sight of the sign Ana had handwritten: "Come and get it! Mexican dessert!"

A couple of the workers sauntered over to the women and the boy. Ana smiled and greeted them, saying cheerfully, "Five cents a custard, and you're in for a treat." She made her first sale, and less than hour later their supply of *jericayas* was gone. Amy and Ana returned home, and together with Franklin, who now would have to remain behind to take care of the ranch, they sat at the table and calculated that, including the ingredients, their labor, the gasoline used for transportation, and even figuring in the ice, they had made more money than they did delivering eggs to stores.

Soon afterward, Franklin went to one of the neighboring ranches to buy a used Chevrolet pick-up truck that he had been offered some time before. He rigged up the vehicle with fixed containers and ice chests so that Amy and Ana could safely transport their goods. Franklin also included a small cubicle where Ismael could take naps during the afternoon while they waited to finish their selling.

The Basts and Ana Calderón worked hard on their ranch and their business as the war years crept by. They remodeled the ranch house to include a large bathroom with a shower and indoor toilet. The bedroom used by Ana and Ismael was expanded so that two beds fit in with space left over for a bookcase and a desk. Franklin negotiated with the Telephone Company, and, after months of waiting, the house finally got a telephone. It was a party line which the Bast house shared with three other homes, but everyone was grateful knowing that it was a luxury during those years.

The only contact that I had with 'Apá and my sisters during the war years was César. It was through him that I learned of how my father had forbidden anyone to utter my name. It was César who told me of Tavo's and Alejandra's wedding, of how everyone had celebrated, and of how my sister went around the house acting like she was a queen.

I usually picked up César when Amy and I were in the neighborhood delivering eggs. He'd wait for us in the alley behind Doña Hiroko's store where we met him. There, he would jump into the back of the truck and take Ismael in his arms, holding him there as Amy and I delivered the flats of eggs.

César was only around twelve years old at that time, but he seemed much older. He was a tall boy, so much so that most people thought that he was at least four or five years older than he really was. He liked this, and he tried to act like a grown-up. I noticed also that he was using pachuco *words he had picked up in the barrio. When I questioned him about the way he was speaking, he laughed, telling me that the girls ran after him because of it.*

Even though he looked like a teenager, my brother was still a little boy during the first years of the war. If I ever forgot César's age, something always happened to remind me of it. I realized how young he was, especially at the end of our runs when it was time for him to get off the pick-up and head home. Each time he'd cry as he hugged me goodbye. I used to think it was kind of funny that such a big boy cried so easily, but it helped me remember that he wasn't as grown up as he looked.

Later on, when Amy and I started traveling to Long Beach to sell our food, César came along, too. He loved the ships anchored at dockside, and he jabbered with the riveters and welders. He was always full of questions. "Ana, why don't you become one of these workers instead of making desserts and frying chickens to sell?" This was one of his favorite ones, and I tried to tell him the truth. "Because I feel freer at what I'm doing, César. I haven't forgotten what it's like to work in a factory."

After saying this to him, I wondered if I was really free. Now, I doubt it. I don't think I was free because there wasn't a day that went by without my thinking of Tavo. After César told me of him and Alejandra, I found that I couldn't sleep. I

*felt jealous and angry, and I visualized them in bed, kissing
and holding one another.*

*This went on until a year after, in the spring of '43, César
told me that Tavo and Alejandra had had a big fight. He said
that it had begun as an argument, and no one had paid attention because they always bickered. Tavo then left, slamming
the door and swearing never to return.*

*César said that he did come back later that night when
they were all in bed, and that he was drunk. Tavo pounded on
the front door, shouting for Alejandra to come out to talk to
him. When she did, they screamed at one another, waking up
most of the neighbors. She tried to scratch his face, and he
slapped her so hard that she fell off the porch. 'Apá tried to
help Alejandra, but Tavo, crazed with rage and whiskey, hit
him, too. When he realized what he had done, he ran away
and didn't return.*

*A few days later, César told me that they had heard from
Tavo. Still drunk and not telling anyone, he had enlisted in
the Marines. When he wrote to Alejandra to tell her of his
whereabouts, he was in training at Camp Pendleton near San
Diego. A few weeks later, he was shipped out to fight the
Japanese in the South Pacific.*

*When I heard this, I became more nervous and agitated
than ever. I hardly slept at nights and I found it hard to eat.
Tavo's face was engraved inside of me so that every time I
closed my eyes I saw him. Sometimes, trying to get relief, I
took Ismael in my arms, hoping to fall asleep, but it was
impossible. It wasn't until one night when I held my son close
that a feeling buried deep inside of me floated out. I recognized it. I was wishing with all the strength of my soul that
Tavo would be killed over there, so that he would never
return. Despite the shame I felt because of that longing, I was
finally able to sleep.*

Shortly after midnight on a sweltering Saturday in June,
1943, the phone rang in the Bast house. Franklin, still in his
undershorts, answered. When he knocked at Ana's door she
was already in her robe and heading out to the kitchen.

"It's for you."

She couldn't explain the feeling of fear that gripped her; she picked up the phone, nonetheless. There was silence at the other end of the line even after she had spoken into the receiver several times.

Finally, a voice stuttered, "Ana, it's me..."

It was Alejandra's voice, shaky, filled with tears. Ana's first thought was that Octavio had been killed. She braced herself.

"¿Qué pasa, Alejandra? Where are you calling from?"

"He's dying...beaten...he's calling for you..."

Her mind reeled trying to focus in on what her sister was saying. Her thoughts scrambled in different directions, unable to grasp whom her sister was talking about. She had expected to be told of a death in battle, on a ship, or in a plane crash.

"Who, Alejandra? Who's hurt? Is it 'Apá?"

"No! It's César! Some of his friends brought him in, and I think he's dying. He's over at the house...I'm calling you from the liquor store."

"How? What happened?... Alejandra, I can't understand what you're saying! Stop crying, and talk to me!"

Her sister's words were garbled by hysteria, and they were incomprehensible. Ana could hear her other sisters wailing in the background; she also heard male voices jabbering loudly. Trying to piece things together, she concluded that they must have run across the street to the only phone available. "Alejandra, did you leave César alone? Pass the phone over to somebody else. Do it, right now! Do you hear me?"

After a pause of a few seconds, the voice of a young man came on the line. "Ana, it's me, Memo Estrada."

"Memo, what happened? Tell me slowly so I can understand you."

"We were out on the street..."

"Who, Memo?"

"Just a few of us guys. It was Oscar, Carlos, your brother and me. We weren't doing nothing, I swear! We had just come out of the dance hall, when some *gabacho* sailors started beating us up, then some guys from the other side of town got into it. It was a mess! I couldn't tell who was beating who..."

Ana's blood rushed to her head. It pounded with such force that for a second her hearing was blocked and she was having difficulty catching the words coming to her over the thin black wire she was twisting in her left hand. The earlier part of the evening flashed through her mind.

César had come to visit. He had come with his friend Memo who had driven in a car borrowed from his uncle. At first glance, Ana had a difficult time recognizing her brother because he was dressed in a zoot-suit he was wearing for the first time. She had never seen him dressed that way. Not knowing what to say, she invited both young men to come into the kitchen. Franklin and Amy were speechless at seeing César looking like a grown man. He obviously had come for their benefit, so that they could take in the outfit of which he seemed so proud.

César's zoot-suit was sharp, Ana admitted to herself. It was tailor-made of pin-striped sharkskin fabric, bottle green in color, and its wide shoulder pads accentuated the boy's already broad back. The coat hung gracefully nearly to his knees, and the slacks draped to a narrow fit around his ankles. César's shoes were of cordovan leather; they gleamed in the defused light of the kitchen. His hat, which he had deliberately left on, because without it the get-up was incomplete, was light green, and its wide brim was turned up slightly on the left side, giving César a cocky, daring look.

"*Esa, carnala.* How do you like my *tacuche?*"

César's improvised sing-song accent left Ana speechless for a few seconds. Recuperating, she said, "It looks pretty good, César, but I think that you're too young to be dressed like that. And what's with this jive talk? Has 'Apá seen you dressed up like this, and talking like a *pachuco?*"

"Nah. The *jefito* would have a heart attack if he saw me. I keep my threads over at Memo's. Right, *ese vato loco?*"

Ana was having difficulty dealing with the change in her brother's looks and his manner of speaking. She had noticed words creeping into his language before, but never so marked. She realized, however, that he had come over to impress her, and that he felt good about his new style but, she told herself, he was too young.

"Where are you boys going tonight, all dressed up this way? I hope not out on the streets." Franklin had stepped over to stand in front of the two young men, and when he saw them make a face, he reminded them, "Haven't you heard what happened the other night? Some marines put a couple of the guys from your neighborhood right in the hospital." He was referring to the attack that occurred in the center of town a few days earlier.

"Nah, Mr. Bast. That won't happen to us. We're just going to push some trucks around tonight, that's all."

Memo, also in a zoot-suit, giggled loudly at what César had said.

Amy sucked her teeth in irritation because she didn't get the joke, but Franklin turned to her, "It's an expression that means they're going dancing."

Ana took César by the arm and led him out to the front porch. Memo followed. When she looked back, she saw Franklin and Amy return to their bedroom, shaking their heads in disapproval. She patted her brother on the shoulder to let him know that she thought he was handsome in his suit, and she tried to smile.

"You look real good, *hermanito*, and I'm glad you came to show me your new outfit, but I think that you and Memo should go back home and stay there. It's Saturday night, and you don't know what's going on out there."

"Are you kidding, Ana? Tonight's a big night. The chicks are just waiting for us. Right, *ese vato*?"

Ana didn't let Memo answer. "César, cut it out. You're only thirteen years old! I don't care how grown up you look dressed this way! You're still too young to be messing around with girls. Now, do as I say, and go straight home!" Turning to the other boy, Ana blurted out, "Memo, how old are you?"

"Nineteen."

"I think that even you are too young. Come on. Be good and go home. César, Amy and I will be out in the barrio on Monday around eleven o'clock. I want you to come with me. In fact, now that school's out, I want you to come with us everyday."

Crestfallen because he had not received the praise he had expected from his sister and because she had spoken to him as if he were a little boy, César hung his head, nodding despondently. He turned to his friend and jerked his head toward the car.

This had happened a few hours earlier and Ana now spoke into the telephone as the pounding in her head subsided. "Memo, how badly is he hurt? You didn't leave him alone, did you?"

"Nah, the old man stayed with him. Ana, I think your
brother is in real bad shape, but your *jefito* doesn't want us to
take him to the hospital. He says that César will be all right
by himself."

"I'm coming over."

Ana hooked the receiver onto the goose-necked telephone.
When she looked up, she saw that Franklin was dressed and
that the keys to the pick-up were dangling from his hand.
"Amy will stay with Ismael. I'll do the driving."

She darted into her room without saying a word. She
came out dressed in gray slacks and a black cotton blouse.
She had on the high top shoes she usually wore around the
ranch. Amy stood by the sink, an anxious look flickering in
her blue eyes. "You two be careful. I'll have breakfast when
you return."

Franklin and Ana traveled in silence westbound on
Whittier Boulevard toward the barrio. It was past one in the
morning, so they hardly encountered any cars. When the
headlights of their truck flashed on the sign indicating
Humphrys Avenue, Franklin turned right, stopped on the
dirt shoulder and turned off the motor. "I'll wait for you here,
Ana. Take your time, but call me if I can be of help."

She patted his right forearm and jumped out of the truck;
her feet created a transparent puff of dust. Without looking
to either side, she approached the house to which she had not
returned since the day her father had beaten and chased her
away. All the lights were on. She took a few seconds to take a
deep breath of night air. She was scared; she knew that she
had been forbidden to return by her father, but her desire to
see César overpowered her fear. She walked up the three
steps onto the wooden porch and she rapped on the frame of
the screen.

Rosalva opened the door. "Ana!" Her voice was loud, shrill
and it made the other voices stop in mid-sentence. A deep,
threatening silence followed. It seemed to Ana that everyone
inside had suddenly vanished and that if she entered, she
would find an empty room. She was trying to gather her
thoughts as to what to do next, when the screen door suddenly slammed painfully against her forehead. Momentarily
stunned, Ana swerved backward as she tried to regain her
balance.

"You here! Haven't I prohibited it?"

Rodolfo Calderón had rammed the door against her with all the force of his arms, but as she backed away, her eyes made out his face in the darkness of the porch. She saw that it was filled with fury and rage. He had not changed; hatred for her still dominated him.

"'Apá, let me see César! *¡Por favor!* For the love of 'Amá!" Her voice didn't betray her fear; it was strong and steady. She opened the door and stepped inside.

"*¡Lárgate de aquí!*"

As he commanded her to go away, his large hand lashed out, landing squarely on Ana's nose. Blood gushed out of both nostrils; in the gloom, it glittered like black liquid. She jerked her hands to her face, elbows up in defense against other blows. She had backed out the door and off the porch. She stood her ground, feet spread wide apart on the weedy dirt.

"'Apá, please!..."

Rodolfo jumped off the porch, by-passing the steps. Ana saw this and retreated toward the street, moving backward while not turning her back to her father, who was charging straight ahead in pursuit of her. She stumbled, then fell. She saw him coming toward her, his face distorted with wrath.

Ana began to writhe on the ground blindly, anxiously groping for something with which to defend herself. Her fingers finally landed on a rock, and even though it was large, she was able to cup it in her right hand. As her father loomed directly above her, Ana sprang to her feet and lunged toward him. She raised her arm and brought it down with all the force in her body. She felt it crash on his forehead. He reeled and fell on his haunches.

Franklin had run up to help Ana and was now by her side. He held her, trying to lead the way out to the car, but by now Rodolfo, though stunned and swaying, had gotten back to his feet. He was hysterical. He rolled his eyes from side to side, their whites gleaming menacingly in the dark. He held a hand to his bloodied face, and with the other he gestured violently towards Ana.

"You cursed whore. For raising your hand to your father, I curse you and your children again. Now get out of here!"

As Franklin led Ana through the front wire gate, she closed her eyes and cupped her hands over her ears, trying to drown out her father's words that again cursed her and her son, this time because she had raised her hand in anger against him.

César died that day and nothing was ever done about it. 'Apá refused to call the police because he said that nothing they could do would bring my brother back to life. So there was a wake held at the house that night followed by a mass the next day. I was forbidden to be with my sisters, but I made sure to be at the back of the church during the service. Franklin and Amy drove me to the cemetery later on to see where César's body was buried, and I thought of Jasmín and of my brothers who never made it through life. 'Amá seemed to be next to me; I thought I heard her crying softly.

Two years passed before the war ended. Many of the boys from the barrio were killed, and others were badly wounded. Reyes Junior was one of the ones who died, and his friend, Henry Miranda, lost one of his legs. When Henry returned home, the government paid for a car specially geared for him. Tavo was not wounded nor killed. He returned with two medals for bravery in the battle of Iwo Jima.

During those years, the Bast chicken farm grew. When I told Amy and Franklin that I wanted to return to school to get a diploma, both of them insisted that I stop working on the ranch and that they would pay for Ismael's and my expenses. After that, instead of making desserts and food, they decided to set up a poultry store on Whittier Boulevard. That idea went over so well that soon they expanded it into a large market.

We heard that Doña Hiroko's store was seriously damaged after a fire bomb was thrown through the front window. She was alone because her three sons had enlisted in the Army and were fighting the war in Europe. After that she was so afraid that she sold her store, her house, and all her things and willingly went to Tule Lake, where she said that she would at least be with others like her.

Ismael had grown mischievous and energetic during those two years. He ran after the chickens, shouting and filling the house with laughter. He was beautiful; his hair had taken on chestnut tones and his skin was white, despite the sun. Amy and Franklin took care of him during the hours that I spent in the classroom, and soon Ismael grew to love them as if they had been his grandparents. He even called Amy "Abuelita," and Franklin "Abuelito."

'Apá died just before the war ended. He neither spoke to me nor allowed me to come near him when he became ill. I wondered at that time if he understood how much I wanted to see him, at least to ask him why he hated me so much. I had hoped to tell him that there was still time for me, and that I would do something special with my life, so that it would erase the shame he had felt when I had Ismael without a husband. But he died taking his hatred for me to the grave.

I got my high-school diploma in June, 1945. Amy and Franklin had a graduation party for me, and my sisters came—all of them except Alejandra. I still have the photograph of me, Ismael and the Basts on that day. Shortly after that, Pilar called to tell me that Tavo would be receiving his discharge sometime in late August. When I hung up the telephone, I asked myself what would I do if suddenly I saw him again. What would I say, I wondered; how would I act? I didn't think about it anymore because I realized that I no longer felt anything for Tavo. Where there had been love, now there was nothing.

છ⊱⊰ઝ

When the last of the boys returned from the war by the end of August, most of the families of the barrio got together for a celebration picnic at Echo Park. The Delgados, Ledesmas, Leyvas, Sotos, Calderóns and others brought food and drink to share with one another. Most of the men still wore their uniforms, and the crowd was dotted with the field green of those in the Army, bottle-green of the Marines, and sailors in Navy blue.

Games of softball and volleyball were organized as well as three-legged races. There was singing and a lot of hugging, but most of all there was telling of stories, each man vying to out-talk the next one. War experiences were exchanged, and some of them grew more exaggerated with each swig of cold beer.

After a long time of loud guffaws and slapping of thighs,
people became tired of listening, so most of the groups went
back to their own conversations. Over at the Calderón table,
however, things were different because only Octavio and
Alejandra were seated at it, and they were not saying anything. He sat with his chin cupped in his hand; he seemed to
be thinking of other things. Alejandra, too, was distracted as
she looked into a hand mirror, fixing her hair and make-up.

Octavio was even more handsome than before the war.
His body had filled out with hard muscle, his shoulders were
broader and his waist leaner, and he had returned from the
Pacific wearing a mustache that emphasized his eyes as well
as his teeth.

Alejandra had also changed. She was still beautiful,
although she looked older than twenty-two. People said that
it was because she had inherited too much responsibility too
soon. She had married at nineteen, and barely had that happened when Octavio left her for the war. With Ana gone from
the house, Alejandra, as the gossips put it, was left alone
with a stern father and four younger sisters to look after. She
had grown bitter, some said, because Octavio had not left her
at least with a first child.

Octavio had come home a few weeks before the picnic.
Officially, he was still based in Camp Pendleton, where he
stayed Monday through Friday. Even though he lived with
her only on weekends, their relationship was already
strained. They had gone through several arguments, which
usually ended with shouting and his storming off to the base.

This time, the bickering began because Octavio was
teaching Cruz how to jitterbug. At first Alejandra seemed
happy as she changed the record so that the music would go
on, but she gradually became irritated when she saw how
tightly he held her sister's waist. Cruz was now seventeen,
and she and Pilar had turned into beautiful girls. The twins
had developed exceptional bodies with slim waists, rounded
hips and full busts. Alejandra had noticed that, physically,
they surpassed her; only Ana was more beautiful than all of
them, and Alejandra admitted this only to herself.

As she looked on as Octavio swirled and danced to the
strong beat of the music, Alejandra saw how much he was
enjoying himself. She saw that Cruz danced along, following
his lead, dazzled by his strength and rhythm. She seemed

charmed by his smile, which she returned with her eyes. It occurred to Alejandra that her sister's glances were inviting Octavio to come closer, and when he stepped forward, she saw that he drew Cruz up against his body so tightly that her breasts bulged against his chest. The move had happened quickly, but Alejandra caught it.

She became furious. She suddenly pulled the record away from the player, smashing it against the wall. Alejandra's move had been so quick and unexpected that the crashing record startled Octavio and Cruz, and both flinched in surprise, involuntarily shrinking and shielding their face from the broken pieces that showered them. A terrible argument followed which ended only when Cruz ran outside crying. The other two, however, did not speak to one another all that evening.

Now, despite the laughter and playing around, Octavio felt bored with the picnic. So he stood up without saying anything and walked away from the table, leaving Alejandra alone. He wanted to be by himself to sort things out. He walked along the small lagoon under the tall palm trees for a while, then over a hill, down to where he saw a small corral which housed ponies. When he got closer he saw that there was a line of people, most of them with children, purchasing tickets.

He smiled when he saw the small track, and he walked over to watch the kids ride the ponies, enjoying their squeals of excitement. He stood there for several minutes, looking at each new rider that entered the track. Octavio's body suddenly tensed when he turned again to the ticket office and noticed a young woman standing in line. He blinked several times as if trying to get rid of a trapped eyelash, then he rubbed his eyes. He finally realized that he was staring at Ana, and that she was holding a little boy by the hand. At first, Octavio didn't know what to do. He knew that she had not seen him, and that he could easily stride off without her knowing that he had been there. He felt compelled, however, to get near her, to say hello, and he was also pulled by the sight of the child. He decided to approach her.

"Hello, Ana." His voice was soft as he pronounced her name. When she heard someone talking to her, she turned to see who it was. It took her a few seconds to adjust to the surprise of seeing Octavio standing in front of her. While she

gazed at him, he was able to see that she had become lovelier
than he had remembered. Her hair was longer, and it glim-
mered in the afternoon sun just as it had when they played in
the cove off Puerto Real.

Octavio looked at Ana's dark complexioned face, at her
slender neck, the full bust, the waist and hips emphasized by
slacks that flowed softly to her feet. Looking at her filled him
with joy and with an intense desire to take her in his arms.
He took a step towards her, but he hesitated when he saw
that she moved back and away from him.

Without returning his greeting, she turned to her place in
line. Seeing Octavio so suddenly and unexpectedly set her
mind reeling, and she felt her heart beating wildly. Ana
scolded herself for being there, on that day, at that time, forgetting that she brought Ismael to the pony rides every
Sunday, that it was his weekly treat. She fought to regain her
composure, and when it was her turn to buy a ticket, she
calmly put the dime on the counter as she took the small chip
from the cashier. She was hoping that her aloofness would
put off Octavio and that he would walk away.

Taking a firmer grip of Ismael's hand, Ana made her way
toward the entrance of the track, but she was aware that
Octavio was walking behind her. She helped put her son onto
the small saddle, making sure that the safety belt was in
place. When the assistant led the pony onto the track, Ismael
let out a howl of excitement. She took a deep breath and
turned to face Octavio, her face frozen and expressionless.

"When did you return?"

"A few weeks ago."

"Great." She muttered the word with finality; it said
goodbye.

Octavio had no intention of leaving. "You look beautiful,
Ana. Honest to God, you do. You don't know how much I
thought of you when I was over there." He stepped closer to
her, so much that she shifted, moving away from him again.

"I have nothing to say to you. Please go away." Her words
sounded hard, harsh, and he flinched as if she had slapped
his face. He saw that she meant for him to leave, but he
decided to pretend not to have heard what she said.

"He's beautiful, too." He pointed his right index finger at
Ismael's bouncing figure, "and I can't believe that he's mine,
too."

It was Ana's turn to wince. Turning fully to face Octavio, she put her clenched fists on her hips and said, "Ismael is mine, all mine! You have nothing to do with him and I have nothing to do with you. Now, leave me alone! I don't want to talk to you!" Her words squeezed out of clenched teeth because her heart had filled with fear when she caught the strange look in his eyes as he pointed at Ismael. It seemed hungry, greedy.

The pony carrying Ismael rounded the track and trotted up to the end; the boy was red-faced and laughing. As the assistant was unfastening Ismael's safety belt, Octavio bolted towards him with long, quick strides, leaving Ana behind. He took Ismael out of the saddle and into his arms. The boy looked at him, wondering who he was. But he didn't show fear because he soon saw his mother by his side. Before Ana could do anything, Octavio kissed Ismael on both cheeks as he told him, "I'm your daddy."

When the boy heard this he recoiled, kicking and straining to be put on the ground. Ana grabbed her son, wrenching him away from those stiff, hard arms. As she did this, she saw that Octavio's eyes were filled with tears. The sight only provoked her. She was outraged at what he had told Ismael.

Taking the boy by the hand, Ana ran over to the parking area. She didn't look to see if Octavio was behind her. Fumbling through her bag, she finally found the keys for the pick-up, and even though her hands were shaking, she was able to jump in, put Ismael on the passenger side, insert the key into the ignition, and crank on the motor. The tires screeched as she backed the truck out. She saw that Octavio was still standing where she had left him. He looked so rigid that it flashed through her mind that his feet were buried in concrete.

☙◊❧

We stayed up most of that night talking about what had happened in the park. Amy and Franklin knew all about Octavio from the beginning, and, like me, they hadn't expected him to come back into my life. We also knew that he was married to Alejandra and that they were without children. This

thought now worried us most of all. As for myself, there was
something else. After the strange fire I had seen in Octavio's
eyes when he looked at Ismael, I felt terrified. But I didn't say
this to Franklin or Amy because I didn't want them to feel
what I was feeling.

We sat at the kitchen table, talking until we finally decid-
ed to take the incident for what it was: a chance meeting, a
coincidence that more than likely would not happen again.
Now I see how foolish we were, and we found out soon that
this decision was our biggest mistake.

Next day, I went to work at the store and I forced myself to
plan for Ismael's first day of school, which was still a few
weeks away. In the meantime, he stayed on the ranch with
Franklin during the day while Amy and I looked after the
store. As I did the work of sorting, ordering and taking stock
of the inventory, I put the encounter with Octavio out of my
mind. I fell into a kind of lull, telling myself that everything
was just as it had been before I had bumped into him at the
park.

❧

Several days after the picnic, Alejandra faced Octavio.
Her body was rigid; it seemed in conflict with the soft over-
stuffed sofa where she sat. She was glaring at him as he
squatted on a small chair in front of her, elbows supported on
his spread-out knees, his hands clutched together and his
head hanging low. He was quiet now, but his words still
echoed in Alejandra's ears. Finally, she spoke.

"Maybe 'Apá was blind to it, Octavio, but I knew all along
that you and Ana were messing around. You think this is big
news for me, don't you?"

Octavio didn't answer her question. He seemed to be
bracing himself for battle as he clenched and unclenched his
fists. After a while, he covered his face with them.

"I suspected right away that she was pregnant. I'm the
one who told 'Apá to check her out. I'll bet you never thought
of that, did you?"

He still did not speak, and his silence made Alejandra
press him more. Her tone took on an air of triumph. "It's been

a long time, Octavio, and now you slither in here telling me that you're the father of Ana's kid. As if I didn't know all along!"

Even though her voice grew huskier with each word it was controlled; it didn't betray the rage that was thrashing her. She shifted her body forward, crouching slightly, trying to see his face. She could hear his hard breathing.

"Why, Octavio? Why are you telling me now?"

His head jerked up suddenly. His eyes were feverish and his skin had grown darker than usual. "Why? Because I want to be honest with..."

Alejandra sarcastically cut him off. "Honest! You? Don't make me laugh! You don't know the meaning of the word."

Stung by her words, Octavio reacted. "Okay! The hell with you! I'm telling you right now because I saw the kid the other day, do you hear me? I saw him and I want him! That's all there is to it! I don't have to explain anything more to you or to anybody else! He's mine, and I want to keep him!"

Alejandra was stunned by the tone of Octavio's words, but even more by what he was saying. His confession of fathering the boy was one thing; his intending to take possession of him was different.

She sprang to her feet, hovering over Octavio. She stood so close to him that he was forced to push his head back so that he could look at her face.

"What? You're crazy! What's got into you? You want him! I can't believe what I'm hearing! All of a sudden! Why?"

He got to his feet, turning his back on Alejandra. His voice, even though tense, had calmed down. "I told you. I saw him, and I can't stop thinking of him. The thought of him is driving me crazy. He's my son, and even though I had never thought of him before, now I want him more than anything else. He's going to be just like me. A man. And I want him to grow up with me."

"Well, you can't have him!" Alejandra was shouting now.

He spun around to face her. "No? Why not?"

"I'll leave you Octavio! I swear I will!"

Unruffled and showing that he thought her words were an empty threat, he only scowled at her.

Alejandra retreated as she looked at his face, and she lowered her voice. "I won't have someone's else's brat under the same roof with me!"

Octavio moved over and stood very close to Alejandra. The vein on his forehead was bulging, and his mouth was a menacing slit that grotesquely separated his chin from his nose. He spoke and his words seemed to come not from his lips but from somewhere else in the room.

"He's my flesh and blood, and if you know what's good for you!..."

"What, Octavio, what will you do to me? Come on, I'm waiting to see how you're going to scare me into doing what you want!"

He turned away from Alejandra, apparently shaken by her challenge. He remained quiet for a long while and then, without turning to face her, he spoke. "You'll take in the kid because Ana did what you've never been able to do. She had my baby. You—you're dry, withered up, and you hate her for it. You hate her so much, Alejandra, that you can't resist the chance of hurting her."

Alejandra's body suddenly seemed to have lost its strength and she plopped noisily back onto the sofa. When Octavio moved around to look at her he saw that her face was strangely cocked to one side. It was ashen-colored and her eyes were half closed. Like a mask, he thought, a cagey, sus-picion-filled mask. He was so engrossed in what he was see-ing that she surprised him when she spoke.

"What makes you think that Ana will give up her son just like that?" She raised her hand attempting to snap her fin-gers, and even though there was no sound, Octavio saw her gesture. When he didn't answer, she added, "Ana will kill you first."

He moved toward the front door and, placing his hand on the knob, he said, "We'll see about that."

Alejandra bolted out of her place and again began to shout. "You'll grow tired of the boy. You don't have what it takes to be a father."

"Look who talking!" His mouth contorted into a mocking sneer.

In an attempt to keep him from leaving her, Alejandra said, "What about my sisters? They live here, too, you know. What makes you think they'll accept the kid?"

"Because they will do anything you tell them to do, that's why. And because they hate Ana, too. Your father taught them how to do it. Remember?"

Octavio turned away from Alejandra as he kicked open the screen door. He walked out of the house leaving behind only the shrill sound of squeaking hinges.

∂⌘

I was speaking to a customer when I looked up to see Octavio standing at the entrance. I closed my eyes hoping to resist the surge of blood rushing to my head, but I felt hot all over, and my hands became wet with perspiration. I forced myself to concentrate on what I was saying to the customer until she left. Then I spread my feet apart and placed my hands, palms down, on the counter. It gave me a sense of balance.

∂⌘

Octavio moved silently toward her as he looked around, making sure that no one else was present.

"Hello, again."

Ana ignored his greeting. "Get it straight. I don't want to have anything to do with you." Her voice was calm; she enunciated her words slowly and clearly so that they conveyed her restrained anger.

"You really know how to get to the point, don't you? Okay! Fine! I'll do the same thing..."

She didn't allow Octavio to go on. "Please leave! Right now!"

"Get off your high horse, Ana! We're not kids anymore, remember? You still act like you're a queen or something. You're just like the rest of us."

Ana shifted her position and began moving from behind the counter in the direction of the office in the rear of the store.

Octavio took her by the arm. "Look, it's simple. I'm not here to see you. I'm here because I want my son..."

Again Ana interrupted him. This time her eyes, wide open, reflected the unspoken fear that had crept into her heart when they had faced one another in the park. "You want your son! You want your son!" She repeated the phrase as if trying to understand words that had been spoken in a language foreign to her.

She slid back behind the counter, putting a barrier between Octavio and herself. She stared unabashedly at his face, and a thought flashed through her mind: she had once loved that face above all other things and people. Now it was the mask of the enemy. She swallowed a large gulp of saliva before she spoke.

"You can't have him. Remember that you abandoned me and him. I don't know why you've had this change of mind. All I know is that you gave up whatever part you had in Ismael a long time ago. You gave it up when you stood by watching my father beating me for what you...yes, you...and I had done. You gave it up when you left me waiting like a stupid fool at the church."

Octavio didn't interrupt Ana as words poured out of her mouth. But his jaw showed the tension that was gripping him, and his lips were pressed into a tight thin line. When he finally spoke, his face took on a scowl that reflected his turmoil.

"I didn't come to be preached at! I came to tell you that you've got to understand that a boy needs a father, and for Ismael, that's me. You're only a woman and..."

"What? Excuse me! What are you saying?"

Ana's outburst cut him off, leaving him startled and groping for words. Her voice was loud, menacing, and her face had turned dark brown.

"Look at me, Octavio! I know what you're getting at, that I'm just a woman, and that without you I'm nothing. Right? That's what you mean, don't you?"

She pointed her stiff index finger, nearly grazing his nose. "Well, look at me, because you're seeing a woman who did it on her own, with the help of these people who took pity on me." She pointed to the rear of the store. "Where were you when we had to sell eggs, a dozen here and there, just to make ends meet? Where were you when I screamed for hours giving birth to my son? Answer me! Where were you? Gone! That's where you were! And why? Because you're a coward and a liar, that's why!"

Octavio seemed to have been struck dumb; he could only glare at her as she pounded him with her words. Her chest was heaving with pent-up rage. She was reliving the thread-bare life that had been made tolerable, even happy, only because of the shelter and protection given to her and Ismael by the Basts. Ana was flooded by repressed anger and hurt at having been cast out of her house by an unjust father who hated her because she had not been a son, and because she had allowed herself to love and receive nothing in return.

He finally regained a measure of balance, but instead of dealing with Ana's words, Octavio chose to attack the Basts. "Ha! Those two old *gabachos*! What do they know of loving my son!"

"*¡Ay, cabrón!* You have no right to call them *gabachos*! They've been everything for Ismael. They're his grandparents. Franklin is more than that; he's my son's father!"

By now Ana was screaming. She had not noticed that several customers had come in, and she didn't see Amy rush out from the back office. Octavio, however, suddenly became aware of the presence of those people and he appeared to be intimidated by them. He backed away from Ana, but not before muttering so low that only she could hear, "He's mine, and I'm getting him back. You just watch and see."

Octavio left the store and Ana ran to the back office, sat down at the desk, and buried her face in her hands. As soon as the place emptied, Amy closed the front entrance and went to Ana. She saw that she wasn't crying, but that her body was shaking.

"Don't worry, Ana. There's nothing he can do. Ismael is ours and there is no way on earth that man can pretend that he's the father. There's nothing—not a certificate, not a witness—that will prove it. You've got us who remember how you were thrown out of your house while he watched. If he was so concerned about his baby, why didn't he speak up there and then? No, Ana, I don't want you to be scared."

Amy's voice was calm and her words were spoken carefully, but her eyes betrayed her alarm. She had been able to catch a glimpse of Octavio's face, and she was just as frightened as Ana, who continued with her face clutched in trembling hands.

"Let's close up the place and go home. Franklin should know about this mess."

Ana wasn't able to speak, so she followed Amy's instructions in silence. When they arrived at the ranch, the pick-up had not yet come to a stop before Ana leaped out of it and, without shutting the door of the truck, rushed into the house where she found Ismael at the table eating a cookie. He was so startled by Ana's sudden appearance that he dropped the piece that was in his hand. She knelt down beside him to help pick up the crumbs, but when he came near her she took the boy in her arms. It was only then that she began to cry.

Franklin had been in the parlor, but rushed into the kitchen to see what the fuss was about. Amy took him by the arm, and together they disappeared into their bedroom. A while passed until Ismael moved slightly away from his mother. When he saw that she was crying, he wiped her face without speaking. The touch of his hands flooded Ana with serenity, and as she held her son at arms length, she told him, "I'm just a little tired, *m'hijo*. Come on, I'll get you another cookie."

That evening after Ismael had been put to bed, Ana, Franklin, and Amy talked until midnight. They pondered on the likelihood of Octavio's threat to take the boy from them. Would he dare do such a thing, and if he did, how could he get away with it? They thought of calling the police to ask for help, but decided that it wouldn't be of any use.

At the end of several hours, they came to the conclusion that the only thing they could do would be to take extra precautions with Ismael. They agreed that at no time would he be allowed out of the company of at least one of them. Ana figured out a plan to alert Ismael's teachers against Octavio coming close to the boy when he was in school.

Once in her bedroom, when Ana put out the lights, she went over to her son's bed, made sure the covers were right, and kissed his cheek. She went to bed, but she passed the night without sleeping.

Octavio stole Ismael. A thief, he intruded into our house, and he robbed me of my treasure. He let months pass so that I would be fooled into believing that I had been mistaken about him. In my stupidity, the man I had once loved now carried away the only thing that had given me happiness. Nothing could have transformed me, deformed me, as did the loss of Ismael: not my father's hatred and rejection, not even Octavio's cowardice and betrayal. With Ismael, Octavio Arce ran away with my soul. And in its place he left bitterness and hatred.

❧❧

The door slid sideways on the track as its bars cast flickering shadows on the interior of the cell. A sturdy nudge by the female guard finally shut the door with a loud bang. Ana stared vacantly beyond the bars; her eyes were fixed on the opposite cell. She reached out, clutching a bar in each hand. Its steel felt cold and frozen. When she looked down at her body, she took in the drab, oversized prison dress that emphasized her thinness.

"Scuttlebutt says you plugged your old man, honey."

Ana heard the voice of her cellmate, but she ignored it because her tongue refused to speak. Instead, she remained rigidly clinging to the bars, her back to the woman. Ana's eyes closed hoping to dispel the nightmare.

"Oh, believe me, I understand. They can be bastards, can't they?"

The woman's voice was graveled by the effects of cigarettes and alcohol, but it had a soft lilt as she spoke, obviously attempting to convey her sentiments of compassion. Ana did not answer; she was lost in a world of hatred and confusion. Her ears began to pick up sounds that came to her from what had happpened only a few weeks earlier. A vision of Franklin flashed in her mind, his pupils dilated with horror. She heard the awful words he stuttered, "He's taken Ismael!"

Ana leaned her throbbing forehead against the cold bars. She felt a sob tearing at her insides as it made its way up, but the cry never made it to her throat and out of her mouth. It clung to her ribs and pounded at her back. She gasped for air to relieve the pain. It sounded like a sigh to her cellmate.

"No use wasting sighs on a son of a bitch, honey. Believe me, I know."

Ana heard the woman, but couldn't answer because she was breathing through her mouth as her chest heaved. Her mind flashed back, reliving what had happened. She saw herself as she grabbed the keys off the hook in the kitchen and dashed into Amy's and Franklin's bedroom. In the closet was kept the .22 calibre rifle used to kill rats and gophers. The weapon was in her hands before she knew it. Next, she was crashing through the front door and leaping onto the running board of the pick-up. The key went deep into the ignition and the motor cranked on. As the vehicle careened into a U-turn, Ana's last glimpse of Franklin and Amy was through a cloud of dust that shimmered in the light of the declining sun.

Now, in the cell, there was hardly anything Ana could remember of the trip between the ranch and the house on Humphrys Street. All she recalled was the prick of the wire gate on one hand and the weight of the rifle in the other one as she crashed into the yard. She remembered herself running up the stairs and pounding on the wooden screen door with the butt of the weapon.

"Octavio-o-o-o!"

In her memory, her voice sounded like the wail of a mad woman as she banged on the door over and again. Looking back, she remembered that she had turned and leapt from the porch and, facing the house, she again screeched out his name.

"Octavio-o-o-o! Alejandra-a-a! Give me back my son!"

She recalled that somewhere in the recesses of her mind she was aware of curious, frightened neighbors who peered through kitchen windows and from behind window shades. Her screaming went on, rising in pitch.

"Octavio-o-o-o! Come out and face me if you're a man!"

Ana tapped her forehead against the bars as she envisioned Octavio's image coming from behind the screen door; she heard its hinges squeak. He was dressed in an Army undershirt and rough khaki pants, and his face was gaunt, drained of color; its expression was menacing. She could see that his nerves were breaking.

"Shut up and get out of here!" That was all he said to Ana before turning his back.

"*¡Cobarde!*"

Ana's voice rang out just before the rifle blast. Octavio was hurled against the screen door by the force of a bullet that penetrated his back. He crumpled onto the wooden floor of the porch, unconscious.

There was silence for a few moments, but then the quiet

was ripped apart by shrill police sirens. Scanning spot lights gave an eerie glow to the night. There was commotion in the barrio. There was screaming, running, banging of doors, and finally there was Franklin, who had come in one of the patrol cars and who was taking the weapon from Ana's inert hands. She felt his arms gripping her, holding her body steady, sensing that she was at the point of collapse.

The voice of Ana's cellmate yanked her back to the present.

"Aw, come on, lady. Quit the moping and sit over here with me. You're making me nervous! Remember that you're in here for just a couple of years. Put yourself in my place, for cryin' out loud! I'm here for a nickel and a dime."

Ana's hands unclenched and fell limply from the bars. She turned to look at the woman who was speaking to her and saw that she was sitting on the bottom bunk bed. She was visible only from the neck down, her head enshrouded in the shadow cast by the upper bed. A cigarette ember glowed in the darkness. Without responding, Ana climbed up to her bed and laid on its uncovered mattress. Its rough material smelled of disinfectant. Reclining her head on the thin pillow, she closed her eyes as she listened to the words of the judge that rang with a hollow, painful echo.

"Because this court has heeded your defense, and because it, too, finds that your past comportment warrants leniency, you are hereby sentenced to only two years imprisonment for the crime you have committed. Bodily assault with the intent to kill is a serious crime, indeed. Nevertheless, the court will show you clemency."

Ana stood in front of the judge. Looming far above her was his white, rigid face, glowering at her. His voice boomed out the sentence. "Furthermore, insofar as the child is concerned, the court is convinced that you have, by your violent and irrational behavior, proven yourself to be an unfit mother. On the other hand, the plaintiff has survived your attack and has asked the court to withhold full punishment on the condition that he be granted custody of the child.

"It seems obvious to me, therefore, that Mr. Arce, a man who has only recently proven his valor defending his country, a man married and settled, is the rightful party to bring up the child whose paternity he has now acknowledged. I, therefore, remand the boy to his care.

"It is the judgement of this court that you serve your term

at the women's correctional facility on Terminal Island. After the completion of the two years, be aware that this court will have also placed a five-year injunction on you. That is, if within that period of time you are ever found within two square miles of the Arce family, you will be liable to further incarceration."

Ana's body flinched at the bang of the judge's gavel signaling the end of the hearing. Then, her body became numb as if paralyzed. When she became aware of the hand of the female marshal nudging her toward the door to the holding cells, Ana turned to look behind her. To the right of the large room she saw Amy and Franklin. They sat rigidly, with their heads hanging low. There were tears running down Franklin's cheeks.

When Ana turned to the left, she made out Octavio,who had been recently released from the hospital. He was sitting behind a large wooden table. Her eyes focused on Alejandra, who stared at her unabashedly showing her hatred. Octavio avoided Ana's glaring eyes; he fidgeted with the tip of his tie.

My mind returned to the cell and to the bunk bed where I lay staring at the ceiling. My thoughts had cleared and I realized that Octavio was not the only one to blame; my sisters had also taken part in the kidnapping of Ismael. They had been in the house, and none had tried to intervene or to help me. Rancor for them gagged me, and I vowed never to forget what they had done.

My spirit drifted, going beyond the cell, recalling that the prison was on an island and that I was surrounded by water. This thought gave me a sensation of plummeting downward, of spiraling headlong into a bottomless watery hole. Then my mind returned to Ismael, thinking of how he must cry out for me, and I shivered when it occurred to me that soon he would begin to forget me.

Ismael was happy to go with the man who said he was his father. The boy liked the stuffed toy he was given, and he went willingly when the man promised to take him to ride the ponies. The man took him, not to the park as Ismael had expected, but instead to a house to which he had never been. Ismael became frightened, and called for his mother. Several women appeared. One of them seemed to him to be the most important one. The only difference Ismael could see between them was that the main one had a white face. The others were brown.

Ismael did not want to be with those people, even though the man patted him on the head and offered him cookies. When Ismael saw that it was growing dark outside, he became alarmed and thought he would walk home. As he opened the front door to leave, one of the women took him by the arm and told him that he could not do that because he would get lost or run over by a car.

Ismael sat on the sofa, looking around him. Everything was strange and unknown to him. He saw that the women and the man were talking loudly; they often pointed at him and wagged their heads. The man kept saying yes again and again, but Ismael could not make sense of what it was the man wanted. The talk finally became so loud that he knew that they were fighting. At one point he saw the man push the white-faced woman against the wall. Ismael knew that the blow had hurt her.

After a while, Ismael was certain that he had heard his mother's voice coming from somewhere outside. Everyone inside stopped talking; they listened. When Ismael was sure that it was his mother calling out, he jumped from the sofa and ran towards the door. He was about to shout for his mother when the woman with the white face cupped her hand over his mouth and prevented him from making a sound. He gagged but could not free himself from the hand which was stronger than both of his own hands.

While he was struggling with the big hand, Ismael saw the man go outside despite one of the other women trying to stop him. He pushed her away and opened the door. Ismael heard a squeak as the man disappeared behind the door. The hand was still pressed over his mouth when Ismael was startled by a loud blast, and then he caught a glimpse of the man's face. Ismael heard him groan as he slipped down while his cheek scrapped against the screen of the door.

Then there was wailing and screaming. The hand had suddenly let go of his jaw, but Ismael was too afraid to move. He looked around him and saw that the women were the ones screaming. They lunged toward the door, but he knew that they couldn't open it because the body of the man was blocking it.

Ismael held his hands to his ears; the shouting, mixed with the screeching of a loud noise outside, hurt the inside of his head. When the women were finally able to shove the door open, he peeked out and saw red lights. He felt his heart pounding as people ran from one side of the front yard to the other. Hoping to escape from what was happening outside, Ismael ran into another room. He knew it was the kitchen when he saw a table, a stove, a sink. He looked straight ahead and he discovered a small door and a space; it was open and just big enough for him. He crawled into the box and rolled himself into a ball. He closed the door, and in the darkness he leaned his cheek against a cold pipe; he felt its dampness. Although there was no light in the box, he liked it because he felt safe.

He didn't know how much time passed because he had fallen asleep, when suddenly the door was flung open and one of the women peered into his box. She took hold of his hand and helped him out. He was cold and shivering, so she put a long sweater around his shoulders. Soon the other women came into the kitchen and started fighting again. This time it was the other ones against the one with the white face. Again they pointed at him, shaking their heads. Finally, the four left the kitchen for a while, and when they walked back into the room with the sofa, they had bundles and boxes which they took out the front door. Ismael never saw those women again.

He began to hate the woman with the white face because he felt that she rejected him. After a few days passed, the man returned; he had white bandages on his back and chest and it seemed to Ismael that he was very angry. He and the woman fought almost always. Ismael was taken to a new school. He didn't like it there, so he pretended to himself that he was with his mother and his grandparents. The teacher scolded him for not paying attention like the other boys and girls, but he didn't care because in his mind he preferred to be looking at his mother's face.

Ismael knew that the teacher was displeased with him, especially when she went to the house to report him. The man and the white-faced woman seemed to agree with the teacher, and Ismael thought that he heard them promise something to her. Still, he didn't care because all he wanted was to return to his mother and his *abuelitos*, so he never listened when he was in class. Once the teacher punished him by putting him in the cloak room. He liked that because he could be alone to think, but then he began to cry because when he tried to see his mother's face, he no longer could remember it. All he saw was her body.

The weather became less warm and then it got cold. Christmas came along. After that, the air began to smell like flowers and Ismael thought of his mother and *abuelitos* less and less. The man and the woman never stopped fighting; it happened every night. They stood facing one another, screaming, pointing at him. Sometimes they even pushed one another. Once the man slapped the woman so hard that blood came out of her nose. When the fighting began, Ismael tried to escape to his hideaway. Most of the times he slept there the whole night.

He knew that things were going to change when a woman wearing glasses came to the house. She, the man, and the white-faced woman sat on the sofa, talking for a long time. They made Ismael sit on a chair while they gestured toward him. He saw the woman he hated shake her head again and again as she said, no! no! Finally, he saw the woman with the glasses give the man a paper for them to sign.

A few days later, the woman with the glasses came to the house again, but this time it was to take Ismael with her. The man insisted on going with them, although the woman disagreed. Ismael was happy to leave that house, even if the man did come along anyway.

Ismael, the man, and the woman with glasses rode in her car until they got to a big building. He liked it because it had several layers of floors. When they went up the big stairs, the woman took his hand and led him to a small room where he saw a tall woman and a man by her side who was even taller. When he got near them, he had to put his head all the way back to look up at their faces. He was able to see that their eyes were the color of the sky. He liked them and the way they smiled at him. All the while, the other man stood by without saying anything to the two strangers.

The woman with the glasses bent down to take a closer look at Ismael as she spoke. "These people are your new parents." Her voice echoed in his ears as if she had been speaking from far off. "You mustn't forget that they chose you from among many other boys and girls."

Ismael looked at the man and woman, and they smiled at him. The man said, "Hello, my name is Simon Wren, and this is Bertha. You can call her mother ,and me, father."

The woman with the glasses was speaking again, "You're going to live in a city called San Francisco, which you'll like very much. And now you'll have a new name, too. From now on, you'll be called Terrance Wren. Isn't that a lovely name?"

Then she turned to the other man, "Mr. Arce, you can be sure that the boy will be in excellent hands." She paused, and turned to the Wrens. "Remember. As the three of you have agreed, you will communicate with each other consistently regarding the boy's welfare."

The next day, Ismael struggled against falling asleep because he didn't want to miss out on the scenery. To the left, the whitecaps of the ocean delighted him, as did the soft brown hills to the right side. But the gentle swaying of the train and the rhythmic clanging of its iron wheels were forcing "Terrance Wren" to fall asleep.

He was leaning against Bertha, the woman he was now to call mother. The boy liked the feeling of her arm and the softness of her chest against his cheek. He was aware that she and Simon were speaking about home, San Francisco, and his school, but Terrance allowed his eyes to shut for a moment. He was happy that he no longer was with the man and woman who fought with each other, and he was glad that he didn't have to hide under the sink and lean against the cold pipe all night long.

Terrance opened his eyes to see his new father smiling at him. The man reminded him of someone; the white face and glasses provoked a picture in his memory. It was his *abuelito* Franklin. He couldn't separate their faces because they seemed identical. The boy sat up on the stuffed bench as he looked up at his new mother, and he was surprised that the same thing was happening. She was his mother, except before she used to be brown and not so tall.

He leaned back while his hand touched the blue velvet

seat cover. He was wide awake now; he felt the train slowing
down and saw that several of the passengers were standing
to take bags and suitcases down from the upper racks. The
boy felt his father's hand on his arm, "Look, son. Over there
on the ocean side."

He responded to his father's words, craning his neck to
look out the window to where his father had pointed. He liked
the sound of the word *son*.

"That's more or less where we live. You'll have a room
that looks out to where the sea gulls feed. Your mother and I
think you'll like it."

৶৵৹

*One year after I was put in prison, Amy and Franklin
were facing a dilemma. Later on I realized that they had discussed it for several weeks because neither of them could tell
what would be best for me. On the one hand, they knew that
being trapped behind bars meant that I couldn't do anything
to fight back once I found out what had happened to Ismael.
On the other hand, they realized that I would sooner or later
find out on my own and hate them for not having told me the
truth.*

*They were brave. They decided to be the ones to tell me
everything. Years later, Franklin let me know that before visiting me, they rehearsed over and again how they would tell me
that Ismael had been put up for adoption, that he was gone
and that no one could get the information as to where he had
been taken, or by whom.*

৶৵৹

Visiting Sunday came, and Franklin and Amy sat nervously on the steel chairs provided for visitors. They had
their elbows placed on the metal table as they faced the
screened divider. On the other side were chairs for the
inmates. Amy held a small bundle wrapped in brown paper;
it contained new underwear and a couple of combs for Ana.
On the table next to Franklin was a shoe box with jars of fig

preserve which they had canned. They fidgeted, making
small talk, and as they looked around they saw that, as
usual, there were other visitors waiting to see a daughter or a
wife or a sister.

When Ana appeared, she seemed pleased to see them,
and she smiled broadly as she slid both her hands through
the separation between the table and the bottom of the
screen. No one spoke; they only squeezed each other's hands
for a few moments. Then Amy signaled the woman guard to
hand Ana the parcels.

They chatted about the weather and the ranch. Franklin
said that they were planning to sell the market; it was time
that he and Amy began to relax, maybe move back to
Cherokee County in Oklahoma with family. They spoke this
way for a few minutes until Ana asked her usual questions.

"How is Ismael? Have you seen him recently? I can't
believe a whole year's gone by. He must be a big boy now."

They looked at one another nervously, but it was Amy
who spoke. "Ana, you know that man doesn't let us get within
five miles of his place. How could we see Ismael?"

As they had foreseen, Ana's questioning had signaled the
right moment for what Amy and Franklin had to say.
Clearing her throat and re-arranging herself in the chair,
Amy got to the point. "Ana, do you remember way back, just
before Ismael was born, we discussed Hagar and her son?"

Ana looked at Amy with an expression of not knowing
exactly what that long-ago conversation had to do with her
present condition. "Yes, I remember. What about it, Amy?"

"Well, good God, Gertie, wouldn't you know it! The reading came up again the other night and we got to talking even
more. We thought that you'd like to know what we said.
Didn't we Franklin?" She turned to her husband for corrobo-
ration, sounding slightly out of breath. Franklin nodded ener-
getically.

Reaching into her sweater pocket, Amy pulled out a folded sheet of paper. She carefully spread it out on the table as
she took her reading glasses from her bag. Ana waited
patiently as this went on. She glanced at Franklin, who
returned her gaze with a sheepish look. Amy began to read.

"'Hagar departed, and wandered about in the desert of
Bersabee. When the water in her bottle was gone, she left the
child under a bush. Then she went and sat opposite the place,

for she said, 'Let me not see the child die.'"

When Amy looked up to take a breath, she saw that Ana's face had become pallid, and that the color of her eyes seemed to dip to pitch black. She realized that she was being misunderstood by Ana, so she quickly blurted out, "That's not the real part! I mean, that's not what we spoke about the other night."

Swallowing hard, Amy spoke nervously. "This part right here is what we were concentrating on, the part when the good Lord again speaks to Hagar. Just listen, Ana, please. 'The angel of God called to Hagar from heaven and said to her, what is the matter, Hagar? Fear not, for God has heard the boy's cry in this plight of his. Be assured in his regard, for I will make him a great nation.'"

Amy's voice trailed feebly as she read the last words; she was frightened by the intensity of Ana's eyes and the expression that framed her mouth. Franklin and Amy shifted in their chairs. No one spoke for a long while. It was Ana who finally broke the silence.

"Amy, you're trying to tell me something." Her voice was calm but they could tell that she was controlling fierce emotion. "Is my son dead?"

"No!" Amy and Franklin answered so loudly that the other visitors and inmates turned to see who had shouted. At the same time, both of them reached in to take hold of Ana's hands which were cold and clammy. Liberally interpreting what she had read, Amy said, "We mean that even if Hagar's son was taken from her, the good Lord promised to make something great of him."

Understanding flashed in Ana's eyes as she sensed the truth behind what she was being told. Ismael was gone. He was beyond her reach, and any hope of getting him back was, for some reason, now out of the question.

Ana's eyes were closed tightly when she finally spoke. "Amy, please say it! I want to hear it in straight, simple words."

It was Franklin who responded in terse phrases; his voice was husky. "Ismael's been adopted. He's now with a new family. They're a good family. That's all we know. We know neither their name nor where they live."

Amy and Franklin clamped their spread-out hands, palms down on the table, and waited for Ana's reaction. The three of them seemed to be frozen; no one spoke, no one moved. Franklin felt perspiration trickling down his back.

Amy moved her hand closer to Ana's. "God will take care of him." Her trembling voice was so thin that it was hardly audible, but she continued whispering. "You'll find him again, Ana, and when you do, you'll remember the good Lord's words."

Silently, Ana stood up and moved toward the door leading back to the cellblock. The guard opened the door for her, and she disappeared behind it.

Hope of regaining Ismael had given me reason to live while in prison. Now I was empty. There was nothing inside of me except hollowness, and hatred for Octavio and my sisters. I passed sleepless nights remembering my father's curse. Maybe, I told myself, Amy and Franklin were mistaken about what had happened to Ismael. How could Octavio give away his own son? Why?

I became obsessed with a desire to break out of that cage. I felt that the prison walls were closing in on me, suffocating me. Soon I convinced myself that if I were to crash through the trap that held me, I would be able to hunt down Octavio and force him to tell me where Ismael had been taken.

It was then that I began to work on a plan of escape.

Sensing what was causing Ana to brood almost constantly, her cellmate cautioned her one night after the lights were out. "Keep your nose clean, Ana. Don't get caught up in any of the shit that's flying all over the place here."

When there was no response, the woman spoke up again.

"You gotta remember that some of these gals are real pros. They're two- and three-time losers, and they're tough, believe me." There was a pause in what she was saying. "But still, don't make the mistake of thinking they have the answer to everything. Oh, yeah, they'll come up to you and tell you how easy it is to do this or that. They'll even tell you that you can spring loose. But don't listen to them, kid. You'll only end up in deep shit because here, nothing is for free. You can expect it. They'll ask you to do things that will make you feel like a pig."

Ana disregarded what she was hearing. Instead, she turned over in her bed, thinking of her plan to escape. Her mind worked on it all that night, carefully examining each detail of what happened every morning.

The next day was exactly the same as the day before; nothing ever changed the routine. Just before daybreak the Milk Brigade, as the inmates in charge of unloading the milk van were called, lined up outside the prison kitchen. They stood in line, shoulder to shoulder, waiting for the sound of the whistle that signaled them to begin moving the heavy crates off the truck. They were drowsy and cranky from having been hauled out of bed at dawn, and many of them still had sleep-encrusted eyes.

"Shit! I need this like a hole in the head!"

"Shut up, will you? You say that every God-damn morning!"

A guard cut in on what the women were saying. "Okay, you two! Cut out the yapping! How many times have I told you not to talk while you're on my detail!" Then she turned to Ana, calling out in a husky voice. "You! Number 36! Get out there and whip open those panels. Why do you have to wait for me to say it every day? Come on! Get a move on!"

Ana hated being called by the number she had been issued when she began her sentence, but she had nothing else to do but obey the guard. She went to the rear of the van and, twisting the handles, opened first one door, then the other. The racks of crates holding the milk bottles loomed in front of her. She climbed onto the flatbed and began handing boxes down to the line of shuffling women.

The chill of the refrigerated van pierced the thin cotton sweater and dress Ana wore, and her hands ached from the weight of the crates. But she had done the same job for nearly a year so her arms and back had become strong. She was able to keep pace with the others who held up their arms waiting for a crate to lug into the kitchen.

Ana had noticed some time before that there was a small space left over in one of the rear corners of the van where nothing was ever placed. After a while she saw that even when the truck was reloaded with empty boxes, that space

was never filled. Once, when the guard turned to talk to the
supervising officer, Ana slipped over to that corner and tested
it to see if she would fit. She discovered that even after the
interior of the van was filled, she could fit without being
detected.

Ana began to figure out a way to squeeze into that space
after the truck was reloaded. It was possible, she told herself,
to make it to the mainland hidden among the crates, and
once the vehicle made it to San Pedro, she would find a way
to escape. But she needed someone to help her do this unde-
tected. She began to look around for that person, hoping the
price would not be too high.

Every day, after the Milk Brigade was dismissed, Ana
spent eight hours working in the laundry. This assignment
also included mending and sewing the inmates' uniforms, and
it was while working at this job that Ana fine-tuned her plan.
One day, as she was about ready to decide on who her accom-
plice might be, she heard someone talking to her.

"I know what's up your ass, cutie."

On that particular day Ana was, as usual, lost in her
thoughts when the harsh words penetrated, making her
swing around to see who was speaking. She glared into the
face of Lynette Hampton.

"Don't act like you don't know what I'm talking about.
I've been here longer than anyone, and I can tell when someone is planning to spring loose."

Ana turned her back on the woman, deciding not to
respond, but the talking kept up. "I guess if I still had my old
man out there, I'd want to get the hell out of here, too."

Ana finally said, "Leave me alone, Lynette. I don't know
what you're talking about."

"Oh, yeah, you do! I've seen you eye-balling the back of
that truck each time you get the chance. And I know what's
going through that head of yours."

Ana slammed the door of the washer and whirled around
to face the woman. "Look, Lynette, back off! I mean it. If you
don't…"

"If I don't, what's going to happen, Ana? Eh? Come on,
I'm waiting."

Ana, always uneasy in the presence of the woman, found
her more intimidating than ever. She reproached herself for
allowing anyone to even guess what was on her mind. A few

minutes passed before the voice chimed in again.

"Look. I can help if you let me. I've got my ways, you know. I've been here for nearly twelve years and, believe me, I can help you."

Ana was quiet as she slowly folded bath towels. She finally spoke up. "I'm not planning anything. But, let's just say that I was, and let's just say that you would help me. What's in it for you, Lynette?"

"Ha! I knew from the beginning you had smarts." Lynette paused while reloading the washer. Then she moved closer to Ana; her voice dropped to a whisper. "Easy. All you have to do is let me be your old man a couple of times. We can get together..."

Ana's shove against the woman's shoulders was so powerful that she skidded backwards, tripping over a filled tub. She flipped over it, landing squarely on her buttocks, and the impact of her body overturned the container, smearing the floor with soapy, dirty water. The fall knocked the air out of Lynette's lungs, and it took her several seconds to regain her breath. But when she did, she suddenly sprang to her feet and lunged at Ana, grabbing her hair. The two women went into a tangle as they fell on the concrete floor. By that time several inmates had rushed to them, forming a circle, shouting, screaming and rooting.

Ana and the woman grappled, squirming on the wet, greasy surface. Both women were grunting and snorting. Lynette cursed; obscene words squeezed out of her clenched jaws. Ana's lips were shut tight as she pummeled her attacker's face with closed fists. Her opponent's ebony-colored skin began to show gray blotches where the blows landed, but she countered by scratching and gouging at Ana's face. After a while, she was able to gain the advantage and, twisting around, she mounted Ana.

Lynette was the heavier of the two women, and her weight bore down on Ana, who seemed unable to free either of her arms even while she felt the other's fingers tightening around her throat. After struggling and squirming for a few seconds, she was able to jerk up her legs far enough to pound Lynette's back with a powerful knee blow.

"Ahgg!"

Ana took advantage of the fingers being released to contort her body. She grabbed at Lynette's hair, and with a

strong yank forced her down to the concrete. Now it was
Ana's turn to get on top where she battered the woman's face
and shoulders countless times with clenched fists. At one
point, she grabbed Lynette's hand and bit it.

"A-y-y-y! Bitch!"

Lynette began to cry as she screamed out for help, but no
one helped her until a whistle brought several guards running. Even when three of them took hold of Ana's arms and
legs, she kept on thrashing about and twisting, trying to land
more blows on her enemy. When the officers finally forced her
against a wall, she stood dripping with grimy soap. Watery
blood trickled out of her nose and from her forehead. Still on
the floor, Lynette appeared to be really hurt because, even
with the help of two guards and several inmates, she was
unable to rise beyond a kneeling position.

Ana, chest heaving and her eyes filled with rage,
appeared to have been subdued momentarily. But she surprised everyone when suddenly she lunged at Lynette again.
This time the officers slammed her against the wall, pinning
her down as they waited for the supervising officer to appear.

Lynette's mouth was wide open and bloody saliva drib-
bled out of it. She began to scream, accusing Ana. "She's trying to escape! I found out! That's why the snake attacked me!
She sneaked up behind me! Try to do it right the next time!
Bitch! Bitch!"

The main officer had arrived at the scene in time to hear
Lynette's accusations, and she approached Ana, who was still
breathing heavily. "What is she talking about, Number 36?
Speak up!"

Ana said nothing. Instead she glared while she sucked up
enough saliva in her mouth to spit at Lynette. The spittle
shot through the air but fell short of its mark, landing on a
guard's high-top shoe. The woman cursed loudly. "God-damn
greaser!"

"That's it, 36! You're in for a treat." Turning to the guards,
the supervisor said "Put her where she can cool off."

Ana was confined to a tiny, windowless cell for a week.
She was taken out of it once a day so that she could exercise
by walking up and down the vast concrete compound for half
an hour. But the session was more painful than helpful to
her. She always returned to the pitch-black cell with a
headache caused by the sunlight, and because of the pain,

she was unable to eat or drink.

When Ana returned to her job in the laundry, she was afraid because she thought that Lynette Hampton would be waiting to attack her again. But the woman avoided her. Ana discovered that she had gained a position of respect from the inmates because she had prevailed over the strongest of them all. She found out that now others looked at her with a mix of awe and envy.

કે•છ

The week of my punishment dragged; it seemed like an eternity. I hardly slept because I was tormented with thinking and asking myself questions. Should I go on trying to escape? And if I did escape, what were the chances of my actually being free? If I made it, wouldn't I be a fugitive all of my life? On the other hand, if I were caught, wouldn't my sentence be extended more years?

I finally told myself that one year had already passed and that a second would pass just as fast. I decided not to try to break out of that trap.

કે•છ

The two years in prison had ended for Ana. She leaned her forearms against the railing of the ferry as it made its way across the narrow channel between Terminal Island and the San Pedro dock. She was dressed in the simple suit, blouse, and pumps provided by the prison supply store. A thin woolen three-quarter-length coat protected her against the March breeze.

Her eyes squinted in the afternoon brightness as her gaze was riveted on the whitecaps. Looking southward, she made out the outline of the Long Beach harbor. She remembered Amy and the food they had peddled on those wharfs. César's face, laughing, was reflected in the cobalt blue as Ana looked down at the swirling water churned up by the boat engines. She looked northward. Her eyes made out the craggy cliffs of Point Fermin Park and its wind-swept, stunted pine trees.

Looking nearer to her, she saw Cabrillo Beach, its round for-
mation reminding her of the secret cove near Puerto Real,
and she saw Alejandra and Octavio, jumping, frolicking, gesturing.

Ana shut her eyes, trying to erase the vision. When she
opened them again, she was thinking of Ismael and that he
would have been eight years old that February. She wondered, as she did almost every day, where he was and just
how tall he had grown; this thought brought a smile to her
face. Turning to press her back on the railing, Ana raised her
face to the soft warmth of the sun. She stayed that way for a
few moments as she thought of her life since her son's last
birthday with her. She straightened her head and looked into
space; her stare was hard.

She thought of the two years she had just finished in jail
and what she had to show for it. Her mind shoved the word
nothing to its forward recesses, but it soon reversed itself.
Ana mumbled, "Not quite nothing." She reminded herself
that she had been allowed to read most of the books in the
prison library for one thing, and she had forced herself to
admit that this had been good. She had also been taught to
operate several types of machines, especially those used for
sewing clothes. More importantly, the prison directors had
placed her in a job at a factory for women's apparel. This, at
least, would give her a beginning.

Ana looked down and stared at her fingers. They were
rough and calloused, just like those of the women she had left
behind. She snorted through her nose as she saw that no
matter how many good things she tried to squeeze out of her
past two years, the truth was that she had hated every second of that time. Nothing could ever make up for the loss of
those months ripped out of her life. She had detested the cell
and the women who had surrounded her. And yet, she had to
admit that they had taught her something. She had learned
how to survive, and how to strike back. Those women had
been her teachers.

Ana was jerked from her thoughts when the boat bumped
against the wharf. It was time to go ashore. As she walked off
the gang plank, she felt her legs tremble slightly. She knew it
was due partly to the sway of the boat during the crossing,
but it was also because she was afraid. She was alone. None
of her family had attempted to communicate with her during

her term in jail, which confirmed their guilt in her mind. A surge of new rage coursed through her, sending energy to her shaky legs.

Her only connection with the outside had been Amy and Franklin. It was they who informed her that Alejandra and Octavio had moved away from Humphrys Street to a house in Monterey Park. They had sold the old place and used the money as a down payment on their new home. Pilar and Cruz had married one after the other and drifted away, each with her husband, and Zulma and Rosalva picked up stakes and moved to New York. No one knew anything about them, either.

Recently, Amy and Franklin had decided that they, too, would move back to Oklahoma. They had at first resisted the move, but circumstances around them were changing so much that they felt forced to begin a new life. Franklin explained to Ana how the end of the war had brought new streets and houses in their area, and that the city had passed rules outlawing the keeping of chickens, ducks, rabbits or pigeons. He said that it was because there were too many complaints of flies and stench.

Slowly in the beginning, then at a more rapid pace, their neighbors had sold their five-, two- and even one-acre spreads to private land corporations. The space was being converted into track homes. So Amy and Franklin, like their neighbors, sold the ranch and the market, and packed their things. After that they said goodbye to Ana, promising to keep close to her with their letters.

Ana walked to the red car terminal thinking of Amy and Franklin, and how they had cried when they hugged her for the last time. She was alone, but she knew where she was going. The prison counselor, the one who had managed to get Ana a job, had also arranged for a room for her to rent. It was located one street away from the factory, on Twelfth and Los Angeles Streets, just in front of St. Joseph's Church.

Ana climbed the high metal steps of the coach and walked down the aisle to sit by a window. As the train lurched forward, she felt blood course through her body and up to her head. She was free, out of the cage and on her own. She found it strange that she didn't mind being alone. On the contrary, she felt that if she followed the right direction she would be able to reach her goal. She blinked her eyes when this thought crossed her mind. Goal? What goal? Ana wasn't sure.

The train swayed, picking up speed, and Ana saw how Los Angeles was changing. They were traveling north, almost parallel to the highway she and Amy had traveled over and again on their routes. She could almost feel the bumping of the pick-up, its tight springs bouncing off the badly paved road. She remembered Ismael seated between her and Amy, his small head jerking from one side to the other. And she saw César, in the rear of the truck, hanging on to its side as the wind swept his dark brown hair back on his head.

Now she saw long tracks of land on which were constructed countless houses; they all looked alike. Where there was still empty space, Ana noticed that new structures were in process, and that almost everywhere there were piles of fresh lumber and sacks of cement. Men seemed to be everywhere, digging trenches, peeping through engineering instruments, waving red caution flags.

The trip from the harbor took less than an hour. When Ana stepped off the train at the terminal in Los Angeles, she asked someone where she was. Sixth and Los Angeles Streets, she was told, six blocks away from her new home.

❧⚶

When I opened my eyes early that morning, it was still dark out and the ceiling of my room was bathed in the yellow glow reflected by the street light. My body felt strange in that new place. I stretched, putting my forearms behind my head while I scanned the small attic room that I had rented. I liked it. The walls were covered with decorated paper, and the floors were of polished wood. It was a corner room with two windows; one of them looked out to Twelfth Street and the other towards Los Angeles Street. I had a view of the twin spires of the church from that window. I smiled, thinking of how different this room was from the cell that had almost become my world.

I felt nervous. Again there would be new faces, a new routine and a new way of working in my life. But my shakiness began to fade away when I told myself that if I worked hard, I

*would one day be able to find Ismael. There was something
else besides this, though. I felt a desire, strong and new for
me, to be able to trace out my own path in life, and to be able
to choose what direction I would take.*

When the eight-o'clock buzzer sounded at the factory,
Ana and two other new women workers were in the locker
room where they had been told to wait for the floor supervisor. Ana was wearing a skirt and blouse she had been issued
in prison, and to cover these she wore a heavy apron. Instead
of the heeled pump shoes, she was wearing loafers and socks
for more comfort.

The three women waited, now and then saying a few
words until the door finally opened and a medium-sized man
with curly red hair appeared. "Morning! My name is Shelly
Feurmann. I'm the floor supervisor. You ladies our new workers?"

The three women looked around as if asking who else
could they be. The man seemed slightly embarrassed and he
spoke rapidly, trying to patch over the silly question. "That
is, of course, I know you're our new people. Well...that
is...just follow me. Wait a minute! I suppose none of you
speaks English, right?"

The three women chimed in, "I do."

Embarrassed again, the man ushered the women away
from the lockers, down a wide corridor and through broad
swinging doors. Ana's eyes opened widely when she caught
sight of an enormous room; it was as big as the prison audito-
rium. The place was lined from side to side with sewing
machines, all operated by women. She looked up and was
amazed at the heavy metal rods that crisscrossed, connecting
vertically from the ceiling down to others horizontally built
into the walls. There were so many that she thought she was
looking at an aerial jigsaw puzzle used for supporting large
bobbins of multicolored threads which intertwined like giant
spider webs. Her ears began to hurt because of the roar gen-
erated by the commotion in the hall.

Each machine was a work station equipped with a table for

single garment parts, and Ana saw that each aisle produced different pieces. One section made sleeves; the next collars; followed by napes and side panels. The women worked with their heads bent low, noses almost touching their deftly moving fingers as their hands worked swiftly, straightening thread and fabric, feeding them into a rapidly stitching needle.

Shelly Feurmann led the three newcomers to their work stations, but because of the noise, he could only point first to the woman and then to the vacant place she was supposed to occupy. Ana was the last one to be seated, and when she settled in, she looked at the machine, then at the piecework for which she was responsible. She thus began what would be a span of years working for Ezra Feurmann and Son, Inc.

The first months were difficult for Ana, mostly because she felt lonely, but also because she wrestled almost constantly with the desire to look for Ismael. Sometimes she scanned the phone book to find Octavio's number and possibly his address, but then she remembered the judge's words warning her, threatening her with a new jail sentence. Instead, she contacted city and county agencies, but the social workers only referred her from one office to another.

She liked going to work because she discovered that it distracted her. At first, she found herself trailing the more experienced operators. In time, she caught up with them, and, after a few months, she was among the most productive operators. This was when she began to notice that they all worked under harsh, unhealthy conditions; the work stations were cramped and lighting was inadequate, as was the ventilation. Breaks were not given, and by the time the lunch period came around, most of the women were exhausted. The same thing happened during the afternoon period. Ana began to think more and more of how they were all underpaid.

In the evenings when she returned to her room, she thought of how strange it was that none of them, including herself, ever complained. She remembered the women who picked tomatoes under the blistering sun in the Valley of the Yaqui River. She also recalled the girls like her who worked silently for the shoe manufacturer, getting pennies in return. What most gnawed at Ana was that no one ever said anything.

The day she blurted out the idea that they should go on strike, Ana caused a furor in the lunch room. Some of the women looked at her as if she were crazy, and others were shocked to hear the forbidden word so close. But most of them, though momentarily bewildered, responded with a smile and a nod of the head once they had regained their balance.

It took weeks for Ana's idea to take hold with her fellow workers while they argued and debated during their lunch hour. After that, when the buzzer ending the lunch period sounded each day, the operators returned to their work stations thinking of one thing: strike. Ana realized that she had touched a nerve, and that even if no one ever spoke up, she knew now that those women were dissatisfied and ready to fight for a better way to make a living. Every lunch hour, and sometimes even after the five-o'clock buzzer ended the shift, most of the women got together to plan.

A few months passed, and when Ana's fellow workers decided that they had a strategy, she was chosen to approach the owner with their petitions. Ana accepted and wasted no time in asking to see Mr. Ezra Fuermann that same day. He agreed to speak to her. When Ana walked into the office, she was feeling nervous, although she looked calm. The older Fuermann, sensing what her visit was all about, decided he would get the upper hand by going on the offensive.

"Now, Missy, I don't want you to be scared." He spoke, looking at Ana over silver-rimmed spectacles. He was a short, stocky man whose bald head was accentuated by tuffs of kinky hair that coiled out from around his ears. He was chewing on the stub of a cigar that wasn't lit.

"Miss Calderón."

"I beg your pardon?"

"I'm Miss Calderón, not Missy, and no, sir, I'm not scared."

"Oh!...eh...I'm sorry, Miss Calderón."

Ana had snatched the offensive from Mr. Fuermann while telling the truth. She was not afraid because she was there to speak up for her fellow workers. As she spoke, she stood erect in the middle of the office, which was cluttered with piles of paper, fabric remnants, newspapers, magazines and file cases with half-opened drawers jammed with crumpled documents.

"Sit down, won't you?...Uh, Miss Calderón. There on that chair." He signaled Ana over to the only chair that was not piled high with something or another. "I know that you're here on a special mission, or something like it. Before you begin, however, I'd like to talk about you." He paused as he gazed at Ana through squinting eyes. He was searching for a reaction, but there wasn't any. "What I mean is that I'd like to offer you a new position, one that would get you away from the machines."

Ana remained serene, as if she had not heard what he was saying. She returned his gaze frankly, steadily, and waited for him to finish what he was saying. She knew he was about to make an offer in an attempt to distract her from what she had come to say.

"See here, Miss Calderón," Fuermann came directly to the point, "I've noticed how well you've caught on to working here. You've been able to manage not only one type of machine, but everything in the whole place. And the thing is that we're having problems with some of the women who aren't as fast as you are. Shelly tries, but he keeps bumping into brick walls. We thought of getting you to help us. What d'ya say?"

She was silent as her mind processed what she had heard. After a few moments, she said, "Maybe you should first listen to what I have to say, Mr. Fuermann. You might change your mind about me."

Ezra Fuermann frowned and reached into his vest pocket for a wooden match, doing it slowly, obviously playing for time to think. He finally pulled out the match and scraped it on the heel of his shoe. The hissing sound filled the silence of the room while he stared at the blue flame for a few seconds. After some minutes, he spoke, "Try me, Miss Calderón."

Looking at him steadily, Ana began to cite the workers' requests. "My companions are unhappy with the conditions here at the plant, Mr. Fuermann. They think..."

"Wait a minute! What's wrong with the place? It has a lunch room, toilets..."

"I thought, Mr. Fuermann, that you were ready to listen, but I see..."

"All right! All right! I'm listening!"

"We have the things you've just mentioned but if you'll take the time to see how cramped the space is around our stations you'll see for yourself that it only causes greater fatigue, which means less production. That's our first request, that you spread out the stations so that each employee can work with less strain."

Ana stopped speaking and looked at Mr. Fuermann, who nodded, letting her know that he wanted to hear the rest of what she had to say. "The ventilation is poor and so is the lighting. We don't get breaks in the morning period nor during the afternoon. Put all of these things together and you'll see why we are unhappy."

"Is that all?" Fuermann sounded testy.

"No, Mr. Fuermann, there's still the most important part. Our pay is not adequate, and we're asking for a raise."

"What?..."

She went on speaking, ignoring his shock. "We understand that the improvements we're asking for will take time, but if you can begin working on it, I know my companions will be happy. As far as the pay is concerned, we're willing to sit down with you to discuss a plan to make the right adjustments."

"And what if we don't agree to your demands, Missy...er...Miss Calderón?" Ezra Fuermann wasn't slouching in his chair anymore. He was sitting up, listening to Ana.

"Requests, Mr. Fuermann. Ours are just simple, reasonable requests, not demands." She paused for a second. "And to answer your question as to what will happen if you don't honor our petitions...well, there's just one word: Strike!"

She spoke with such force and conviction that Fuermann sat up as if he had received a high-voltage shock. He stared unabashedly at Ana. He forgot all about the proposition he had been on the verge of making because he saw in her eyes, in the way she spoke, in the way her body moved, that she would not accept a few more dollars and a softer job in place of what she was asking.

"Oh, now look, Miss Calderón. No one wants a strike. I don't want it. Shelly doesn't want it. Everyone comes out a loser, and you know it."

Ana looked into his tiny eyes without responding. She allowed minutes to pass and yet she remained silent. Fuermann looked at his watch, then out the window. Afterward, he even began tapping his fingers nervously on the desk. Yet nothing came out of her mouth. Ezra finally spoke. "Give us a few days to talk this over, Miss Calderón. It's not going to be easy."

After a few days, Ezra Fuermann called Ana into his

office. "Miss Calderón, Shelly and I have agreed to sit down with you and whoever else to…"

Ana sensed his intention to stall and that he was not planning to negotiate, so she interrupted him. "No, Mr. Fuermann. We've waited long enough, and we want an answer by Friday. Otherwise we go home. We all have things to do around the house."

Ana left the office quietly, but her hands were shaking. She was afraid that she had cut him off too suddenly, without giving him a chance to express what he and his son were willing to propose. It was done, however. Now, she and her fellow workers had to face the possibility of walking out on strike at the end of the week.

Ezra Fuermann called Ana back into his office at the end of the day. When word got around of the impending meeting, all the workers stayed on in the locker room after quitting time. Everyone wished her good luck and told her to be tough.

"Okay, Miss Calderón. Shelly and I are willing to follow your recommendations because, what the Hell, we were going to do practically the same things on our own."

He paused, staring at Ana with his small, incisive eyes, but when he saw no reaction coming from her, he went on talking. "We got the building next to this one a few months ago, so now we can spread the stations out so they won't be so cramped. We're cranking on more electricity to give more light and putting in more windows for better air. We've got a new schedule that includes a morning and afternoon break. The money, well, that's the hard part. We can only increase the pay gradually over the next few months. Anyway, we've decided to do it, so let's see what happens."

Fuermann spoke rapidly, gesturing with his stubby arm. He didn't allow time for Ana to speak. Instead he waved towards the door as if dismissing her. When she turned to leave, he spoke up. "Wait a minute there, Miss! Where are you going?"

"I thought you were finished." Ana looked puzzled.

"No, no. I'm not finished! I want you to do something for me. Listen, Miss Calderón. I want you to help Shelly out there on the floor. We're expanding to the next building and that boy can't be everywhere at the same time. So you're the one. What d'ya say?"

When Ana returned to the locker room to speak to the

other women, she closed the door behind her. The Fuermanns stood at the other end of the hall, craning their neck as they peeped around the corner to see what would happen. After a few minutes of silence, there was a loud burst of shouting, hooting, laughing, and applauding.

❧

I worked as a floor supervisor with Shelly Fuermann for the next two years, and we became friends. I have to admit that I liked him because he was an easy-going person who enjoyed joking, and I could see that he felt good being with me. We had lunch together most days in his office when we chatted about movies or food or gossip we had heard. But I never talked about myself, even though I knew that he wanted to know what I was like when I was alone. Hardly a day passed when Shelly didn't ask me questions that might give him a little information about what was inside of me.

❧

One day as Shelly was peeling an orange, he blurted out, "I'll bet you've read a lot of books, haven't you, Ana?"

Ana was surprised at his question, and she looked at him quizzically. "Why do you ask?"

"Well, you seem to know a lot."

"I guess I've read a few books."

"Like which ones?'

"Mostly novels."

"Which ones?"

"What's in that orange that's making you ask so many questions?" Ana had finished her lunch and was brushing crumbs from her lap as she spoke to Shelly. When he didn't answer, she continued speaking. "There's one by John Steinbeck that I really like."

"Tell me about it."

"Now? We've got to go back to work in a few minutes."

"Come on, just a little bit." The truth was that Shelly enjoyed hearing Ana speak; he loved the sound of her voice and the way she pronounced words.

"It's about a couple of brothers and how one hates the other one because their father loves him more. It's also about their mother, who leaves them to become first a prostitute, then the owner of a brothel. It all happens in Salinas."

"Prostitution! Brothels! My, my, Miss Calderón! I thought you were a nice girl, and here you spend your time reading seedy novels." Shelly teased her, hoping to get more talk out of her. He didn't want her to leave, but she was packing her thermos and lunch bag. "What other novels can you tell me about, Ana?"

She had slid to the edge of her chair. With her elbows on the desk and cocking her head sideways, she looked at him inquisitively. "Such interest in novels all of a sudden. What's going on?" She smiled and said, "Well, there's Anna Karenina. She was a rich woman with a boring, bossy husband. She fell in love with someone else, and for that she was punished by everyone: her husband, her friends, her relatives. He—the lover, that is—wasn't blamed for anything."

Shelly was staring at Ana, obviously weighing what to say next. Then he raised his arm and spoke in a melodramatic tone, "Ah, sex, sex, sex! It maketh the world goeth around." He laughed out loud, seemingly enjoying what he considered a witty remark. When he noticed that she was not sharing the joke, he blurted out, "Ana, have you ever had sex?"

She stood up and made for the door, incensed by his question. As she put her hand on the doorknob, she hesitated, then turned to face him. "None of your damned business!"

"Ha! I love it! You've got guts! Ana, you're great! Really! You're right, it isn't any of my business." Shelly's eyes were filled with admiration and affection for her. He thought she was the most beautiful woman he had ever seen.

Before walking out, Ana narrowed her eyes as she looked at him, deciding what next to say. "If you're wondering how a person like me ever had the time to read those novels, I'll tell you. I read them while I was doing time in prison. Terminal Island." She didn't allow Shelly to speak because she abruptly left the room. She knew that ice water thrown in his face would not have shocked him as her words had done.

At lunch time next day, Ana joined Shelly because she didn't want him to think she was upset with him. He seemed surprised to see her come into the office, but in a few moments he showed that he was happy that she had returned.

They ate their sandwiches almost in silence. At the end, Shelly said to her, "You know, Ana, I think you ought to go back to school." When he saw her surprise, he went on. "No, really. I mean it. You've got something special."

Ana shrugged her shoulders and smiled cynically. "Really? What's so special about me. I told you yesterday I was a jailbird."

"Don't talk that way. I don't care about that, and I don't even want to know why it happened. All I'm saying is you're a smart woman and you ought to do something with those smarts."

"I'm too old. I'm nearly twenty-nine years old."

"Hey, I'm thirty, so if you think I'm going to let you tell me that's old, you've got a fight on your hands! No, kid, listen to me. Remember when you went into the old man's office and laid out what the workers wanted? Had it been anybody else, whoosh!" Shelly made a sweeping motion with his hand and forearm. "But did he bat an eye at you? Of course not! And why not? I'll tell you why. You've got something special. It's built-in, and all it needs is to be let out. Polished. Trained. Use whatever word you want, but I think that with a little bit of schooling, you'll go places."

Impressed by his sincerity, Ana was looking intently at Shelly as he spoke. She didn't appear to be surprised; it was as if he were saying something she had heard before, or thought before.

"Where can I go? I've already done high school."

"College!"

"Col...College? Now I know you've lost a screw!" Ana was incredulous, and she laughed at the idea. "College is for rich white boys. Not someone like me!"

"Not anymore, lady. Up to five years ago—maybe. Look, Ana, there are new colleges cropping up all over the place. They're called junior colleges. Why don't you look into it? You could take a couple of courses, at night, maybe. Classes in— oh, hell, I don't know. Something like business, or economics, or what about accounting? Yeah, that's it! Accounting. The old man would go bananas if he didn't have to depend on those shysters who screw him every time they feel like it."

Ana silently stood up, but before leaving she placed her hand on his shoulder. She wanted to let him know that she took him seriously and that he, inadvertently perhaps, had reached into her, breaking through some of the layers that had caked over her after Octavio had betrayed her. All that night she considered what Shelly had said because she often felt that there was something inside of her waiting to be freed from its cage.

She checked around and found out that there was a new junior college in East Los Angeles, located close to where she had grown up, out where the tracks of flowers used to grow on Floral Drive. She decided to move close to the school, and found a small apartment in a two-story building on Brooklyn Avenue, almost across the street from the college. It didn't matter that now she would have to take a bus to work. What was important, she told herself, was that now she could take courses every Monday, Wednesday and Friday nights.

↪↪↪

Nearly two years passed while I worked with the Fuermanns and took courses. Although I kept in touch with Amy and Franklin with letters, I knew that I was alone. I could have had friends, but something inside of me didn't want to be with other people. I could have allowed Shelly to love me, but I was afraid, and whenever I asked myself why this was so, a door inside of me closed so that I never answered my own questions.

I liked attending classes and I didn't mind spending most of the money I earned on books. Some were for subjects I was studying, but others were those that attracted me with their title, or even their cover. After work and classes, I read for hours during the night, and most of the time I reached the end of the textbook before the assigned class time.

As the months passed, I became more interested in the factory. I saw that there was something about me that was liked by the workers, both men and women. Up to that time, I hadn't realized that others wanted to follow me. I saw that they listened to me, so I kept close to all the workers. My job as a supervisor made it easy for me to stop at their stations to ask how things were going, or what needed to be changed or fixed.

Maybe it was because of this that Mr. Fuermann began to

depend on me more and more. One day, he asked me if I would be willing to keep the company books. But I had to tell him that it was too soon, that I had to study more. He laughed and told me to hurry up because he couldn't wait for me much longer.

Shelly and I went on being friends. Sometimes I accepted his invitation to go to a restaurant and a movie on Saturday nights, but most of the time we talked and joked during lunch breaks or after work. I liked him, and perhaps we could have been more than friends, but we never got the time.

The Korean War broke out in 1950, and Shelly was called up from the list of reserves. At that time, his father was so upset that he was absent from work for three days. Shelly, however, laughed it off, saying that he would win the war single-handed. He joked that if the enemy hadn't plugged him in the last war, they wouldn't do it in this one.

All of us at the factory got together and had a farewell party for him. We sang and ate cake in his honor, and we even gave him a pair of flannel pajamas to keep him warm over there. The day came for him to leave, and Mr. Fuermann asked me to accompany him and Shelly to the ship that was going to transport him. When we said goodbye, he kissed me. I liked the sensation of his lips on mine, but the feeling stayed there. It never reached the rest of my body.

Ezra Fuermann and Son, Inc. experienced a surge of new business during the first months of the Korean War. Ezra had commissioned Ana to make contact with the small stores that were appearing along First and Spring Streets in an effort to create new outlets. He was certain that her style and ability to communicate with the merchants in Spanish would prove to be an asset. He was right. Orders increased to the point that he saw that he had to expand.

Although Ana was now involved with marketing, she continued with her classes. Since her salary had gone up, she was able to buy a used car, giving her more time to concentrate on her books as well as on company business. It turned out that she thrived on work, and everyone around her wondered how she could keep up with her responsibilities, which increased with each day.

Ana underwent a visible change during that time. Instead of denim pants and loafers, she was now smartly outfitted in tailored suits or dark dresses, and she always wore high-heel shoes. The heavy net or bandanna that used to hold her long hair in place was replaced by smart hats, and she wore gloves whenever she went outdoors.

Ezra Fuermann often joked that he had found the woman with the touch of Midas because whatever the contact might be, if Ana did the transaction, it meant more money for the company. Because of this, Fuermann now included her in most of his major decisions regarding investing in new space and additional machines. She also became instrumental in devising new methods of packaging and transportation of products. It was Ana's idea for the company to expand into baby apparel, a line that soon turned out to be the most successful.

Ezra was happy during that time, but it ended eleven months after Shelly left. One day, Ana was called to the main office. When she knocked on the door there was no response, but she went in anyway. She found him sitting at his desk, his back to the door, staring vacantly out the window. She stood by the desk for a while, but when Ezra still didn't turn around, she cleared her voice, hoping that it would alert him to her presence. When she saw that even that did not stir him, she decided to say something.

"Mr. Fuermann. You asked me to come by?"

When he didn't acknowledge her, Ana moved around the desk to have a better look at him. She saw that tears were coursing down his cheeks, and that he held a crumpled telegram in his right hand. She knew instantly what it was, and she closed her eyes for a few moments, hoping to get courage from somewhere within her. She leaned against the edge of the desk for balance, but she still couldn't speak.

Impulsively, Ana reached over and took the message from Ezra's hand. She read that Shelly was dead. He was killed during an assault on a machine-gun nest.

No one as close to her had been killed in war. She remembered Reyes Junior, but he had been distant, not as close to her as Shelly had been. She recalled how she had wished that Octavio would have been killed, and was not. Then she thought of César, and that he, too, had died in a war waged in the streets of their barrio.

The factories closed for three days in memory of Shelly Fuermann. His body was flown to Los Angeles from Korea, and from the airport a long cortege of cars filled with friends and fellow workers accompanied Ezra and his son to the Veterans Cemetery in Westwood. There was a large gathering of people at the grave site, but Ana was singled out by Ezra to sit at his right hand while the Rabbi spoke of Shelly's bravery and worthiness as a son.

As she listened, she was transported to César's death. That time she had been forced to stand at the rear of the church and had been forbidden by her father to take part in his funeral and burial. Now, as Shelly Fuermann was being lowered into his grave, she felt the rage against her family more than ever. She was struck by the irony of having been blocked from her brother's presence, whereas now she was in a place of honor, sitting next to someone who had been a stranger three years before. Ana felt affection for the man seated next to her, as if Ezra Fuermann had been the father she had longed for, someone who respected her and found in her something valuable.

When the service ended, Ana turned to Ezra and realized with a shock that he was struggling, fumbling with his vest. She saw that he was trying to stand, but that his feet were instead tracing tiny, jiggling steps that failed to give him balance. His head swiveled grotesquely toward her and his eyes, which were bulging, seemed to implore her to do something. Saliva was dribbling from the corners of lips and his face was turning dark purple. As she reached out to take his hands, Ana realized that his body was stiffening, becoming rigid with each second.

By then others had noticed what was happening, and several men rushed to help her. They took hold of his shoulders and waist, but he wobbled out of their hands and collapsed on the damp grass. By the time the ambulance arrived and Ezra had been taken to the emergency care of the hospital, he had suffered a stroke that left him in danger of dying.

*Ezra didn't die, but the stroke left his left side paralyzed.
The doctors affirmed that his mind was unaffected and that
in time he would be able to regain most of his speaking ability. But even when he recovered consciousness and he could
speak again, I saw that he was a changed man. It seemed that
his soul was paralyzed with the grief of having lost Shelly. I
tried to distract him with my visits, first at the hospital and
then when he was taken home, but he was silent and withdrawn most of the time, and it wasn't until weeks later that he
began to notice me.*

*I visited Ezra every evening, taking time to tell him details
about the business of the day that I thought would be of interest to him and sometimes might even make him laugh. I wanted to bring only good news. In the beginning, he hardly
responded to my attempts to cheer him up. In time, he was
normal again, and I thought I noticed that he was beginning
to care more for me each day.*

*It was nearly Christmas by the time Ezra was able to
overcome most of the slurring of his speech, and he and I
talked as we used to before the stroke. Gradually, our conversations became more personal, like those of a father and a
daughter. What I mean is that before his illness our words
had been filled mostly with the details of business or wise
cracks or sometimes even sarcasm. But now our conversations
were simple, unaffected. I think that when we spoke to one
another now, we were not afraid to say what we were feeling.*

෨෧

On one of those evenings, Ezra was seated in a wheel
chair next to the fireplace; his lap was wrapped in a colorful
afghan. "Ana, do you have a family?" The brief silence that
followed his question was filled with the crackling of twigs
underneath a larger piece of wood. "I mean, like brothers or
sisters?"

Ana looked at Ezra and felt a deep fondness as she gazed
at his face, its left side inert. The thought crossed her mind
that the same question would have been offensive to her had
it come from anyone else. Instead, she smiled.

"Yes. I come from a big family. I'm the oldest of seven

girls, and we had a brother, too. He and one of my sisters died a long time ago."

"You never mention any of them. Anyway, not in front of me."

Ana was quiet as she stared at the fire because she was remembering her sisters. The thought of them made the pit of her stomach contract. She knew that it was resentment that was yanking at her guts.

"I'm sorry. If you don't want to speak about them, tell me. I don't want to intrude. Oh, hell, what a liar I am!" He interrupted himself abruptly; his voice was hoarse and he spoke slowly, trying to control the muscles in his tongue. "First, I start poking around your insides, then I pull the old 'I'm-so-sorry' song and dance. It's just that you've never said anything about them."

"Yes, I know. It's something I never speak about to anyone." Ana stared at the log in the grate and saw that it was beginning to smolder. "I even had a son, once."

Ezra's small eyes locked on her face. He didn't speak, but his expression was filled with surprise mixed with curiosity. When Ana returned his stare he looked away, embarrassed that she had been able to see his emotions.

"The boy's father was scared to tell the truth, and I had the baby by myself. That is, with the help of two friends, Amy and Franklin Bast. My son was with me for a few years, then..."

Ana had not felt the knot forming in her throat. So, when her voice cracked, she stopped speaking. She was surprised and afraid that she would cry. Ezra, not knowing what to say, squirmed in the chair as he awkwardly slipped his right hand under the afghan along with the other one. She suddenly sprang to her feet, making him think that she was going to leave. But instead she went to the fireplace and threw a log into the fire. After that, she returned to her place and began to speak again.

"My son's father stole him from me. It happened just after the war. He was able to do it with the help of my sisters."

She was speaking tersely because her voice had grown husky and it was hard for her to talk without croaking. Her heart was beating so fast that she was sure that Ezra could hear it pounding from where he sat. She was amazed to think that she had not told anyone about Ismael, except for Franklin and Amy. Ana didn't realize it at the moment, but she was clasping her hands around the wooden arms of the chair where she sat so hard that her fingers and knuckles had turned a brownish white.

When she stopped speaking, Ezra swallowed hard and said, "Kid, I'm sorry. I had no idea. You've always look so... so..."

"What, Ezra, what do I look like? Dumb? Stupid?" Her voice took on a sharp edge that cut at the old man, making him recoil in the chair.

"No, Ana! No!" He seemed hurt that she should think that he would see her that way.

Ana released her grip on the chair, grinding her elbows into the arm rests and putting her hands under her chin, palm against palm as if she were praying. Her voice was calming down. "I'm sorry, Ezra. I guess I'll never get over it."

They were quiet until he spoke. "Well? What did you do about it? I can't even begin to imagine a woman like you letting that happen to her without doing something."

"I got a gun and shot him!"

"You shot!... Who did you shoot?"

"The bastard! The guy who kidnapped my son!"

"Christ!... Ana!"

"I didn't kill him, though. That's my only regret, because I had to pay for it anyway. I did time on Terminal Island along with hundreds of other women who had done just about the same thing as I did. When I went to work for you and Shelly, I had just got out." She paused, then said, "That's why I never speak about my family. I hate them all!"

The crackling sounds in the fireplace bounced off the high ceiling, accentuating the prolonged silence between Ezra and Ana. Neither of the two spoke until he sucked in his breath as he shook his head. "You'll have to forgive them one day, you know..."

"Why?" Ana cut off his sentence as resentment flooded her.

"Because your insides will freeze up on you if you don't, that's why. I had a brother that I never forgave. He went to his grave that way."

Ana was staring at him because she had never heard Ezra mention anyone except his wife, who had died years before. She was listening intently, still smarting from the idea of forgiving Alejandra and her other sisters.

Ana said, "Some things are unforgivable. I don't think I'll ever be able to forget that my own sisters helped to hurt me so..." She abruptly stopped speaking, as if thinking of something else. A few moments later she spoke again. "But then, my father hated me. Maybe that's why it was so easy for the others to do the same."

Ezra was staring out the window. Evening had set in, and the garden was wrapped in darkness. The right side of his face twitched slightly, as if trying to carry the weight of its inert side.

"Your father hated you?"

"Yes."

"Why?"

"For years I thought it was because I wasn't a boy. I was his first child, and I was convinced that his disappointment at my being a girl was too much for him. But later I saw how much he loved my other sisters, and I knew it couldn't have been just because I turned out a girl."

She was quiet. Then, moistening her lips with her tongue, she said, "Others told me that I had ruined my mother's womb because all the boys she had after me died. Except for the last one."

Shaking his head, Ezra said, "Oh, come on, Ana! You're too smart to swallow that one. Besides, how sure can you be that your old man really hated you? Sometimes a kid can misunderstand her father, you know."

Her head snapped towards Ezra. Her face had reddened. "How do I know? When he discovered that I was pregnant, he tried to kill me. He nearly beat my brains out, and he would have gotten what he wanted, except some neighbors stopped him. He cursed me and my baby, too."

Again shaking his head, Ezra said, "I'm sorry, Kid, I really am. Rotten things happen in a lifetime, but you know..." He interrupted himself as he looked at her, his gaze was intense. "...I still think that forgiving them for all the crap they've handed you is the only way."

Ana let out a snort through her nose; its sound was charged with sarcasm and mockery. Then she shook her head so hard that the dangling earrings she wore made a tinkling noise. She muttered one word—"Never!"

Ezra didn't speak up right away, instead he nibbled at his right upper lip. "You and I have something in common, Ana, despite our differences: age, and who knows what else. But there's something in each of us that I'm afraid will one day bring us right down to our knees. I think Shelly's death has already done that for me."

She kept quiet because she was picturing herself on her knees. "When I was a little girl, my aunt took me to the Shrine of Guadalupe in Mexico City where I saw a woman on her knees. She was crying and her puffed eyes told me that she had been sobbing for days, maybe even weeks. My aunt told me that the woman had surely committed a grave sin and was now penitent. The image of that woman has stayed with me ever since."

Ezra shifted his bulky body in the chair to get a better look at Ana. The left side of his face seemed to sag more than ever, and the reflection from the fireplace accentuated the deep cracks that rimmed his lips. He sighed deeply. "I wish that I were a religious man, but I'm not. I know the words *sin* and *penitent*, but I don't understand them. I just know one thing. I don't want you to go on hurting. Let go of it, please. I mean, let go of the pain and the hate."

త~ళ

I didn't let go of the pain or the hate because I had already wrapped myself inside of those feelings, as if they had been hardened skin that nothing could scratch, much less pene- trate. I felt alone, even in the company of others, and although I tried to awaken the attraction for men that I had once felt for Octavio, I couldn't. I was empty and dry. It was as if I had become sexless. No one, nothing aroused me.

When Ezra asked me to take responsibility for the accounts of the business, overlooking its cash flow and expansion plans, I was happy to plunge into the Fuermann business, working intently, hoping to forget the dryness inside of me.

As the years passed, my position in Ezra's business expanded and I gradually became wealthy. I liked it very much because I discovered that having money helped me for- get what I had lost. I bought a town house in the Fairfax

District and moved out of the small room I used to rent. I was glad about that, too, because it took me far away from the barrio that brought me bad memories. Nevertheless, I often thought of the palapa where I was born and of my mother's soapy arms as she stuck the chocolate-colored nipple of her breast into a baby's mouth. And no matter how much money I made, the image of my mother's open legs and a tiny head appearing from between them hardly ever left me.

No one knew these things about me. No one imagined where I had come from or that I had been a prison inmate just a few years before or that I had been forced to struggle for a living on a bleak chicken ranch. No one dreamed that I had a son who had been taken from me.

But when I looked in the mirror, I knew who I was, and hardly a day passed that I didn't remember the details of my life. If I abandoned myself to the agitated business of work, it was only to still those memories. Whenever I sat in conference or interviewed an employee or traveled to other parts of the world, it was to fill the emptiness inside of me. The desire for fashionable clothing, jewelry, and fine surroundings—a feeling that intensified in me with each year—was just another thing that helped me forget the bitterness that welled up inside me, especially at night.

The fifties crept by and disappeared. Ezra continued living, and now that I look back, I'm convinced that it was because of me. He hoped, I think, to live to see me happy. But he died in 1962, leaving me with the memory of being loved by him. He also left me his enterprise and estate.

ঌ৹ঌ

By 1965, Ana had become very wealthy; her friends and associates suspected that her fortune measured in the millions. Calderón Enterprises, as her corporation was now called, had tripled in size and output since the days of Ezra Fuermann. The company now included high fashion in both men's and women's apparel, and new plants were set up on the East Coast as well as in Chicago, New Orleans, Houston and San Francisco. This growth culminated in the erection of a twelve-story building located on Wilshire Boulevard. It became the corporate headquarters for the business.

Although she surrounded herself with energetic profes-
sionals who could have run the enterprise for her, Ana managed her affairs directly, and she seemed inexhaustible as
she dealt with one task after the other. She kept personal
control of the finances of the corporation as well as the hiring
and firing of upper management. Friday morning was the
center of the business week for Calderón Enterprises
because, beginning at 7 a.m., Ana held private sessions during which her managers reported to her. They presented
themselves in groups. First Personnel and Resources, followed by Communications and Transportation. After these
came Finances and Marketing.

She had made a singular reputation for herself among
her staff members. On the one hand, Ana was perceived as
willing to help and always open to suggestions; on the other,
it was known that if contradicted or dissatisfied, she was
prone to harshness. It was common knowledge that she de-
manded directness, honesty and promptness. If she asked for
a report and gave a time and date for its presentation, she expected her request to be honored exactly. When someone
hedged or sidestepped one of her questions or doubts, she cut
him or her off curtly. She often said that she had no patience
for pussyfooting.

Her associates and employees had a high regard for her
but they realized that they knew little about her and that she
was for the most part enshrouded in mystery. No one knew of
her beginnings or of her family. It was known that she was
unmarried, and curiosity was common regarding her past
and whether or not she had ever had a husband or children.
Everyone around her knew that she was intensely reserved
and they could only guess at what she thought. One thing
was certain: no employee had ever been taken into her confidence or into the inner aspects of her life.

To all appearances, Ana lead a sumptuous existence, and
her personal attire was the first proof of this. She was forty-
five years old, yet she had retained a youthful, slim figure
and her face had become more beautiful. To match her looks,
she wore clothing exclusively made by leading fashion design-
ers; her suits and dresses were always fabricated of imported
silks and linens. Her love of quality jewelry intensified,
prompting the secretaries surrounding her to remark among

themselves that if what she wore sparkled, it was a true diamond; if it glittered, it was solid gold.

Another sign of the elegance of Ana's life was the mansion she had recently constructed on the bluffs overlooking the Pacific Ocean. It was a sprawling, white stucco Spanish-style house which had large plate glass windows as its mark of distinction. There was hardly any area in the place from which the ocean could not be seen. Behind the building Ana had a small stable where she kept horses, because riding had become her favorite pastime over the years.

Ana now owned a limousine and a Rolls Royce, and each automobile had its assigned driver. For cross-country trips, she had a private plane accommodated with conference, dining, sleeping, and dressing areas, and it was aboard this plane that she conducted much of her business. Both at home and at travel, she had a private secretary, a woman, who accompanied her and was at her service any time of day or night.

This was Ana Calderón, the successful business woman everyone saw; the one admired and respected by most people, envied and hated by a few. The private Ana, however, was unchanged from her early beginnings. At night she still wrestled with her memories of poverty and hatred, and during the day, whenever she was alone, she turned inwardly, scrutinizing the steps that had brought her to the present.

What gnawed at Ana stubbornly was her failure to find Ismael. For years she had poured money into private investigations, individual detectives and sometimes even entire agencies in the hope of tracking down her son. Each time the answer had been the same: the files were sealed and inaccessible. Every lead had failed; each clue had turned up empty. She often thought of finding Octavio to question him, but the idea of even knowing of his whereabouts sickened her.

Ismael had vanished from the world, her world, but even after years of searching and probing, Ana still harbored a secret hope that she would one day locate him. The thought that he was now a grown man filled her with greater anxiety because she wanted to see him and be part of his life.

One day, Ana was absorbed in these thoughts as the elevator silently ascended to the executive suite. It was a crisp, autumn morning and she was scheduled to meet with Larry Whiting, the Communications Officer. After that she had appointments, a luncheon, and finally a fund-raising dinner at the Biltmore Hotel. When she stepped out of the elevator, a secretary met her with the usual list of obligations.

Ana listened as she walked toward her private office; she was removing her coat and dark glasses. The young woman recited the time and item to be dealt with beginning at ten that morning.

"...Eleven thirty: interview candidate for accounting position. After that, lunch..."

Ana stopped abruptly and looked at the secretary with a questioning expression on her face. "Accounting position? Which one?"

"Oscar Rubalcaba's position. Remember? You fired him last week, and we're searching for a replacement."

"Oh, I forgot. Hmm... Eleven-thirty. Will I have enough time to make it over to lunch? Maybe we ought to cancel...no...better not. We need someone to fill that slot soon. Do we have more than one applicant?"

"There are three others, but I've scheduled them over the next few days instead of all at once. We don't want you to get too tired."

Ana caught the humorous sarcasm in the secretary's voice and responded, "You got that one right, Sandra. Tell the applicant to be patient if I get tied up with Whiting. Sometimes he talks too much."

At eleven-fifteen the intercom on the secretary's desk sounded. "Sandra, I'm finished with Whiting. Is the applicant in?"

"Yes, Miss Calderón. You'll find his file on your work table. Let me know when you're ready to receive him."

Ana went to the table and found several neat stacks of file folders, each clearly designated. Under a note indicating the accountants' applications, she took the top one and returned to her desk. She put on her reading glasses, opened the file and scanned the front page. BA in economics, Stanford. MBA, Northwestern. Experience, six months at State Industries Corp. Age: 25. She picked up the receiver and pressed the button, "Show him in, Sandra."

Experience had taught Ana that she had to interview every applicant carefully before making her final choice, because even after scrutiny, sometimes the person employed turned out to be inadequate. She leaned back in the high-

backed leather chair as she swiveled it around to face the
window. It was a clear day; she could make out San Pedro
and the bridge that now connected the mainland to Terminal
Island. When she heard the secretary clearing her throat,
Ana spun the chair around to its original position. "Miss
Calderón, this is our applicant, Mr. Terrance Wren."

The man was obviously nervous and he awkwardly
reached over the desk in an effort to shake Ana's hand. She
glared at him, not knowing exactly why, and it took her a few
seconds before she lifted her hand to return the gesture. She
felt his hand clammy against hers. "Thank you, Sandra." As
the secretary turned to leave, Ana spoke out to her, "Will you
please let me know when the car comes by? I don't want to be
late for the luncheon. Please, Mr. Rye, take a seat."

"Wren, m'am. Wren."

Ana took several moments as she stared at the young
man. He was tall; over six feet. His skin was white and
healthy looking, and his hair was the color of chestnuts. He
had a broad forehead and eyes that were large and brown.
His nose was regular, not long, not short, and his lips had a
tiny upward curve at either side. He was dressed in a dark
suit and tie; his shirt was a pale blue.

Terrance Wren returned Ana's gaze frankly, innocently.
His nervousness continued and it showed in his hands, which
he clenched and unclenched. She looked down at the file and
began to speak. "I see here that you have all the necessary
credentials, Mr. Wren, but very little experience. What
makes you think you can cope with a highly demanding job,
such as this one?"

He opened his mouth to speak, but nothing came out. He
placed a cupped fist up to his lips, cleared his voice and tried
again. "Well, you're right, m'am. I just worked for six months
up-state for a small outfit, but I think that if you give me a
chance, I'll be able to keep up with the load."

"I see that you're originally from San Francisco. Right?"

"Yes, that's it. My folks live up there, too."

"Why would you leave the place where you grew up, as
well as your parents, to come down here?"

He smiled broadly, showing a row of straight white teeth.
His face took on a gentle expression that engaged Ana's
attention. His smile made her feel something unusual, a
strange sensation that was quickly flooding her body. Her

mind groped, stumbling as if in the dark, trying to identify what it was that she was experiencing, but it found only emptiness, nothing. She became uncomfortable, and this feeling turned into annoyance, first with herself and then with the jittery man sitting in front of her.

He began to answer her question, "Well, m'am, your corporation is well-known in a lot of places. I've heard good things about it from several buddies, and I'd like to work here. Also, I'll be honest and admit that I love the sun; that's another big reason. And, after all is said and done, Los Angeles isn't all that far away from San Francisco. I'll be home for Christmas, as the old song..."

"Please call me by my name!" Ana's exasperation was growing, and she brusquely interrupted him. When he looked confused, she repeated, this time with irritation in her voice, "Please call me Miss Calderón!"

"Yes, m'am...I mean, Miss Calderón."

She then assaulted Terrance Wren with rapid-fire questions.

"Are you willing to travel out of state on short notice?"

"Yes...Miss..."

"What about late-night work? And I mean Saturdays and even Sundays?"

"Certainly..."

"Are you willing to submit detailed reports to me on the spot?"

"Of course...I..."

"What if I ask you to do an unpaid internship?"

"I think I could..."

"Well, Mr. Rye, I see that you're willing to do just about anything for this job, aren't you? You must be pretty hungry!"

Terrance caught the sarcasm in her voice and the way she had intentionally used a wrong name. He kept quiet, not knowing what to answer. But he didn't take his eyes away from her hard glare.

Ana was surprised and embarrassed by her outburst, but she still could not explain why she was feeling so much anger. Something in his looks, his demeanor, the way he returned her gaze, unsettled her, and she felt herself filling up with resentment. After a few moments, however, she forced herself to regain her composure. She wrinkled her brow and ran her tongue over her upper lip.

"I'm afraid I got carried away, Mr. Wren. Excuse me, please. Give us a few days to let you know the final decision. I must be honest with you in saying that there are several other candidates for the position. There's something else, however..." Ana pointed at her forehead, "I had, up here, the picture of an older man. No offense to you, personally, but you might yet be too inexperienced for the demands expected in this business."

Terrance seemed shaken by the interview, and when she stopped speaking he stood up and walked toward the door. Before leaving, he looked back at Ana. He was obviously confused. He, too, was unable to explain why she had taken such an intense dislike to him. As he opened the door he murmured, "Thank you, Miss Calderón."

꒰ঌ•᠅

Why had I been so angry with Terrance Wren? What had provoked me to rudeness towards him? Why did I put aside the rules that had always guided me? It was unlike me, but I know now that something inside of me had stirred, and I failed to recognize what it was. Instead of forcing myself to understand, and despite my confusion, I decided to give him the job. He was with me for three years.

꒰ঌ•᠅

Ana put Terrance under the guidance of Kevin Tang, the Chief Accountant of Calderón Enterprises. She asked him to give her a weekly report of the new employee, but other than that, she saw him only now and then. A year had passed when he unexpectedly appeared at the weekly session in place of Tang, who was ill that day.

She was dressed in a maroon suit; its lines were tailored to fit elegantly yet comfortably. Her hair, which she wore starkly pulled into a roll at the back of her head, accentuated her eyes and high cheekbones. Simple diamond earrings studded her earlobes, and a gold chain with the initial A hung neatly at her throat.

Ana sat erectly at the head of a large, highly polished conference table. Surrounding her were the chief representatives of the Marketing and Finance Divisions of her firm. When the men entered the room, she was already in her place. Documents were neatly placed in front of her as her secretary gave her information she would need for the meeting.

"Gentlemen, please take a seat."

They were in good spirits, and they smiled at her as they individually returned her greeting. It was 7 a.m. and most of them were energetic and ready to go to work on their reports. When Ana saw Terrance, she asked him, "Mr. Wren, where's Kevin?"

"He's out sick today, and he's asked me to present our report to you, Miss Calderón."

"I see."

Without further talk, Ana launched into the meeting, following the agenda she had formulated beforehand. She went from one report to the next, asking questions of clarification and modification. "How is the program going for the new line, Bramante?"

She was especially interested in the marketing report because the firm had initiated a new line of baby clothes, and at her suggestion, the division representatives were targeting outlets in the eastern sectors of Los Angeles for this product in particular.

"Miss Calderón, as the report I've handed in shows, there's been a noticeable increase in sales out there. I think we're on target."

It was after a lengthy discussion of this topic that Ana closed it as she turned to Terrance. "Mr. Wren, I believe we're ready to hear about our accounts."

Terrance was visibly nervous. He shifted back and forth on his chair and cleared his throat several times. When he picked up the report to refer to it, he dropped it on the floor. Then, as he bent down to pick it up, he knocked over a glass of water with his elbow. When the water splashed over to the next man, he jumped out of the chair trying to avoid being doused, and as he did this the chair fell over on its back. This caused everyone at the table to move or stand, and in less than a minute Ana's meeting was in disruption.

She was the only person who had not moved. When

Terrance looked over to her, he saw that she was trying to stifle a smile, and after everyone returned to their places, Ana said, "Mr. Wren, is there a hidden camera somewhere in here? I mean, are we filming a comedy?"

Everyone laughed out loud at her remark except Terrance, who was so embarrassed he could hardly speak. After the meeting, he stayed behind to apologize to Ana, and he did so with apprehension because he hadn't forgotten her harsh manner during his first meeting with her. To his surprise, she was not upset with him. On the contrary, she seemed to have enjoyed the opportunity to poke fun at him, making the others laugh.

When she walked away from the meeting, Ana was also surprised. The irritation and annoyance he had caused her during their first meeting had evaporated, and just as she couldn't explain her feelings the first time, she now found it impossible to find the reason for her new reaction. She decided to put aside thinking about the matter and went on with her work.

After a while, Ana asked her Chief Accountant to include Terrance in the weekly meetings. Later on, she called on him from time to time, asking for up-dates on certain figures and accounts. He seemed glad to accommodate her wishes, and after some months it got to the point that he could anticipate her next step.

He and Ana began working late in her office, and as time passed this became their daily routine. Whenever she went on a trip to any of the branch factories, Terrance now accompanied her on the plane. Some two years after being hired, he became the employee upon whom she most depended.

❧✦

I began to feel different during those months, and I could tell that others had noticed. I think it was because I smiled more, or maybe it was because I chatted with the office boys and the elevator conductors. Everyone knew that I had hardly done that before.

But the change in me was real. When I woke up in the morning and slipped out of bed, the first thing I did was to draw the drapes away from the windows. The ocean that I hardly noticed before now gave me a jolt of pleasure each time I glanced at it. Everything around me seemed to become more beautiful each day, and I asked myself why I hadn't noticed such beauty before.

During the years of Ezra's illness, and even after his death, my work had become a routine, a mechanical thing that filled up my days. But now I looked forward to stepping out of the elevator to be with the men and women who were my staff, people who had seemed little more than furniture during other times.

I admitted that Terrance was at the heart of what was happening. I was captivated by his sense of humor and the way he was able to transform a column of zeros and fractions, making them not only interesting but charming.

I liked his company, and I was impressed by his intelligence and personality. Sometimes I found myself thinking of his looks because I found him handsome. At those times, however, I forced myself not to think of him that way, and instead I concentrated on his skills as one of my most productive employees. But I slipped often because I felt good noticing that he was engrossed with me, too. I often caught a look of admiration for me reflected in his eyes, and I liked that very much. Sometimes I would unexpectedly look up from whatever I was doing to find him gazing at me with a faint smile that lingered around his lips.

I knew what was happening to me, but whenever a faint voice inside told me that I was getting too close to Terrance, I stifled the idea by telling myself that he was necessary for the operation of the firm. Whenever I was forced to recognize that he was filling most of my thoughts, I rushed to concentrate on other matters. I was able to sweep away the nagging voice this way.

戣扇

On the way home one evening, Ana was forced to confront her relationship with Terrance. As her driver managed the car through traffic on the Harbor Freeway, she sat back on the leather seat. She reclined her head, eyes closed, as if she had been asleep. But she was thinking. Something had occurred between the two of them that afternoon.

When she opened her eyes, the headlights of the on-coming cars made her blink while she thought of how her body had trembled when Terrance inadvertently touched her hand. A vibration had streaked through her body with a powerful sensation, and she knew that she had not felt anything like it since the times when she had lain with Octavio. The feeling caused by Terrance's hand so unsettled Ana that she abruptly cut off their work without explanation.

The vehicle sped south as she wrestled with her thoughts. Her mind reached out, hoping to find an explanation, anything that would dispel the confusion she was experiencing. Then she looked out the window, staring at the span of twinkling harbor lights, and she thought of Puerto Real. Suddenly, this image connected with others. The number of years that had passed since she was a girl flashed through her memory, and she remembered that she was old, too old for Terrance. Certainly too old to feel what she thought she felt. Ana closed her eyes as she allowed this realization to seep into her. She forced her mind to concentrate and to let what she had just thought of take root.

Ana suddenly sat up. She thought that she had found the answer. She told herself that she had been mistaken, that she was beyond the age of feeling such things. She leaned back, fixating her mind on this idea. A while passed before she felt the car glide onto the long driveway leading to the carport. By the time the driver stopped the car and opened the door for her, Ana had convinced herself that she had imagined what had happened that afternoon.

The next evening when Terrance came to her office, his arms loaded with reports and papers, Ana felt afraid, but she resisted her fears and reminded herself that she was a professional woman, above such nonsense. She sensed an awkwardness in him, but she nonetheless launched into working until they were reminded of the time by a delivery boy who brought them sandwiches and coffee. After the boy left, Ana decided that they had done enough work, and they went to the coffee table at the far side of the office where they chatted as they ate.

Terrance often told her of his childhood, of his school days and even of his years in college. She liked listening to him because he had a charming way of telling of his experiences.

Ana was grateful, especially that evening, for any small talk that might lighten the stiffness that had grown between them with each passing minute.

Instead of his usual lighthearted adventures, however, Terrance began to tell Ana of an unhappy memory in his life. "I remember that sometimes I used to sleep under a sink with my face pressed against a cold pipe. Isn't that strange, Ana?"

"Under the sink? Are you sure you weren't playing a game?"

"Hmm. Maybe. The truth is that I can't remember anything else. I don't even remember people or things, just the dumb cold water pipe. Sometimes I think that it was just a bad dream."

Ana was looking at him intently. "I wish I had known you then. I'm old enough, you know."

"Yeah, I guess."

Nervously changing the subject, Terrance said, "Hey! Did I ever tell you about the first time I got drunk? I was a freshman in college and..."

Again he stopped suddenly and turned to her as he took her hand. She was surprised, but she didn't resist because she was instantly overcome with emotion. She looked at his face and saw that it was beautiful, and that the vein in his neck had thickened, and that it was throbbing. Neither of them spoke as they drew closer to one another. She knew what was happening, and although the inner voice tried to scream out to stop, that she was too old for him, that something was wrong, she suppressed it when she felt his lips on hers. She tasted his tongue, and submitted to him.

Ana removed her clothes and watched Terrance as he did the same thing. Then he reached out, cupping her still firm breasts in his hands, and he lowered his face to kiss her neck. She returned his caresses and kisses as she drew him towards her, and when they laid on the carpet, they remained still for a few moments, feeling each other's body. Then they rolled over each other, tumbling over and over as if wrestling until, almost out of breath, Ana wrapped her legs around his waist and surrendered to his penetration.

*The earth was quaking beneath me, and I knew that I had
never loved anyone as I did Terrance. My body and mind and
heart exploded, catapulting me into a world so sublime and
beautiful that all the hatred and anguish that I had tasted
vanished, and in its place there was only beauty and pleasure.
When I gave myself to him, I forgot everything. I forgot my
age, my loneliness, and everyone who had ever entered my life.
We were lovers for nearly a year before our happiness ended.*

୧ৡବ৶

It was raining in Los Angeles that early December morning. Ana and Terrance sat in the airport lounge waiting for
his flight to New York; they were checking last minute
changes to the report he would be presenting on arrival. She
looked happy, serene, and the only thing that disturbed her
was that she wasn't able to go with him because she was
scheduled to fly to Houston.

When the announcement was made that his flight was
ready for departure, Terrance moved closer to Ana and kissed
her lips. He didn't say anything, but his eyes told her that he
loved her. After a few moments, he said, "I'll return in three
days. We'll spend Christmas in San Francisco."

She smiled at him and pressed his hand against her
cheek. *"Buena suerte.* I'll be waiting."

Terrance took his briefcase and went to the exit where he
turned to look at Ana. He smiled again and waved goodbye.
As he walked away from her, she moved over to a window
where she could see him make his way across the blacktop to
the ramp leading up to the plane. She watched him as he
pulled his hat down in an attempt to shield his face from the
drizzle, and she kept her eyes on him until she saw him climb
the steps and disappear into the small entrance of the plane.

Ana remained looking at the plane for a long while. Then
her eyes scanned the runway that glistened with the moisture of soft rain, and she smiled as she recalled the days she
and Terrance had spent recently in Santo Domingo. As she
watched the plane begin to move, she remembered the tropi-
cal sun on her face and the emerald-colored water that had
transported her back to where she had been born. She, with

Terrance by her side, had lived the most beautiful days of her life on the island where, for the first time, she had felt free. They had passed days in which they danced, loved and conversed.

Ana returned to her office later that day and she worked without stopping for lunch. She dictated several letters, received representatives from competing firms, and met with three plant managers. As the sky began to darken, she noticed that it was still raining, and she paused for a few minutes for a cup of coffee. Terrance was on her mind.

When her secretary walked in with the evening newspaper, Ana was startled by the shocked expression on the woman's face. Ana stared at her for a few moments, and then without saying a word, she took the folded newspaper and spread it out on the coffee table.

Jet airliner en route to New York goes down in snowy Iowa corn field. All aboard perish.

Ana looked at the secretary, trying to find a contradiction on her face of what the newspaper was telling. But the expression that she saw was a confirmation, not a denial. Ana was stunned, and she refused to accept what her mind was beginning to tell her. She rushed to the desk where she fumbled clumsily, scattering papers onto the floor while looking for her reading glasses. When she finally found them, she dashed back to the newspaper and scanned the report. Her index finger slid down the center of the fine print as she mumbled out the name of the airline, the flight number, its place of departure, its scheduled place of arrival.

The details confirmed that Terrance was dead, but still Ana resisted. She looked first at the secretary's blanched face, then back at the newspaper. The headlines leaped from the newsprint, wrapping themselves around her throat. She began to choke, to suffocate. Breathing became difficult. A throbbing began in her head; initially it was a dim, dull pulsation, then it expanded, growing, enlarging, until she felt that the pounding would destroy her brain and kill her. She raised her hands to her head in an attempt to relieve the pain.

"Miss Calderón, maybe you ought to lie down...here..."

"Please leave me. Please! Nothing more. No calls...no one...Please!"

The woman left the room and closed the door silently,

leaving Ana with her hands clutched to her head. When she was alone, she felt that her body was losing strength. She had no control over it as it inertly fell to the floor. There she rolled into a tight, round ball, knees tucked under her chin.

๛๛

My hands and forearms would not let go of my head. Flashes of my short time with Terrance blurred with those of my childhood and with the memory of my father's curse. I understood that the pain I was now feeling was greater than the punishment inflicted on me by his fists, and that it surpassed even his hatred. This thought forced my mind to stop, to look around and to remember that I had once before experienced an agony equal to this one when Octavio had wrenched Ismael away from me.

๛๛

The distant ringing repeated, four times, five times. A voice interrupted the sixth ring. "Hello."

"Mr. Wren?"

"Yes."

"Mr. Wren, I'm calling from Los Angeles. My name is Ana Calderón. Do you know of me?"

During the seconds of silence that followed, Ana could hear distant voices crisscrossing, mixing, blending on the line. She could also hear the man's breathing at the other end.

"Yes, Miss Calderón. Our son spoke often of you, of his work and of Los Angeles. But especially of you. He wanted us to meet you soon."

She felt her throat on the verge of exploding. She had not allowed herself to weep, but she knew that sooner or later she would have to cry, if only to relieve the pressure that was growing in her chest.

"Yes...thank you. I'm calling to extend my condolences to you and Mrs. Wren. I'm also at your service. I mean...if there's anything I can do for you." After a long pause, she added, "How is Mrs. Wren?"

The man sighed deeply, but his voice was steady. "She's having a hard time. He was everything to us."

Ana wanted to tell him that Terrance had been everything for her as well, but instead she said, "I would like to accompany you and your wife at this time."

"And we want you to be with us. We've decided to have a simple graveside service with only the people closest to Terrance and to us. You're one of them, of course. I'll notify you as soon as the time and place is settled."

Ana was listening keenly. There was one more thing she needed to ask. "Mr. Wren, what about his body?"

"It's en route at this moment. My wife and I will be at the airport to receive it."

"Thank you. I'll wait for your call." Ana returned the telephone receiver to its cradle. She was home; she was alone because she had instructed her staff to leave and not to return until she called them. She walked out to the front terrace, where she stood gazing vacantly at the ocean; it was a massive sheet of grayish slate. She stood for a long while in the drizzling rain, feeling its moisture chilling her burning skin.

Two days later at the airport in San Francisco, Ana walked over to the waiting car after leaving her plane. She was dressed in a plain black woolen suit and a small hat that curved down shading her eyes. As she slid onto the stuffed leather seat, she asked the driver if he knew his way to the cemetery. When he affirmed that he did, she sat back and closed her eyes. She had not slept since the news of the plane crash, nor had she been able to eat, and she had not reported to her office. Isolation was the only way she could deal with her grief.

The rain had stopped, giving way to dense fog as the limousine approached the inner area of the cemetery. The car glided slowly up to the grassy knoll where the gatekeeper had directed them, to where Ana saw a small group of people. They were dressed in black, and they huddled around the coffin which had been placed on a bier. The vehicle was still moving, but her eyes were riveted on the box piled high with flowers.

The car slid up to the curb and stopped. The driver walked around to open the door for Ana, who was already scanning the group, trying to identify Terrance's parents. Her attention was caught by a tall man wearing metal-rimmed glasses, and next to him stood a woman whose face, which was sad but composed, told Ana that she was Terrance's mother.

Ana got out of the car and moved toward the mourners, who had already seen her and seemed to be waiting to greet her. She found walking difficult because the heels of her shoes sank into the moist sod with each step. But as she approached the Wrens, she put out her hands to greet them. No one said anything because they understood that they shared the same loss. It wasn't until moments later that Mr. Wren spoke to Ana.

"We thank you for being with us today. It means a lot to the both of us."

She managed a weak nod in recognition of his words, and she was grateful when the minister asked them to take a seat in front of the coffin so that he could begin the service. As he read from the Bible, Ana's mind drifted back to the chicken ranch and she saw Amy reading from the book with black covers, her face illuminated by the bluish light cast by the kerosene lamp. When Ana's attention returned to the present, the minister was reading a psalm that told that no one need fear because, like the shepherd who seeks out the lost sheep, the Lord will come to the rescue.

Ana winced at the irony she perceived in those words. Her heart welled up with resentment, thinking that life had taken her on different paths, but each one had ended in loss because there had been no shepherd; nothing but emptiness and pain.

When the minister finished his prayers, he went over to the Wrens to console them as he patted each one on the shoulder. He handed Mrs. Wren the small crucifix that had been placed on top of the coffin, and with that he left the mourners, who began to break up into small groups of twos and threes.

Ana was about to make her way back to her car, when she recalled that she had not said goodbye to the Wrens. She turned to approach them and saw a man, someone she had not noticed before, talking to them. She lowered her eyes for a few seconds, but then returned them to the man. She blinked, then focused her gaze, trying to see more of his face because there was something about his body and its movements that reminded her of someone. She turned away, wrinkling her brow in concentration. A few moments later she knew. It was Octavio Arce. He was stouter, and his hair had receded, but she knew that it was him.

She was overcome with confusion; she could not explain his presence there, nor his connection with the Wren family. She gawked at him, not noticing that he, too, had looked in her direction and that when the Wrens moved away, he began to approach her with a look of surprise on his face.

"Ana..."

Octavio extended his hands toward her, but lowered them when he saw that she had no intention of returning his greeting. He appeared to be intimidated by the way she was looking at him.

"What are you doing here?" Her voice was a hoarse whisper; it was charged with rancor.

Resenting her tone, he changed his attitude, and instead of answering the question, he fired another one at her, his voice also harsh. "How did you find out?"

"Find out? Find out what?"

Octavio responded bluntly. "That these are the folks who adopted Ismael. I've kept in touch with them all these years."

Ana, who by now was standing next to her car, fell backward, but was stopped from landing on the concrete by the support of the limousine. She glared at Octavio, her mouth agape, her eyes opened so wide that they looked like pools of black water. Only seconds passed, but her mind had already grasped the pieces of the puzzle, putting it together. Years of searching had led to one dead-end after the other. The files had been sealed, she had been informed, but now she knew that Octavio Arce had been given every detail, and he had known the truth all along. She clamped shut her eyes. Ismael was Terrance and Terrance was Ismael. Her son!

Fearing that she would be sick in front of the others, Ana opened the rear door of the car and stumbled in headlong without closing the door behind her. Octavio followed her move and crouched down on his haunches. He saw that her eyes were shut tightly, and that her head was bent back against the seat. Her skin had become ashen.

"What are you doing here, Ana? How did you know?" When she refused to respond, Octavio frowned and bit his lip. "Are you the woman who was his employer? The one he was crazy about?"

He glared at Ana. Her head was still pressed against the seat, and she was holding her arms close against her stomach as if to relieve intense pain. Her silence forced him to piece things together, slowly at first, but it wasn't long before his face betrayed his understanding of what had happened.

Shocked with what his mind was telling him, he asked, "You didn't do anything wrong with him, did you?" Ana's mouth was clamped shut, and her prolonged silence compelled Octavio to pursue questioning her. "How far did you go with the boy, Ana?"

The impact of this question struck her in the center of her being, making her shudder. Without thinking, she shouted, "Leave me! Get out! Go away!"

The driver, who had been standing, waiting for her next instructions, thought that the man crouching next to the car was assaulting Ana, so he ran to Octavio and, taking him by the nape of his coat collar, dragged him back. Octavio lost his balance and fell on his buttocks, but he was able to get to his feet almost immediately. Struggling, he shouted, "Get your hands off me, you son of a bitch!"

Another chauffeur came to assist Ana's driver, and both men grabbed hold of Octavio's arms and forced him to his knees. As he grappled with the two men, his coat and shirt hanging in disarray, he managed to wrench himself partially loose, and he turned to Ana. She was sitting rigidly against the seat, her jaw set and her eyes dilated.

"How far did you go with him? I'm asking you a question?"

Octavio's voice was high-pitched and nearly hysterical, but instead of responding, Ana glared back at him, inciting him to scream even more. Ugly words sputtered from his mouth.

"Oh, you dirty, filthy woman! You slept with him! You! His mother! You actually did that with him! And you poisoned him, too, didn't you? Just like all the others, you killed him with your poison! Not even God will forgive you this time! Pig! Go blow your brains out! That's what you should do! You bit..."

Someone, an unseen hand, slammed the door, shutting out the obscenities that Octavio was vomiting.

❧❦

I was oblivious of everything except the sight of his bloated face and neck, which were deformed by hatred and which I could see through the sound-proofed window. I saw that his contorted, muted mouth was spewing words that were riddling my spirit.

When the driver returned to the car, he was red-faced and sweating. I asked him to take me to the airport, where I boarded my plane and headed back to the shelter of my home.

❧❦

It was the twelfth of December in Mexico City. Ana was kneeling on the rough concrete courtyard leading up to the Basilica; her knees were bare and unprotected. She wore a loosely fitting black cotton dress, and a mantilla designating her as a woman who had committed a grievous sin. As she looked in front of her, she saw that there were hundreds of other people also on their knees. When she turned around to look behind her, she saw that there were as many others back there, too. She was surrounded by penitents, men and women who were about to make their way across the immense plaza of the Basilica on their knees until they reached the altar of the Virgin of Guadalupe.

She looked up at the facade of the building, scanning its intricate design of coils and loops and niches. Ana's eyes, blinking in the vivid sunshine, made out statues of saints, martyrs and virgins, their limestone faces eroded by centuries of exposure to wind and rain. She looked at the pigeons and how they moved around their nests, craning their necks to peep down on the mass of people beneath them.

Over to her right, Ana saw Indians dancing in homage to the Virgin. The dancers were resplendent in their headdresses crowned with long, green quetzal feathers. The loincloths worn by the men were decorated with metal patches, and the womens' dresses were of white cotton decorated with rainbows of color. Rattles and strings of dried pods were wrapped around the dancers' ankles, and as as they moved to the

cadence of drums, they pounded their bare feet against the
ground, creating a rhythmic clatter that rose to the far sloping hills fringing the expansive valley of Mexico.

Her knees were beginning to ache, but Ana forgot her dis-
comfort as she looked in every direction and saw thousands of
brown-faced people, their hair shining jet-black in the rari-
fied air. The men had sparse beards, and their moustaches
were stringy tuffs that hovered above long, tapered upper
lips. The women she saw had round, flat faces, and their eyes
were slanted and bright. Most of them had children with
them, some lashed to their backs in a shawl.

They were jammed into the open courtyard facing the
Basilica. Ana knew that the mass of people spilled out beyond
the churchyard, clogging city arteries that led to the shrine
like spokes hooked to an axle. Her eyes took in every imagin-
able color: white and turquoise balloons; magenta, royal blue
and green *sarapes*; brown, tan, gray *huaraches* and
sombreros. There was food and drink and sweets everywhere,
and in the center of that mass of human beings were the penitents who waited their turn to crawl all the way to the altar
to fulfill the promise that would cleanse them of their sins.

Ana's mind drifted away from the din and chanted
prayers to the days that had passed since Terrance's burial.
She had returned to the protection of her home, but she had
been unable to sleep or eat because of what she had learned.
Her confusion was so great that she could not think clearly or
make sense of what had happened to her.

Her son had been taken from her and she had found him
only to lose him again. Unknowing, she had become his lover,
and this perplexed and depressed her. She was far from
understanding why this had happened to her. The world was
large, inhabited by millions of people, and yet the most
unlikely, improbable thing had happened to her. Her son had
returned to her by accident. There was a void inside of her.
For days, she floundered, struggling to keep from drowning
in a sea of blame that filled her mouth with bitterness, chok-
ing her as if it had been caked mud sticking in her throat.

The day came when she could hardly breathe, and the
idea of suicide began to obsess her. She sat for hours staring
at a gun; its bluish glint seemed to seduce her and yet fill her
with fear. At night, she became afraid of the darkness.
During the day the light made her seek refuge in the gloomi-

est corner of her house. She felt defeated by the memory of her sin because no matter how much she resisted, she was constantly assaulted by recollections of Terrance, of his kisses and caresses.

Ana knew that to remember was to sin all over again. But she was incapable of not thinking of him and of the love they had shared. She understood that by clinging to the memory of her love, she raised her fist in the face of God. But Ana could not erase the image of Terrance's face or the sensation of his body inside of her.

Driven by desire to be forgiven, she made her way to Mexico City with the intention of approaching the altar of the Virgin of Guadalupe. There, she was convinced, she would find the absolution that would keep her from losing her mind. Ana remembered again the penitent woman, and she now understood her grief. Her own misery, she told herself, had begun when her father had cursed her and Ismael.

She was suddenly jolted from her thoughts by prayers that signaled the penitents to move forward. Hail Marys blared from gigantic speakers, and people began to weep and shout words that she couldn't make out. There was a surge of bodies, and they pushed at one another roughly as they began to hobble their way across the pavement to the entrance of the church. Ana, trying to keep up with the crowd, began to lose her balance. Sweat coursed down her back and between her breasts as the *mantilla* wrapped itself around her neck. She felt a flash of searing pain which made its way from her knees up her body, and she realized that her legs were bleeding.

People began to sing hymns in honor of the Virgin. These merged with mumbled prayers and weeping, and with petitions that were yelled out. Body odors mingled with the pungent smell of incense and the smoke of the candles inside the church. The heat was stifling. Pain in her knees forced Ana to crawl on all fours. Then she realized that her hands were smeared with blood from those ahead of her, and she knew that behind her others were wiping up her own blood.

As she groveled toward the altar, Ana was overwhelmed by her nothingness. Her money, her success in business, the respect and admiration of her associates, her massive business with its corporate headquarters paled as her father's curse echoed in her mind. She was, as he had predicted, a sinful, wretched woman who had lain with her son.

When it was finally her turn to kneel at the railing that towered above her head, Ana looked up to see the frame that housed the image of the Virgin of Guadalupe. She murmured, *"Virgencita, perdóname."* She held her breath, as if expecting the image to speak, forgiving her.

Ana froze as she clung to the railing. Soon, people began to push her, grumbling that she was taking too long, and that it was now their turn. She didn't pay attention to any of them, although she was vaguely aware that a custodian was approaching. She knew that nothing could drag her away until she was given an answer to her prayer. But there was no answer. There was only stillness and emptiness inside of her. The Virgin was silent and there was no miracle to calm Ana or to help her rid herself of the disgust and shame that had stalked her ever since she could remember.

After a while, she got to her feet, turned and dove head-long into the crowd, elbowing through the tightly squeezed bodies without pausing to look back. She could not wait to get out into the sunlight and fresh air. When she emerged from the dark interior of the church, she saw a young woman seated on a mat. She was selling fruit. Ana gave her the shawl that had covered her head, saying that it was a gift. The girl took it gladly, her face showing that she was puzzled by the strange woman who did not stop even to be thanked.

⊱⊰

It could be said that my story ended that day in Mexico City, but it didn't. I returned to Los Angeles convinced that like other people I would continue to live my life with unresolved doubts and questions. This thought made me feel shallow, and because I couldn't think of anything to fill the emptiness, I threw myself once again into my business.

During those years I still received letters from Amy and Franklin who had grown old but seemed always to watch over me despite the distance that separated us. A letter came from Franklin in 1975. It was brief, but what it said affected me as I hadn't imagined possible. Amy had died in her sleep, he said. There had been no pain. When he discovered her that morning, he could tell that her passing had been serene.

He ended his letter saying, "Amy has left you something that I'll mail you soon. I want to tell you, also, that hardly a day passed in which we didn't speak about you and Ismael. You were the daughter we never had; he our grandson. And, Ana, just recently, we remembered Hagar all over again. Just before going to bed one night, Amy said to me, 'If ever I die before you do, Franklin, I want you to promise me that you'll remind Ana of Hagar.'"

When I finished reading the letter, I sat up until past midnight. I stayed in the dark watching the images of my life drift by me. I reached far back into my memory to my girl- hood, when I played and danced outside the hut with the palm roof. The faces of the campesinas *of the tomato fields seemed to melt off the white plaster walls, and I saw Tavo's face as the setting sun wove strands of gold into his hair. I felt his caress- es and kisses, which blurred with those of Ismael. I saw my- self sitting at the kitchen table as I listened to Amy's high- pitched voice reading from the pages of the Old Testament. And the enigma of Hagar swirled around me, unsettling me as it always did.*

As Franklin had promised, a package came from him some weeks later. I put the bundle on the coffee table and sat for a long time staring at the brown wrapping paper and twine that held the parcel together. I knew what it contained even without opening it. I could tell by its weight and by its shape, because I had held it in my hands countless times.

When I finally unbound the ties and ripped the paper away, the worn edges of Amy's Bible appeared. I noticed the faded leather marker, and I knew what I would read when I opened the book at that place. When I stuck my fingers between the pages, the book opened to the verses telling of Ismael and Hagar.

I closed my eyes to calm my nerves. When I looked again, I focused on those lines that had been underlined over and again with different shades of ink, as if Amy were trying to tell me something. I took the book in my hands and read the words. "You are with child and shall bear a son; you shall call him Ismael because the Lord has heard you in your humilia- tion."

"The Lord has heard you in your humiliation." These words hit me with such force that I think I stopped breathing.

I searched my memory, recalling the night that Amy had read about Hagar. Had Amy skipped that verse? I couldn't remember. I put the book aside, but the turmoil inside of me went on for days, and my agitation grew with each hour. My mind groped and floundered until I decided to return to the place of my birth, hoping to find the answer there.

I left Los Angeles not knowing what I would discover in the land of my childhood. When I arrived in Puerto Real I went to where the palapas *had stood and found that in their place were condominiums and hotels. There was nothing left of the hut in which I and my sisters had been born. There wasn't a trace of Tía Calista's house, either, or of anything that might have reminded me of my childhood days when I sat gazing at the sea, dreaming of becoming a dancer.*

I returned to the cove of my childhood only to find it crowded with bathers and skiers. I was surrounded by people and children who shouted as they played games, as well as by vendors who peddled coconuts and fried fish. I left and returned next day at dawn, hoping that it would be as it used to be.

It was still dark that morning as I walked from one end of the cove to the other. I was alone, waiting for the sun to rise. I felt excited because I had not seen the sun come out over the gulf since the day we had left to go to the Valley of the Yaqui. I sat down and buried my toes in the black, moist sand as I watched the yellow ball begin to peek over the horizon.

My mind recreated the steps that had taken me away from Puerto Real, and those that had brought me back. I remembered when my father cast me away from him, as well as the loneliness from which Amy and Franklin Bast had rescued me. I felt Doña Hiroko's gentle hands, and I saw Doña Trini's face.

I looked out toward the rising sun and my heart filled with memories of César and my sisters. I felt my heart beating faster because Ismael, still a baby, was walking by me. He was so real that I saw his footprints on the sand, and when I reached out to him I saw that he was grown, and his name was Terrance.

I raised my hands to my eyes to get a closer look at them, and I saw that they were spotted, and that the veins bulged against skin that was beginning to wrinkle. I felt under my chin, running my fingers over the loose layers around my neck. I had grown old, and I knew that only now was I beginning to see what before had been blurred shadows.

I listened to the early sounds of people beginning their workday, and it struck me that I would be one of them if 'Apá had not taken us north. I thought of the people I would not have known and the moments I would not have lived. Then I tried to visualize my sisters and Octavio just as we had been at the time we trudged, single file, over the very sand I was sitting on. I tried to see our faces as they had been when we were children. Finally, after some minutes, I was able to draw up that picture.

The sound of the ebbing waves receded and Amy's voice suddenly sounded inside of me. She was repeating the Hagar verses, those telling of the slave girl being cast out into the desert, and of her fear because she desired to live. I closed my eyes, partly because the sun was now coming over the horizon and its brightness was almost intolerable, but also because I was straining to reach farther into my memories, trying to unravel the mystery of Hagar and what meaning it had for me. I wanted to return to the ranch and to the kitchen table where Franklin and I had sat listening to Amy.

I gazed at the emerald-colored water as it connected with the deepening blue sky, and then I looked into myself, remembering the words I had uttered while I was still a young girl. "It seems to me that the Lord saved Hagar because she was important on her own, because she was who she was. She came first, and God needed her so that her son could exist. That means that Hagar was more valuable than her son."

My body stiffened and I yanked my feet out of the sand when I remembered how Amy had answered my interpretation of the verses. "Well, now, I'll just have to give this whole thing a bit more thought." Yet, she never again said what she really thought. Not until now, after her death, when she finally showed me the verses that told of Hagar's importance; that she had been heard because she was she, and because her distress had meaning, even if Ismael had not existed.

I began to see that what Amy must have meant was that despite my father's hateful curse, despite Octavio's betrayal, despite my sins, and even after finding Ismael only to have him disappear from my life, still, like Hagar, it was for me to choose to go on living because I was given a life to live. This thought coursed through me. It gradually flooded my being, freeing me at last from the desert of worthlessness into which I had been cast by my father's disdain.

I rose from the sand and stood with my face lifted to the morning sun. I felt its warmth bathe my forehead and cheeks. After a while, I turned away from the water's edge and began to make my way back home. I was at peace because now I understood that I had lived and loved, and that I had discovered the value of who I am.